Lander Blue

Fate, Turquoise Treasure and Survival

Lander Blue

Fate, Turquoise Treasure and Survival

A Novel

Richard Ryan
Gail Douglas

Santa Fe

Sunstone books may be purchased for educational, business, or sales promotional use.
For information please write: Special Markets Department, Sunstone Press,
P.O. Box 2321, Santa Fe, New Mexico 87504-2321.

eBook 978-1-61139-657-7

Library of Congress Cataloging-in-Publication Data

Names: Ryan, Richard, 1953- author. | Douglas, Gail, 1943- author.
Title: Lander blue : fate, turquoise treasure and survival : a novel / Richard Ryan, Gail Douglas.
Description: Santa Fe : Sunstone Press, [2022] | Summary: "A mystery novel, set in Nevada and New Mexico, follows a grandson trying to solve a treasure hunt for ten million dollars worth of Lander Blue turquoise hidden by his grandfather for him to find"-- Provided by publisher.
Identifiers: LCCN 2022001253 | ISBN 9781632933744 (paperback) | ISBN 9781611396577 (epub)
Subjects: LCSH: Treasure hunting--Nevada--Fiction. | Treasure hunting--New Mexico--Fiction. | Turquoise--Nevada--Fiction. | Turquoise--New Mexico--Fiction. | LCGFT: Detective and mystery fiction. | Novels.
Classification: LCC PS3618.Y3434 L36 2022 | DDC 813.6--dc23

LC record available at https://lccn.loc.gov/2022001253

WWW.SUNSTONEPRESS.COM
SUNSTONE PRESS / POST OFFICE BOX 2321 / SANTA FE, NM 87504-2321 /USA
(505) 988-4418

This book is dedicated to the turquoise mines
of the Southwest and the stories they have to tell.

CONTENTS

Acknowledgments

We want to thank our families for their support and tolerance while we wrote this. Special thanks to Glynis Edgar and Rhonda Reed for their editing, and to Penny Jost for making us feel like we wrote an entertaining story.

Introduction / Lander Blue Turquoise

Turquoise is the premier gem of the American Southwest. Some collectors think that in its purest form, it is one of the rarest gemstones in the world. It is the stone of choice for local Indians and cowboys, well-to-do visiting Dallas women and vagabond kids passing through. The color symbolizes calming energy that brings wisdom resulting in serenity.

Many Indians thought it represented touching the sky. As lore goes, as you bond with the sky stone, the good luck and protection it provides brings emotional balance and ultimately happiness. In many ways this story supports that theory.

In numerous places in the Southwestern United States Anasazi Indians used rocks and sticks to probe and pry apart turquoise pockets they saw in cliff faces or rocky gully washes. Even they knew to follow the vein. This sometimes led them further and further into a dug embankment, until they needed something more than sunlight to see what they were doing. Like everything, when it is first discovered and man has not had a chance to greedily overharvest or overuse it, it's hard to imagine the size and quality of what they found.

The few known stones dating back to that time are usually large and many times refined to a point of only starting to reveal their beauty. Some of those ancient excavations are still mined today. Instead of a crazy Anasazi miner, it's a crazy old hippie or rich businessman that has the same dream of finding the big vein like their ancient ancestors did.

A rough chunk of mined turquoise is a combination of copper, iron, aluminum and phosphate. This combination in different proportions is why there are so many different types of turquoise. This chemical drip fills and hardens in any rock void or fissure that it finds. Too much running water and the turquoise cocktail will wash away, never having a chance to solidify.

Because of this creation process over millions of years, each type of turquoise has a specific name and home due to the host rock that it found in which to solidify. Stones from each mine typically yield one or maybe two distinctive looks due to the matrix. The rest of the rock, the turquoise part, gets its color from the amount of copper or iron present when it solidifies. The more vivid the blue, usually the more copper in the mix. Blues range from the iconic soothing delicate Tiffany to the sometimes almost black Bisbee.

Moisture-sucking dryness is the final condition that makes for an ideal turquoise incubator. The fortuitous addition of silica or quartz usually comes with this, resulting in harder stones and better quality. Battle Mountain, in Lander County Nevada, where this story begins, has all of this.

There are over four hundred registered turquoise mine claims in Nevada. This story is about the turquoise taken from one of those mines, the Lander Blue Mine. It was located south of downtown Battle Mountain. This mine has been the dream and envy of turquoise miners everywhere.

The Lander Blue was a "hat mine" meaning the turquoise deposits could be covered with a normal sized hat, like a fedora. The deposits were small, but centrally located and concentrated. The gem-stone quality had not been seen before in the turquoise world.

It is the unmistakable black spider-web veined stone. Even an untrained eye can see the difference. The creamy dark blue is endless when you stare into it. The thin randomly streaming black matrix leads your eyes around like an unseen guide that wants you to get lost.

This gift from the land was mined out over the course of ten years and several owners. At that time, the supply of the finest gem quality turquoise in the world stopped. Because there will not be any new Lander Blue, it is the rarest and most valued turquoise in the world today.

Stones over ten carats are hoarded and rarely traded. The four hundred dollars and up carat price is irrelevant to many collectors. Approximately one-hundred-eight pounds of turquoise was recorded as the amount taken from the Lander Blue Mine.

This is where the make-believe story starts. Until recently only eighty-eight pounds were accounted for by collectors and high-end turquoise traders. Many an hour has been spent over a beer at the annual mega gem show in Tucson contemplating where the missing turquoise might be. This story is about that remaining twenty pounds or approximately ten million dollars of Lander Blue that recently reappeared, solving the mystery and shaking the world turquoise market.

Prologue

I'm Michael Hamilton. After two tours in Afghanistan, I am a recovering Marine. I am the third M in this story. I live in Santa Fe, New Mexico in the old part of town. My best friend since childhood is a Native American named Willow Gantry. He has my back in this story and helped me solve Clue 1.

My family was wealthy. They were different. I guess I am different in this regard too. I wish that my Grandfather had been my father. I am pretty sure he felt the same. My parents didn't like me, especially my father Mel. He is the second M in the story.

This story begins with my Grandfather Mort, the first M. He was a piece of work. His life was shaped by fate, a random stop at a diner in Battle Mountain, Nevada. At that time, he was a marginal young man with a five-year-old son he did not know. After that day in Battle Mountain he turned into a magician, a riddler, a Santa Fe personality and a world-renowned Native American jewelry dealer.

Mort owned Hamilton's Southwest Jewelry on the Plaza for many decades. It was an international destination for serious turquoise and silver jewelry traders and consumers.

Out of love for me and spite for my parents, before he died, my Grandfather set up an unexpected life-changing adventure for me. Along the way I met Rita Owens, who changed my life. I also made a new friend, Detective Cecil Soledad.

This story spans forty-seven years. The last three months shaped my future. Kierkegaard said, "Life can only be understood backwards; but it must be lived forward." I agree. This is a story laced with fate, irony and forging forward without fully understanding why most of the time.

1 The First M

Hunger is a universal motivator and this afternoon Mort Hamilton's empty rumbling stomach is motivating him. He is driving from Burns, Oregon after visiting a woman he met in Santa Fe, New Mexico, where he is currently residing. Residing, meaning he has returned to the place where he fathered a son five years ago. He had found a place to sleep and shower at a friend's house in the old part of Santa Fe, behind a stucco courtyard wall. Mort can walk to the plaza and his favorite local bar. For now, the primary criterion for choosing a place to stay is that he doesn't have to pay for it.

This afternoon, however, he is heading south to see a friend in Las Vegas. He had been asked to leave Oregon after a couple of weeks of crashing and taking advantage of another short-term female acquaintance. A cup of black coffee he quickly poured into a used paper cup he retrieved from his car before he scurried out the door this morning had served as breakfast.

He stops at a small diner located on the brick paved main street of Battle Mountain, Nevada. The sign above the window next to the entrance door is hanging crooked. There is a slim triangle of unbleached stucco that apparently has just recently been revealed on the left side. It will soon be baked like everything else in northern Nevada. Mort thinks even the people get bleached and eventually look the same.

He has heard from his friend in Vegas that if you want to disappear, or at least get lost in the landscape, this is a place to do it. It is one of the reasons that people are coming to Lander County. From what Mort had seen of the last hundred miles of Highway 80, anyone who wants to come to this place for that reason can have it. It isn't for him.

Unsurprisingly, the diner is full of locals eating a casual lunch. Small town America in 1973 is on full view. Some are there to catch up on local gossip, with lunch being the excuse. Others are there to eat and quickly close a deal on cheap property to the south where they can start digging a new turquoise mine. Before reaching for the door, Mort automatically adjusts his crotch and pulls a cheap black comb out of his back pocket and runs it through his wavy brown hair. Whatever the reason, once Mort walks through the door, this diner has a familiar feel. It also has an enticing smell.

No one looks up as the door slams shut leaving a couple of frustrated flies buzzing around, still waiting to sneak in. If the patrons cared they did not act like it, but Mort knew there were several sets of suspecting eyes watching him when he was not looking. A strange man dressed in a suit in this town meant you were selling something or looking for somebody. Mort knows people think it is unusual to travel in a suit. He thinks it makes him fresher, that he pays more attention to his driving. His car has an air conditioner. Even so, his friend in Santa Fe thinks he is crazy to wear a suit to drive a car in the summer. It is a habit he developed working as a driver, general handyman, enforcer and sometimes do-gooder for Domingo Flores, a high school friend.

Domingo's empire was upended one winter afternoon when a husband came home early to find his wife hunched over a kitchen counter with her legs spread and her skirt around her waist. Both she and Domingo stopped panting and looked up when the husband opened the door. Domingo was loaded, but not with bullets. He didn't have a gun and the very irate husband did. The police did not like Domingo. They called it justifiable homicide. By process of elimination, Mort was out of a job.

The suit habit stuck with him. He knows he looks better than everyone else in the place. He always likes this kind of attention. He can reinvent himself every time he enters a new place for the first time. He personally chooses to act mysterious and like he has money for any new audience.

He deliberately perches on a stool between two empty stools, the only remaining seats in the place. Perfect, no one on either side. His feet are now on the foot rail and his elbows are lightly resting on the counter. He is ready to order. He is also ready to get up quickly and depart if necessary. He smiles to himself. A quick departure is his primary consideration when he decides where to sit in another chicken shit little diner in another chicken shit little town.

He likes sitting at the counter. It reminds him of being at a bar. He almost feels the greasy smell of the grill. The four-foot hunk of gas-powered steel in this diner has been a provider of food bliss for a lot of years. It is the machine that creates the expected Battle Mountain Diner taste. The grill is being used like a trusty cooking tool by a woman with a red apron bound tightly around her shapely backside.

Her blonde hair is cut like Jane Fonda's in the movie Klute. It's called a shag, he thinks. Mort likes long hair on a woman, but most of the time, their hair isn't what matters. The cook's shag is held in place by a black net that Mort can barely see. This has an interesting and unexpected appeal to him. So far, this stop is working out nicely.

As he checks out things other than what is under the red apron, he notices a sign taped to the mirror away from the cooking area that says "Turquoise Jewelry for Sale. Real silver. Real turquoise. Next door." There is a picture of a large deep blue piece of turquoise mounted on a thick smooth silver wrist band. The band is on a woman's wrist attached to a hand mysteriously appearing out of a completely black background. Below the hand it says "Lander Blue" in big square-edged black letters, "The BEST turquoise in the Southwest." The flyer is noticeable because it isn't sun faded and crinkled, like most of the other things taped to the mirror in the dedicated area.

Mort orders a chocolate shake. He wants the blender to whir causing the patrons to instinctively raise and lower their voices in unison and in harmony with the blender. They won't even know it, but he will. In the mirror on the wall across from the bar he can see himself. He can also see if anyone comes up behind him. Another habit cultivated from doing things that make this type of precaution a daily part of life and a few times, survival. He swivels slowly on the stool.

There is a row of booths against the wall. Hanging on the wall at each booth are photographs of either miners or mines. Mort assumes they were taken in the area. Some of the pictures look old and yellow. One booth has a big picture of what looks like a giant mine. The road circles and circles forever into a gigantic hole. He nods to a couple of people that look up. He never changes expression. He hopes he is being perceived as mysterious. His vanity has created this irony. He likes that. He is a man who wants to be noticed, but not too much and on his terms.

Mort tastes the still-steaming hamburger. The cheese escapes messily from the perfectly toasted bun. The bun is done like it is supposed to be. Left on the grille in the patty grease till the edges turn brown. It crunches when he takes that first bite. He knows why he has stopped to eat lunch at this little diner. The same thing that has guided his life for about twenty of his thirty-five years has put him here, fortuitous luck.

The burger is almost gone. The shake is now a pleasant memory. Mort is just about to order a cup of coffee to go with the apple pie now sitting in front of him when the diner door opens just a crack and someone peeks in. The sunlight blaring through gives the illusion of a shadow trying to enter. Apparently, feeling the coast is clear, a woman pushes the door open and steps into the packed diner. She is dressed in tan overalls and heavy work boots covered with dust. She even has a smudge of dirt on her face. But what a face. The woman is stunningly beautiful even though she is dressed like a construction laborer.

She smiles as people start to look up. They are quiet just for a second. A man in a blue leisure suit with shiny white leather shoes sitting at the table nearest the door says, "Hi Suzy." Soon after, several patrons, between mouthfuls of chicken fried steak, greasy hamburgers and very salty fries, mumble "Hi Suzy" and then quickly resume eating. Suzy walks to the stool to the left of Mort and asks if he minds if she sits there. Without hesitation, he smiles and stands slightly, catching his napkin in his lap. Mort says, "Sure. Why not?"

2 A Delightful Conversation

Suzy effortlessly slides onto the stool to Mort's left as the woman occupying the stool to her left looks up and smiles. She quickly turns away and resumes her conversation with a much younger longhaired man to her left. When Suzy sits down, a small plume of dust pops out of her right back pocket and settles on the floor. It is just enough to be noticeable. Mort keeps looking at his pie, but smiles to himself, because he can tell she is embarrassed. As with any new situation, he instinctively goes for his comb, but resists the temptation. The habit is a tell for when he is nervous and entering an unfamiliar situation. He knows it but didn't care enough to change. Besides, he likes his hair. He doesn't know her name, but God, whoever she is, she is built like a brick shit house. He didn't care for a lot of hippie slang, or hippies for that matter, but in this case, the term fits.

When the waitress finally makes it over to the woman, she carries a glass of water in a red plastic cup that has been washed so many times it has a gray hue on the outside. The word "Diner" is all that remains of the lettering on what was a new glass four years ago. She expertly puts it down on the worn, what looks and feels like copper, countertop, a safe distance from her newest customer. Mort's mind strays while the woman chats and eventually orders. Apparently, the waitress knows her. Mort overhears the waitress say, "Have you found any new veins lately?"

When he hears the unusual question, he snaps to. He has been wondering why places that you need ice in a drink the most, because of the blast furnace summer heat, were the places where they typically were the stingiest with the ice. This thought is triggered when he notices how much ice is in the dingy glass. It is a glass of ice with some water added. This is another sign of a good place to eat in his opinion.

As she is ordering a bacon cheeseburger and a glass of milk, Mort looks at her. He wonders what kind of veins a waitress would be asking someone about who is wearing dirty overalls and covered in dust. "Sure, she's a doctor," he thinks to himself. No, it must be something else. After she orders and the waitress goes back to scrambling around behind the counter, she looks at Mort. "Milk is a shake without the ice cream." She smiles like she has said something smart. "I'm Suzy, Suzy Goodhap. You're not from around here, are you?" It didn't happen often, but Mort is immediately taken. Suzy's looks pop him a good one. Then her voice knocks him out. Mischievous and sexy already, after only a handful of words. This is the only way he could describe her.

It takes him a second to say, "No, just passing through. Driving from Oregon to see a friend in Vegas. I'm Mort." She adjusts her overall straps up her shoulders revealing parallel clean stripes on what appears to be a silk blouse. The marks are noticeable. More noticeable to Mort is that the pulling up of Suzy's overalls draws his attention to her chest hiding under her dusty overall bib.

If her chest is half as good as her face, she is a cut above what he is used to or feels like he even deserves. Her voice is girlish, but so confident that it doesn't come off that way. After Mort takes a sip of coffee, he flirtingly asks, "I assume you are from around here or did you bring the dust from somewhere else?" When she turns to answer his question, her right sleeve slides up her arm revealing a giant turquoise and silver bracelet. It is the bracelet in the picture on the flyer taped on the mirror behind the bar. It is unmistakable.

The stone in real-life is much more engaging and beautiful than in the picture. Suzy sees him looking down at her wrist. "I found this piece of turquoise the third day after I filed my claim. My heart skipped a beat when it broke off from the deposit." Mort looks at her. She sees the look on his face. He chuckles openly. "So that is the vein the waitress was talking about. Is it a turquoise vein? You're not a weird dusty doctor?"

With that question she swivels on the stool. She is directly facing him, her knees almost touching his. Smugly, "It's from my claim south of town. It's the best one in Lander County by far." She holds the bracelet up for him to inspect. Every now and then she looks around the room like she is sizing up a situation. Mort got "How" out, and she started again. "I was out for a walk by myself late one afternoon in the foothills east of Long Peak. I would do that occasionally to forget about my real job as a blackjack dealer at the Copper Kettle Casino."

"That afternoon I took a trail up into the rocks above my favorite trail and just happened to see several small chunks of turquoise on the ground next to this washed off cliff face. The face looked normal, except for this dark spot about as big as a human head. The dirt had fallen away. If the wind hadn't been blowing the scraggly sage in front of it, I would have missed it."

She catches her breath but is not going to stop. "At the time I didn't know it, but I had found one of the best veins of turquoise ever found. I covered the spot up. Right there I prayed no one else would find it. I don't even remember floating back to my car and driving home I was so excited." She takes a drink of her milk leaving a light lipstick ring on the glass and a faint milk mustache on her upper lip. She wipes her mouth quickly. "I learned in two days how to file a claim for a turquoise mine on public land, and I did."

The waitress brings Suzy's burger and sets it down in front of her. The heavy white oval plate met the copper countertop with a dull thud. "You sure you don't want any fries?" The waitress' voice trails off as she walks away. She knows the answer. Suzy daintily cuts the burger in half. She proceeds to take one of the biggest bites from it that Mort had ever seen a female mouth take. After she finishes chewing up a second bite, the same amount, she looks at him. "So, what were you doing in Oregon?"

For some reason Mort feels like telling the truth to this woman instead of making up a bigger-than-his-life story, like he usually does. "The woman I visited just bought the Silver Spur Motel in Burns. I first met her in Santa Fe, where I..." He slows. "Where, where I live right now. She invited me out there to help her get it set up." He smiles sheepishly. He looks right in her eyes, "After a couple of weeks she didn't feel like I was helping enough and asked me to leave." Suzy smiles, looks straight back into his eyes. "You mean she kicked you out."

Instead of denying it Mort says, "Yep. I really had it coming. It started out fun, but she was too busy to spend time with me. She expected me to help too. I mean, help with the motel." He made the last statement so seriously as Suzy takes a drink of milk, she laughs into her glass with a loud gurgling sound. A couple of drops of milk splash on the counter. Some goes up her nose. She lowers her glass slowly and wipes the milk off her nose with a food stained napkin. "I like you. You are too honest, too funny."

Between slightly smaller hamburger bites, she tells him that she needs something to laugh about right now. Cal, her husband, is a local loan shark in cahoots with the casino. Worse than that, he is an asshole.

"The only thing good about the son of a bitch is that he is gone most of the time." They both laugh briefly and then look at each other. It is silly. She sounds mean, but they both know she isn't.

As they finish up, Mort notices she leaves a five dollar bill for the waitress. A nice tip for a $2.50 burger and glass of milk. Without looking down he quickly slides the three quarters he left under the edge of his empty hamburger plate. The remaining grease has congealed in the center and does not look so appetizing now.

They both get up slowly not looking at each other. She adjusts her overalls. Very quietly Suzy asks, "Can I talk to you in the parking lot?" She doesn't wait for an answer and walks toward the door. This game is not new to Mort, but totally unexpected. He instinctively waits and adjusts his pants. He makes sure he leaves all remaining food from his lunch on the counter or the floor, not on his pants or clean white shirt. Once he puts his comb away, he turns and starts for the door. Just like when he came in, he makes minimal eye contact and takes the most direct route to the door.

He quickly puts on his sunglasses before the door has a chance to close. The two o'clock Nevada sun is blinding and blistering. He rounds the corner of the building and just starts to look up. It takes a minute for his eyes to adjust enough to see Suzy at the far end of the lot leaning against a baby blue Cadillac. Mort is not surprised. She may have been in overalls and dusty as hell, but his bet is that the woman has money. He seems to have an intuition for determining that about women.

When he finally reaches her Suzy stands up straight. "Would you like to see my mine?" At first, he thinks she said, "Would you like to see mine?" He wistfully thinks how great that would be, but quickly realizes that was not what she said. Just like when he saw her for the first time sitting on the stool next to him, he replies, "Sure. Why not? I've never seen a mine." Suzy nods. "Follow me, but stay back some as we go through town. We are going south for about five miles."

3 Going to a Turquoise Mine

Mort looks back at the diner. No one is going in or coming out except a young Mexican man with a black bandana wrapped around his head. The young man dumps a giant trash can into the dumpster next to the back door. Then he disappears back inside quickly, slamming the screen door to the kitchen as he reenters. Mort opens the dusty door of the Cadillac for Suzy. Where he grabs the chrome door handle he leaves a clean spot, or at least a lighter spot. He wipes the sandy grit from his hands by rubbing them together while he watches her maneuver into the dark blue leather seat. Once situated, she starts the car, quickly looks at herself in the rearview mirror and pushes the air conditioner "ON" button. The big Cadillac engine slows for a second when the air conditioning comes on. Then it starts purring like a big cat again.

He doesn't say a word. He turns and quickly walks back to his new black Mach 1 Ford Mustang parked in the only shady spot in the half acre of boiling asphalt parking lot. Mort had pulled into the lot and was looking for a parking spot just as the car parked under the only tree and oasis of shade was backing out to leave. Another little dose of the luck that has been known to follow him around.

He opens the driver-side door and the heat blasts out. Black outside and black inside. The car is cool looking because of the all black, especially with the silver custom rims that came on it. As with most things however, the compromise is worth it sometimes and sometimes not. Whatever his motives at the time of purchase, he knows the black color combination can create a furnace, even parked under a shade tree.

He bought the Mustang at the Ford dealership in Santa Fe specifically for the trip to Oregon. It was bought to impress. When he first saw the car, he thought he was too old for it. He dismissed this idea when he sat in the leather contoured racing seat looking out into the dealer's showroom hungrily wishing he was out on the highway. He thought to himself, "How could I not look good in this?" The purchase was made possible by the dealer's nothing down policy and a very cursory credit check.

Mort had used his gift of persuasion to manipulate the salesman named Ed into giving him the loan. The salesman was decked out in an unbuttoned big-collared orange shirt with a big gold chain around his neck. Mort thought he was trying too hard. He thought the same thing about any man who would wear such an outfit. The loud colors. The gold chains. He made a calculation that he could build Ed's ego up and make him feel obligated to give him the loan at the same time. It worked.

Suzy slowly rolls past the rear of Mort's Mustang. She does not even look at him as she passes. He assumes she wanted to see what kind of car he is driving. She edges up to the parking lot exit and looks both ways before heading south out of the parking lot. The whole time she is fidgeting with a giant pair of red sunglasses. Mort backs out of his parking space immediately feeling the tree's umbrella from the sun disappear. He heads out of the lot slowly too. The Mustang's AC begins working overtime. He can see thick smoke bellowing from the stack on the back side of the diner's roof. With the windows still down, the burning grease smell wafts into the car just for a second before the AC air pushes it back out.

Settling in for the supposedly short drive, Mort raises the windows and turns on the radio. He finally finds an FM rock station out of Las Vegas. He looks at his gas tank and wishes he could fill up before leaving town, but it is too late. When he looks up from his dash, Battle Mountain is in his rearview mirror. If he doesn't pick up speed, he is going to get left behind. The Cadillac is getting smaller in the distance.

The Mustang was made for closing distances quickly. Mort lets the horses run. Soon he can see Suzy waving to him while looking in the rearview mirror. Based on where he thought her mine was, he should have enough gas to get to Austin when he leaves. It is only about thirty miles further south down Highway 305.

Sure enough, about five miles later the Cadillac's right blinker starts. A sign for the Copper Basin Mine is to the left toward the mountain. About half a mile later the paved road veers to the left going to the mine. Suzy veers to the right. They are now on a dirt road. Mort immediately understands why everything about Suzy is dusty. From the direction of the copper mine he sees a dust devil coming their way. As if it did not wish to be seen, the spiraling cloud disappears as he stares at it. The swirling debris is left stranded in the air.

They are now paralleling the northeastern edge of Battle Mountain. The road is not too bad. Mort turns his windshield wipers on a couple of times to get the dust off the windshield. He is now hanging back some to keep from driving blind. It is like being in a grimy gritty dry fog. About a mile down this road Suzy turns left down a worn two-tire path between two giant stands of prickly pear. The path emerges into a small cleared area made for parking.

She pulls into the area as far as she can leaving room for him to park beside her. They are looking at each other in their cars while they wait for the dust to settle. Mort thinks to himself that he is not dressed for this as he pulls his tie off before he even gets out of the car. When his car door shuts, a thick layer of dust falls from the side of the car onto the ground. Some of it lands on his polished brown penny loafers. Mort knows this is a sign of more dust to come.

Suzy gets out and immediately walks over to him. She says softly, "Thank you for coming. I don't show my mine to anybody, but I wanted to show it to you." At this point Mort is unsure whether to be flattered or suspicious. They are out in the middle of nowhere. He has no idea what he is doing with a married woman who is a miner and whom he has known for less than two hours.

There is a path heading off around a rock outcropping about twenty feet from the front of their cars. Suzy nods her head toward the path. "We are going that way. Hang on a sec." She goes to her trunk and pops it open. She grabs a canteen and a couple of old beat up gray helmets with headlamps taped on them out of an old wooden fruit crate. She hands these items to Mort. After digging around some more she comes out with two pairs of worn dirty leather gloves and two short wood-handled picks.

As they start down the path, Mort feels the sweat forming in the middle of his back under his white shirt. He stops at his car and sets the helmets down so he can roll up his shirt sleeves. They are quite the miner couple. Suzy in coveralls and work boots and Mort in dress clothes and polished shoes. After about a hundred feet the path disappears into the rocks. Mort sees a cliff face nearby with a folding chair in front of it. There is a firepit and an old sturdy-looking folding table to the right.

Suzy stops and looks relieved. "I'm always scared when I return here that someone will have raided it or damaged it. I have been coming here almost every day for three months now and that feeling will not go away." Softly, "I probably won't have kids, so this is my baby. This is my Lander Blue Mine."

They set the gear on the table. "Where is the mine?" Mort asks. Suzy motions with her right hand. "We go up a little trail another hundred feet. It's right up there." She breathes a couple of times and wipes her lips. "The trail switchbacks a bunch up to the ridge. It's harder to climb, but the view of the sunset from up there is the best in Lander County, maybe the world."

Mort looks to where she first points and sees a shadow indicating a depression in the cliff face. About two feet into the shadow he sees a series of eight heavy vertical logs set in the ground. The logs are bound together with a couple of ominous-looking chains protecting what he quickly realizes is the entrance to her mine.

The two big shiny round padlocks holding the chains' ends together glisten in the sun. The crude door to her mine is not totally secure, but it is about the best you can hope for out here in the middle of nowhere. He is beginning to see why she didn't bring a lot of people to the mine. In the middle of the logs about four feet up from the bottom is a sign with blue spray-painted letters: LANDER BLUE MINE – NO TRESPASSING.

4 In a Turquoise Mine

They gather the gear from the table and start walking up the last trail to the mine. About twenty feet from the mine entrance there are piles of rock shards and dirt in a row along the trail. Mort thinks the logs at the front of the opening look like a fort on the plains in the 1800s. His family visited a dude ranch in Arizona when he was a boy. It had a stockade for prisoners that was built like this. He smiles as he remembers his parents told him it was for kids that misbehaved. As they get closer, Suzy starts digging around in her left overall pocket for the padlock keys.

She times it perfectly and has the keys ready as they reach the logs. Mort shakes the logs lightly. "Does this really keep people out?" Suzy stops. "It probably wouldn't if someone really wanted to get in. With the sign, so far, it's worked." She says with a smugness, "The turquoise coming out of this mine is so unique that if someone stole from it, they would have a hard time selling the stone because it is not being sold by me."

She unlocks the padlocks and hangs each on a loose chain end. After she puts on a pair of gloves, she bear-hugs the first log on the right, pulling it up and to her chest. Grunting slightly, she swivels and leans it against the cliff face to the right. She does the same to the second log. Removing the second log leaves about an eighteen-inch space to enter the shadowy hole into the embankment. It appears she has dug about eight feet into the cliff. He now knows that the piles they passed on the trail are the dirt and rock she has dug and sifted through. As he turns sideways to enter, he stoops. His six-foot frame needs about six more inches of clearance if he is going to stand up straight.

Suzy hands him a helmet. "We probably can see enough to dig for another two hours. I like using the lamp anyway." Mort looks at her

"Dig?" He notices how perfect her teeth are when she smiles. "Don't you want to find some turquoise?" she says without looking at him. He is now in the hole smelling the musty dirt. "So, this is mining," he says under his breath. His love of the "hunt," for pretty much anything, starts kicking in. He thrives on overcoming the challenges and finding the prize. He wasn't sure what the prize was, but he realizes there is opportunity. He feels his enthusiasm growing. The thought of digging, hunting, and finding a piece of turquoise fits right in with his personality.

Suzy looks around and says, "Not bad for a one woman show, is it?" Mort asks, "Does your husband ever come out here with you?" She holds her pick. "Once at first, but never again. He hates dirt." Mort laughs. "I'm not a big fan of it either." She grabs his hand and leads him to the back of the hole. "Well today you will like it." Mort is surprised how soft her hand is considering the work she is doing. Even after Suzy releases his hand, the connection remains. It is warm in the mine. If she grabs his hand again, it is liable to get warmer.

The sun is lowering and shining through the logs. The spaces between the logs creates a jail bar pattern on the back of the hole. There is just enough light to see a round pocket of dark stone in the upper right. There is another one about three feet to its left. Suzy puts on her helmet. "So far, I've taken thirty pounds out of this hole in about three months. I have sold about ten pounds." Mort has no idea if this is good or bad. It sounds good and Suzy certainly seems proud of it.

Mort has carried the canteen. He doesn't ask, but assumes it is water. He takes a swig. It is. The water is warm as he expected it to be. He feels like pouring it on his head, but he knows the dust will turn to mud. That will mess up his hair, so he doesn't. Before he screws the metal cap back on, he holds it out to Suzy, who takes the canteen. She takes a swallow and turns. "You sure seem to be a nice person." Mort remembers her grabbing his hand. "It takes one to know one," he retorts quickly. He is surprised. He really means it.

There is enough sunlight, but Suzy switches her helmet light on. She looks at him without speaking, obviously expecting him to do the same. Mort puts on his helmet and switches on the light. He hates hats and only wears one when the sun is going to fry his head. He doesn't like baseball or stocking caps either. This helmet is none of these, but it stirs his dislike of having something on his head. They move to the back of the hole. She approaches the dark spot on the right. With her pick she starts working around the hole. Pecking. Removing chunks of dirt and rock. After a couple of minutes of this tedious chipping, Mort can see a little vein of vivid dark blue starting to emerge.

Suzy is breathing softly and steadily. She is working. She isn't talking. Mort starts looking around. It is hard to hide where he is looking with the lamp on. He starts wondering about the possibility of a cave in. This place could be his coffin. No one would know where they are. She reads his mind, having seen his light fixated on the hole's ceiling. Suzy stops her pecking and turns his way. "The rock will support itself. I worried about it at first, especially when it rained. My little mine is as solid today as it was when I started burrowing into this mountain. I don't worry anymore."

After a brief pause, she says, "You want to be a miner? Take the other pick and start opening up this deposit." She puts her hand on the other dark spot. "Be gentle with the pick. Don't hurry. The turquoise deposit will open up and tell you where to dig." Mort rerolls his shirt sleeves up and starts in as he was instructed. It doesn't take long for him to figure out what she meant. After about three minutes of soft pecking he sees a deep blue vein of turquoise about two inches long and a half inch wide.

It is unmistakable, even for a rookie miner. The spot of turquoise is embedded in a shard at the edge of the deposit. As he is staring at it, the fragment naturally separates. It hits the dirt face and starts to fall. Mort drops the pick and catches the fragment like it is precious. Suzy laughs. "That one wanted you. You can keep it to remember the afternoon."

Mort holds the shard in his hand. The light from his helmet reflects off the blue spot in the shard. Suzy comes over. She looks at it. "You got a nice one. Probably about eight carats when it's finished." That doesn't mean a whole lot to Mort, but he is excited about his find anyway. Without even thinking, he puts his arm around her and says softly into her neck, "Thank you." She tenses initially, but then relaxes and puts her arm around his waist. Their heads are close, but neither moves any closer. After a second, they separate. She quickly goes back to chipping away at her deposit.

They don't say anything for about fifteen minutes. Mort steps outside. It feels good to stand up straight again. The sun is setting enough that the back of the mine is getting dark. He leans against the cliff face by the entrance. He marvels at what this woman is doing as he looks around. It is almost crazy. He likes it. A few minutes after he hears her stop pecking, she emerges with a wicker basket. It has five new lander blue shards in it.

He starts to apologize for being too forward, but it is not necessary. She sets the basket down and puts her arms around his sweaty neck. The dirt does not matter. Neither speak. Suzy puts her dry puffy lips on his and pulls him into her. He closes his eyes and goes with it. The kiss is short. The feeling he had when she held his hand is nothing compared to this. She sniffles when they separate. "I needed you today."

He is not quite sure what to say. Maybe he had needed her too. The way he feels now compared to the way he felt this morning when he got in his car to head south, is light years different. He is energized. He feels changed. This is ridiculous. She looks up at the ridge. "You want to see a sunset you won't forget? It's the reason I discovered this. I came up here to get away from my life and I found another one. This little hole in the earth is the most gratifying thing I have right now."

Mort doesn't say anything. She puts the two removable posts back in place and collects the chain ends. Mort hears two clicks as she secures her mine for another day. He dusts his shoulders off as they started walking up the trail to the ridge. His penny loafers are scraped and cut from the rocks, but he doesn't care anymore. He just doesn't want to twist his ankle. After watching him pat himself down Suzy says, "There's only so much you can do. I have learned to live with the dust. It's part of my life now." She smiles and takes his hand in hers again. This time Mort squeezes back. They continue walking.

They round the last short switchback revealing a western view that seems endless. A looming gray thunderhead is parked right over the mountains at the end of the valley. The sun is in front of it and appears to be balanced on the horizon. They sit down close together on a flat clean ledge. This is the spot, Mort thinks. It is like nature knew that this was a good spot to watch a sunset and it provided a bench.

He rests his hand on her thigh. She reacts by scooting closer. He can feel her quadricep muscles contract and expand through her overalls as she swings her feet underneath the ledge. They sit quietly until the sun is gone. The thunderhead remains parked. It will wait until they leave to come east and wash away the tracks they left on their way to the mine.

This is the best fifteen minutes Mort has spent in a very long while. He doesn't remember the last time he watched the sun set. Being there with Suzy is special in a way he is still trying to understand. She is different from any woman he has met. Mort wonders how she feels about him. It has been approximately six hours since she pushed open the Battle Mountain Diner door. He is now sitting peacefully with her on a mountain top. He just saw a magnificent sunset, with a beautiful woman, after mining for turquoise most of the afternoon in the middle of nowhere. All of it is totally unexpected.

Suzy breaks the silence. "Let's go. The rattlesnakes will be out soon and those shoes of yours won't protect your ankles." This was enough for Mort. He snaps out of his euphoric state. He gets up, straightens his pants, picks up his gear and follows her as she starts down the trail to the cars. When they got to the bottom she giggles. "Got ya! I've never seen a snake here, especially at night." They both drop their gear and tussle like two kids play fighting. He picks her up and swings her around playfully. Her feet hit the ground. She keeps her arms around him. They hold each other tight, periodically kissing and then looking at each other affectionately.

5 Getting Clean

They arrive at the cars as it is getting dark. Suzy has been quiet on the way down. Mort is really confused by the afternoon's events and the way he feels about them right now. Once again, he wonders if she feels the same way. He takes off his helmet. He puts it in the crate along with his pick when she opens the Cadillac's trunk. He knows he has helmet hair. He feels the back of his head. He feels the dirty crease from the helmet's worn inner leather band. He pulls his comb out. He thinks about how dirty it will be if he uses it. He puts it back in his pocket. He pretends he never thought about it.

He feels a sense of regret when he thinks about continuing his trip south to Las Vegas. In a short wrinkle of time Suzy has attracted him like no other woman before. Mort wonders if it is circumstantial, maybe just some more good Mort luck. He doesn't know. He looks at her beautiful face. He thinks about how genuine she is and how nice she has been to him. It is endearing. Why? Other women he has known were not at all like this.

As if Suzy reads his mind, "This sure has been a fun afternoon. I still don't know why I wanted to show you my mine. I hope you don't tell anybody. Not that it's a big secret, but the fewer people that know exactly where it is, the better." Mort laughs. "I don't know anybody who would care, much less know what a turquoise mine even is. Don't worry. Your secret is safe with me."

At that they both laugh. She is looking at the moon coming up. It is a full moon peeking over the crest of the nearest western mountain range. It is bright, offering a comforting light in the clearing where they stand. Both are wondering how to end the day.

Mort starts to say he guessed he would continue his journey south.

He waits a minute to see if she is going to say something. She does. She is looking away. "I hate to see this day end." Now she is looking at him. "I've been thinking. Would you like to come to my place about three miles from here and clean up?" She pats some dust off her crinkled sleeve and continues, "It's the least I can offer you." She teases him, "You didn't help much, but you were great company."

Aside from getting to spend more time with her, the notion of getting cleaned up is very appealing. Mort looks at Suzy for a second before speaking. "What about your husband?" As if Suzy expects the question, "I was on my way to see an attorney in Vegas about getting a divorce this afternoon before I ran into you at the diner." Mort is unsure whether to believe her or not. "Seriously?" Suzy responds sheepishly. "I'm not proud of it. I was in a bad place when I made the decision to marry Cal. It hasn't worked. I have to do something." She pushes her hair out of her face. "I will go tomorrow."

Mort is still sizing up the situation. "So where are we heading?" "I have a little place that was mine before I met Cal," Suzy replies. She laughs at him playfully. "I haven't seen Cal in three weeks. He just come around our house in town to take a shower sometimes. He never comes to this place." Mort doesn't make it a habit to pursue married women. He has already decided this is different. He just wants to continue being with her.

Mort changes the conversation back to getting cleaned up. "You sure we need to get cleaned up?" She quickly retorts back. "I don't, but you sure do." That seems to settle it. While Mort feels the Lander Blue shard in his left pocket, she starts for her car. "Follow me again. We get back on Highway 305 and head south for two miles. Take a left at the Prospector's convenience store. We go less than a mile east."

Mort hurries to his car. Suzy has backed out. Her car lights are on bright. They hit him in the eyes as she straightens out. He sure doesn't want to get left out here in the middle of nowhere. The full moon is starting its ascent into a night sky that looks brighter to Mort than maybe ever before. He hops into the Mustang and backs out roughly. Based on where he sees Suzy's lights, she is not leaving as fast as she did from the diner. He is relieved. He isn't spooked, but this is not normal territory for him.

Pretty soon he sees the Copper Basin Mine sign. Suzy is on 305. Maybe he can blow some of the dust off his car. He accelerates. With his lights on dim, the road seems narrower. He is racing his shadow. There is not a car in sight other than the Cadillac. He finds a loose napkin in the Mustang's console and wraps his newly mined turquoise shard while he is driving. He puts it in the console wondering what it might look like under a magnifying glass with a good light. It will have to wait.

In the distance he sees a lone yellow light on the left. It is not moving. It is a beacon for those needing a six pack and smokes or overpriced gas. It is also an oasis for bugs longing for a light to swarm to on a hot summer night. As Mort gets closer, he sees it is the convenience store. About that time Suzy's blinker comes on. As he turns for the final leg to her house, he sees the light is a lone giant bulb. No cover. He smiles, thinking it is bright enough be a beacon for UFOs.

There is a giant metal cutout of a prospector stooping like he is panning for imaginary gold underneath the light. Mort stares for a moment, then turns following Suzy. Other than the fact that he is panning in an asphalt parking lot, it looks like a prospector. The floppy hat and the long beard outline are perfectly to scale. His pan is a shiny silver hubcap which looks out of place because it isn't rusted. When Mort looks back at the road, he sees a right-hand blinker come on in the darkness ahead. By the time he enters the gravel drive of the small white wood-clad house, Suzy is standing at the front door with a key in her hand.

As Mort approaches she opens the screen door. "I'm sorry. I didn't think about it. I don't have any real food. Just some good Swiss cheese and saltines." She raises her voice slightly. "I do have something special to wash it down with. In fact, it will do a real good job of getting the dust out of our mouths and we can toast to your find today." With that she unlocks and opens the door. She reaches inside without going in and flips on an overhead porch light. Suzy steps through the door and a couple of seconds later a warm light in the corner of the front room comes on.

Mort sees that the little house has a nice front porch. There are flowers growing in a bed to the left of the steps up to the porch. The moths have already found the light. He is glad it is at the end of the porch, instead of at the front door. Pretty soon he hears a window unit start. The thought of a cold shower and a cool room makes him happy. He is looking forward to being clean.

Suzy goes to a little refrigerator and retrieves an ice tray from the freezer on the top. She gets two big clear green glasses from what looks like a nicely outfitted cupboard. She puts half the cubes from the tray in each glass. She takes the glasses to a giant bottle of water turned upside down in a stand. The water gurgles out slowly as she fills each. Neither waits for it to get cold. They both gulp a couple of times. They make eye contact. Mort wonders if she feels like a kid too. She leaves the room. He hears a cabinet open and the water come on in the shower.

He tips the glass and swallows the last of the now cold water. He fills the glass again and looks around her place. It is furnished minimally, but with very nice things. It looks like everything needed is here. He sees some black and white photos of the Lander Blue Mine hanging on the wall behind the small dining table.

Soon Mort hears, "Come in here and take a shower first, while there is enough hot water." She pauses for minute and adds, "There is a fresh towel and washcloth on the vanity. Make yourself at home." She is drying her hands on a white hand towel when she reappears. The Copper Kettle insignia is on one end of it. There is a colorful poker chip embroidered on each side of the copper-colored letters. "I am letting the water run for a minute. It's been about a week since I have been here."

The air in the house is starting to cool. Suzy closes the front door quietly and turns off the porch light. Mort takes his glass of water and walks into the bathroom thinking about the shower. As he is closing the door he hears, "I have a bottle of wine that I have been saving. We'll have it after we get cleaned up."

He smiles and shakes his head. Why did this not surprise him? The bathroom is almost as big as the living room he just came from. The sink vanity is white marble. There is a big pink marble standalone tub. The shower is glass and at least four feet by four feet. It has a large shower head. He yearns to stand directly underneath it.

The candles Suzy lit on each end of the vanity provide just enough light. He carefully takes off his dusty clothes and heaps them in a corner. His skin breathes. He walks to a window between the tub and shower and opens it. As he pushes it up, he hears a coyote calling. Another one answers. The shower water is warm, but not hot when he steps in. He lets the water run on his head for a minute and then turns his face up to the water with his mouth open.

He looks at his feet. A stream of brown water flows down his legs and disappears down the drain. As he is picking up a green bar of soap from a recessed holder in the wall, he hears a soft knock on the bathroom door. It slowly opens. For some reason he is not startled. He doesn't assume the fig leaf position. He looks up to see Suzy come through the door. When it is completely open, she stops. "Do you mind if I join you?"

He feels the cold air from the living room rush into the bathroom. The window unit is working. She has lost the overalls. She drops the dusty silk blouse and quickly removes a lacy white bra. One more time, "Sure, why not?" He smiles. "I mean it more than I ever have." Before him, naked and smiling, is the most beautiful woman he has ever been with. He considers himself a good-looking man, but his level of perfection as a human specimen is not even close to the level she has achieved.

Her breasts are more beautiful than he imagined when she pulled her overalls up at the diner. Her nipples are erect and perfectly proportioned. Her pubic hair is thick and perfectly trimmed in a soft looking V. He sees the light from the living room coming through the gap between her legs where they meet the rest of her body. He imagines putting his hands together and running them up between her legs into that gap. He sees skin that makes him want to touch it. Her face and hair are already burned into his brain, and now so is the rest of her body.

He gets an erection before she is even to the shower door. He turns away, thinks about it for a second and turns back around. He is certainly ready for her to join him. She smiles as she enters the shower. She shuts the glass door gently. She places her hands right on him. "I'm glad to see you too." Mort isn't embarrassed at all. He pulls her around so her back is to him. He gently wedges his erection between her back and his stomach by clutching her arms and pulling them around him. He wants her to feel it on her back as the water runs down on them. He cradles her breasts with both hands. He slowly kisses her neck. The top of her head fits nicely under his chin. He can feel her hair through his beard stubble. He remembers how she could easily walk around without stooping today in her mine.

They take turns scrubbing each other with a soapy washcloth. During this cleaning exercise there is massaging, caressing and rubbing of various body parts as well. Like most big showers this glass box has a bench. Mort sits down in the middle of the bench never letting his gaze stray from Suzy's face. There is no talking. Their eyes are streaming good thoughts at each other. Without a word she straddles him, moaning softly as he penetrates her.

He is hard, she is wet. Perfect placement is not an issue. Suzy puts her arms around his neck and leans back into the shower forcing herself down on him. The water is coming down on her face. It is Mort's turn to moan. When she leans back into him, she exhales loudly. His palms are just the right size to perfectly cradle her butt cheeks.

Like her thigh muscles, her butt muscles are firm and defined. He gently pulls her to him. He then gently pushes her away. Down and away, down and away. She pulls his head down to hers. She puts her lips on his. She sticks her tongue in his mouth when he pulls her down. When he pushes her away, she pulls her tongue out. This is too much for Mort. He is about to say we need to slow down or I'm going to come, when she grabs him tightly and starts to move quickly. Her eyes are closed. She is tightening and loosening around him in a hurried rhythm softly moaning.

He pulls her in again. He puts his mouth over her right breast. Suddenly, with a force that almost makes him dizzy, he starts to come. He tries to keep from losing control. They are each into their own experience. They continue moving up and down in unison.

Both are gasping for air. Their slippery legs and arms are still entangled as they both crumple on the bench. Sitting side by side letting the water run on their feet, Mort stares at her breasts and smiles. He sits up straight, trying to stretch his back. He is still tingling. Every now and then he twitches involuntarily like someone pinched him. They embrace tightly and kiss one more time.

6 Twenty Pounds Later

Mort stands and rinses off quickly. His erection is still visible. He steps out of the shower. "I'll leave it with you. Would you mind if I laid down on the bed for a minute before I get some stuff out of my car to change into?" As Suzy shuts the shower door, "I will join you in minute." He wakes from a light sleep to see her coming into the bedroom with a plate of Swiss cheese slices and saltines. He realizes he is famished. The diner hamburger served him well, but it is time to eat something.

Suzy is wearing a black tee-shirt with black bikini underwear. Just as she is about to sit on the side of the bed next to him there is a loud pounding on the front door. They both jump. Suzy looks at him. "I will take care of this." Her face is serious. He can tell the glow of the last hour is dissipating fast. She goes to her purse before leaving the room and pulls out a chrome Colt 45 revolver. It has pink pearl grips. She spins the loaded cylinder looking at it like old west cowboys do before they go to a gunfight. She is familiar with this gun. This is not good.

Mort is wondering what the hell is going on. He had minimized the fact that she is married until now. After she leaves the room he runs to the bathroom and grabs his dirty clothes. He puts on his pants and shoes. He picks up his shirt. He puts his underwear and socks in his pants pocket. He can hear himself breathing hard. He sits on the bed on the side next to the bathroom to calm himself. He is ready to exit quickly through the bathroom window if necessary. He sits and listens.

He hears the knob turn as Suzy opens the front door. He hears the door hit the wall as it is pushed open violently. A man starts cursing loudly. He is in the living room now. He is yelling, "You bitch. You stole from me. Where is the bag from the safe?" There is a brief silence and then he starts again, "You fucking somebody here? Whose car is that out front? Not only did you take the turquoise, but you're fucking another guy aren't you?"

Mort can see their shadows as they circle the room screaming at each other. Suzy growls, "You never delivered. You never fucking delivered. You promised me so much. It would have taken so little. I wanted a baby and you told me to shut up and be happy with what I had. Fuck you." With that, Cal takes a swing at her. Suzy takes a step back. She has her revolver behind her back in her right hand. She pulls it out, pointing it at the floor.

Calmly she says, "The twenty pounds is in my trunk. Get it and leave me alone you fucker." That is enough for the loan shark. Mort hears Cal step heavy. He hears a slap. Cal bellows out of control, "You are going to pay for this." Just as Mort starts for the door to the living room, he hears one shot. It is muffled slightly so it must have been at close range. He hears someone crash into the coffee table.

He stops short of the door when he hears three more rapid shots. They are louder. He hears Suzy gasp loudly. He waits about ten seconds before he moves. He doesn't hear anything else from the room. He smells gun powder in the air. He peeks around the door frame and sees the loan shark with a box-looking pistol in his hand. He is slumped next to the coffee table. There is already a huge red spot on his chest. The color mixes with the big flowers on his gaudy Hawaiian shirt.

Mort sees Suzy slumped back against the couch. He stumbles to her. Her pistol barrel is still warm from the first shot Mort heard. She hit her irate husband directly in the heart. He was right, she was familiar with the gun. Even though the 45 hollow-point slug stopped the left side of his heart cold, Cal was not caught off guard. As he fell, he pulled his own pistol and fired three times in Suzy's direction. It was his last act of streaming consciousness. The second shot caught Suzy in the chest. It wasn't as clean as the shot that took him out, but it was going to take her out too.

Mort sits down on the floor next to her. Tears well up in his eyes. He holds her hand with both of his hands. She opens one eye and says something. He leans in to hear her, "I took that turquoise today from the safe at our big house. I was going to stow it in Vegas after I met with the attorney. I stop at the diner and meet you." She slows and gurgles. Her black t-shirt is now soaked in blood. "I told you he was an asshole." She tries to laugh, but a weak smile is all she can manage. "I have no family. I hate my husband's brother who will inherit my mine. I would rather you have that bag of turquoise." She raises her voice. "It's mine. I mined it. Get it out of my trunk when you leave. You will figure out how to handle it. It's worth a lot of money."

Mort wants to scream. "Stop. What are you talking about?" Her life is draining from her right before his eyes. With all the rabblerousing and dirty work for clients that he has done, he has never seen anyone die, much less someone he cared about. He thinks about taking her to the hospital in Austin, but it is too late. She looks at him one last time. "Thank you for a great day. Take care of my Lander Blue." With that, her head slumps forward. Mort is alone in the room.

He is shocked. He is blubbering to himself. The last three confusing minutes have turned what was probably the best day of his life into the worst. He stands. He looks around the room. His survival instincts kick in. They left the diner separately, so no one knows they met at the mine. They left the mine and then came here. No one knows he is here. Someone might have heard the shots. He knows from the coyotes he heard earlier that sound will carry across this open valley.

Mort forces his mind to slow down. He looks at Suzy's body. He thinks about using the phone in the kitchen by the refrigerator to call an ambulance. He quickly dismisses that idea. The first question will be who are you? Then later, why were you at Suzy's house when she and her husband are both dead? He thinks about going to the store at the turn off and calling an ambulance from the pay phone he assumes they have. He knows it really needs to be a hearse.

Any call will mean police. He doesn't want to wait around or answer any questions. He can get down the road and call the police then. He wonders if there really is a bag of turquoise in her trunk. He wonders if it really is worth a lot of money. If there is, Suzy gave it to him. It is his, even though no one else knows it or can verify it. He decides to get to Austin and then call the police station in Battle Mountain.

He goes to the bathroom and gets a wet hand towel. He quickly wipes down everything he remembers touching in the bathroom. He moves into the bedroom. He has not touched anything except the bed in there. In the living room he wipes down the arms of the chair he sat in for only a very short time. In the kitchen he wipes the counter. He dumps his water glass in the sink. He washes it with hand soap carefully. He dries it and puts it back in the cupboard with the towel. He stops and takes a breath, trying to remember if he touched anything else.

He takes one last look. Out of the corner of his eye he sees the unopened wine bottle sitting on the counter. It is a bottle of 1972 Stags' Leap Cabernet Sauvignon that they never got to drink with the cheese and crackers. He grabs it and puts it under his arm. He finds Suzy's car keys in her purse and puts them in his pants pocket for now. He wipes her purse down just in case he touched it. Feeling everything is taken care of inside, he stuffs the towel in his pocket with the keys.

He kneels by Suzy. He sees the "one of a kind" bracelet on her now limp wrist. He starts to take it but changes his mind. For some reason that feels like stealing. He hopes that what she told him in the mine about the power of turquoise is true. He is not religious, nor superstitious, but he feels like the stone will help her. He holds her hand for another instant. He still feels a strange kinship. That feeling is soon replaced with deep sorrow and a feeling of loss. He looks at her face for the last time. He sighs, "You may have been the someone I could have loved forever."

Mort stands and goes to the door. He puts the towel on the knob and opens it. He peers out cautiously as he opens the screen door. Seeing nothing except the dark outline of a few trees and three cars, he quietly but firmly shuts both doors and walks quickly to his car. He opens the passenger side back door and grabs his jacket on the seat. He holds the wine bottle in front of him for a moment like he is reading the label. He wraps the wine bottle in his jacket and lays it securely on the back seat. He pulls his socks and underwear out of his pant pockets and throws them on the floorboard.

He has wiped the keys already, so he holds them with the towel. He clumsily gets a key into the Cadillac's trunk. He opens it and sees the crate with the mining gear in it on the right side. The moon provides enough light for him to see a white heavy canvas bag on the other side of the trunk. It is not far in, so he knows she probably was the one that put it there. This is the Lander Blue turquoise. The bag is about four shoe boxes big. He picks the bag up with his left hand and hesitates. The last eight hours have changed his life. Is he stealing this turquoise or did she really give it to him? He quickly decides he doesn't care. He undoes the drawstring at the top and looks in the bag. It is too dark to see much. He feels shards in the bag like the one he put in his console, except bigger and individually wrapped in tissue paper.

He wipes the trunk edge and shuts it. He goes to the driver's side door of the Cadillac. He sees several fingerprints in the dust on the handle and around it. He knows some of them are his. Wiped clean it will look suspicious. He takes a handful of dirt and rubs it on the handle.

When he stops, there is a new coating that looks like the rest of the car. He wipes the keys again and holds them with the towel. He sets the bag of turquoise on his car trunk and turns back to the house. He goes back inside. He puts Suzy's car keys back in her purse.

He doesn't want to be in this place anymore. The gunpowder smell is gone but the room has a new ironlike smell now. He quickly leaves. He pulls the doors shut using the towel. He thinks aloud for the last time, "I hope I haven't missed something." If he has wiped everything clean, no one will know he has been there. His heart is heavy as he walks to his car. He leaves the inside light on and the window unit running. Sadly, he hopes someone finds them soon, but only after he is a long way down the road.

He puts the bag in the very back of his trunk. He stacks a couple of old frayed packing blankets in front of the bag. He moves his suitcase in front of the blankets. He is unsure why he is hiding it so diligently, but he goes with it. He doesn't want to think. He is still reeling from what just happened. Suzy's blood is drying on his skin. He grabs a clean white shirt out of his bag. He fluffs it lightly and throws it on. He doesn't button it. He keeps looking around to see if anybody is watching. The night is silent and dark. All he can hear is his head pounding. He wads the bloody shirt up and throws it in the trunk.

It's nine o'clock. It is totally dark to the east. He can see the convenience store light as he starts out. He turns on his lights and stomps on the accelerator squealing the tires as he turns onto 305. As an afterthought, he wonders how smart that is. He doesn't care, he wants to get away as fast as he can.

He stops at a 7-11 about ten miles north of Austin. It is the first sign of civilization he has seen on the road. He fills up the Mustang and buys a chili cheese dog and Coke when he goes into the store to pay. The drive has been through some of the strangest land he has ever seen. It is all shadows and jagged forms. There is no need to speed. He thinks there might be a better chance of seeing a UFO than another car on this road this time of night. That is good and bad. About five miles north of Austin he sees a sign for a Lake Austin one mile ahead. He turns into the deserted campground and parks next to a bank of three dumpsters.

The one on the far side of the three is almost empty. The piles of garbage on the other two closed lids indicate people would rather pile their shit on a full dumpster than walk the extra 15 feet. Mort goes to the end dumpster. He uses his Zippo lighter to ignite a paper bag into which he had stuffed the bloody shirt and the wrapper soaked in grease from the chile cheese dog. He throws it into the back corner of the dumpster. He does not smoke, but several of the women he has courted lately were smokers. His stomach is telling him he should have gotten some Tums for dessert. He finishes the Coke and drops the empty bottle into the dumpster.

The bag is burning now. The blaze happens quickly. The twelve percent humidity helps make that possible. He watches the fire until it burns out. He keeps looking around for approaching lights. It is just him and his dumpster fire. He sticks his lighter in as far as he can. All he sees is a pile of gray ashes. Some are permanently affixed in the corner by warmed dumpster goo. If someone saw it, they might wonder about it, but who was going to look in the dumpster? He doesn't turn the Mustang's lights on as he slowly rolls back onto the road. He looks both ways. If someone is watching, they aren't doing it with a light on.

He stops for one traffic light in Austin. He passes a lit-up filling station and sees a pay phone next to a Dixie Ice box. He thinks about it. "I'm sorry Suzy. I know someone will find you. I'm sorry. I'll make it up to you." He thinks about having to live with the decision he just made. He pushes the accelerator to the floor. The Mustang jumps and his head pushes back into his headrest. He turns the radio up loud and opens the windows. He sees a lone car coming his way on the distant dark horizon.

7 Suzy's Stone

Rattled and agitated Mort arrives in Las Vegas early the next morning. The lonely seven-hour drive on straight valley bottom highway offered plenty of time for him to process what happened. He thinks during a hundred-mile stretch that he has never traveled so far at night without having to dim his lights. When he is not obsessing about the cargo in his trunk, his mind circles back to the loss he feels for Suzy. He replays his steps as he left her house to make sure he didn't miss something. Constantly replaying this in his head exhausts him further. He drives for fifty miles sick to his stomach with the window open. He is too unnerved to stop.

He finally pulls into a filling station at the start of the Las Vegas strip and fills the Mustang again. He cleans the windows. It's hard to tell if the dirt or road bugs are worse. He thinks about the drive to the little mine and how dusty it was. Mort slowly pulls away from the pump to the end of the cashier's little building. He parks next to a new Ford truck. He cracks his front windows and leans back. He pushes his feet against the floorboard and stretches his legs almost standing up against his seat. He closes his eyes.

He keeps seeing Suzy come into the shower. He remembers how she smelled and how she was covered in dust. It is too much. He just wants everything to stop for a few minutes. He can't shake the urge to look over his shoulder. His concern is too burdensome to allow him to relax.

He places a fresh cup of coffee from the store on the top of the black pay phone and dials his friend's number. Six rings and finally a pickup. Based on the clearing of his throat before he says "Hello," he knew he woke Jack up. "Hey Jack, It's Mort." Jack wakes a bit more.

"Hey Mort. You here?" Mort looks at the ground like they are talking in person, "Sorry for the change in plans but I am sick. A cold or something. I just want to get back to Santa Fe." Jack is quiet for a second, "Man, that's too bad. I guess I'll have to continue without you." He chuckles as he clears his throat again. Mort hears him light a cigarette. "Win some money and have a drink for me. Catch you next time I'm through." They both say good-bye, agreeing to talk the next week.

Mort walks around his car several times raising and lowering his arms. He thinks, "Enough of Las Vegas." In an hour he is headed due east. He stops in Flagstaff and gets a chocolate shake at a Dairy Queen. He falls asleep in his car in the parking lot. He is awakened suddenly by three car loads of kids driving through honking and yelling. His nervous energy is about to run out, but he keeps going. A gas fill-up, a hamburger and home-cut fries, a couple of roadside-stop bathrooms and one more cup of coffee. He arrives in Santa Fe late the next night.

His crash-pad friend is gone for another few days, so Mort doesn't have to explain about returning early. He doesn't have to pretend like everything is okay. He hibernates. He only goes out for food. He stashes Suzy's bag in a closet in the guest room he is occupying. He leans his friend's three pairs of snowshoes in front of it. The second afternoon he is back, he removes the bag from the closet. He closes the blinds and turns on the overhead light.

He finds a large white towel in his bathroom and spreads it on the dining-room table. He carefully removes the contents one shard at a time. Each is wrapped in tissue paper. The towel is not big enough. He gets another and spreads it in line with the first towel, flattening all the wrinkles. There are a few chunks the size of the one he mined. Most are bigger. Their turquoise veins are thick and blue. He sees the mysterious black matrix in the veins. He picks up a shard and holds it up to the light. "Wonder how many turquoise stones this will make?" He realizes how little he knows about turquoise, and more importantly, how little he knows about what he now possesses.

After a week of reading, drinking tequila and only going outside into the back courtyard of his friend's house for short times, Mort visits the Santuario de Chimayo. He loves the winding drive from Santa Fe. As a boy he imagined that this valley of strange desert forms was the surface of Mars. He likes to sit on the old scarred wooden benches in the main room of the small yet famous church. The young priest that hangs out in his office at the entrance calls them pews. Mort tries to nod to him when he sees him. For some reason, it matters to Mort that he knows that he is there.

He steps carefully on the uneven rock floor as he enters. The priest's office is empty. He thinks about the thousands of people who cross this dark entrance into the small old chapel each year during Holy Week. He is humbled as he considers his situation compared to the many who come on crutches or in wheelchairs. He wonders if they get as confused as he is. A stand of small white candles to the right of the entrance is flickering. Mort thinks about lighting one of these candles for Suzy but continues to a pew. The bultos spaced along the wall are dusty and their paint is faded. They are imposing and he feels like they are looking at him.

He closes his eyes and thinks hard. He calls it praying. He is unsure as to whom or what, but it makes him feel better. This trip, he thinks hard about not getting caught. It feels selfish. He knows he has done nothing wrong, but it would be very difficult to explain why he has Suzy's bag of turquoise. He thinks about Suzy. He thinks about how meeting her has so unexpectedly affected him.

He hasn't reconciled her demise. It haunts him in the back of his mind, emerging occasionally to unnerve him. His mind wonders what it would have been like if he had met her when he was looking for his first love. Mort has never been prone to daydream or think what if, but he does. What if she had been Mel's mother? He shifts in the old pew as it creaks in the silence. He thinks about his five-year-old son. He has been a poor excuse for a father, but still he is not ready to play dad. That guilt will just have to wait.

He realizes as he sits overwhelmed with these feelings that he needs to change his life. He is not ready today, but somehow things seem clearer. After an hour he starts to lose focus. He nods off a couple of times. The stuffiness is too much. He exits the sanctuary though an adjoining prayer room. He pauses and looks at the crutches and photographs of loved ones, living and dead, adorning the walls. It is wallpaper made of peoples' pain, lives cut short or complicated by physical challenges. Mort is overwhelmed by the sheer number of them. Sadness and hope hang in the air.

The church is non-committal about whether miracles have really happened in this room. Many come hoping that they do. The light from the open exit door at one end of this room shines on a small low doorway on the other end. This door is the entrance to the "dirt room." Mort calls it this because of the hole that contains holy dirt in the middle of the small room.

People from all over the world come to take the dirt. Some share it with loved ones who are sick or need healing. They all hope it will help them. Many put it in plastic or tin souvenir containers that they purchase at the gift shop. Mort thinks about a small tin box containing holy dirt somewhere in his odds and ends. He has had it since he was a teenager. When he is alone in the room he kneels at the hole. He places the palm of his hand on the dirt. He speaks softly, "Please protect and help me."

He returns to his friend's house and continues his isolation. He waits every day for a knock on the front door by a couple of men in black suits from Nevada. After a couple of more weeks, he relaxes some. He has bought a Las Vegas newspaper a couple of times a week since he returned to see whether there is anything more about the homicides. After the initial story, he has not seen anything else. This time in isolation is the first time as an adult that Mort has sat and reflected about his life. He recognizes that he has no roots, no goals. He is a drifter.

Once his friend returns, Mort decides to stay in Santa Fe. He is not concerned about making money. He has always been resourceful enough to get by. He is concerned about being in the same town with a son he has not made part of his life. He knows he can change this, but he wonders if he will. He admits to himself that he doesn't really want to try. He doesn't care much for his opinionated sister either. This adds to his guilt. For now he will keep sending her a check each month so that she will continue caring for his son.

He rents a casita at the end of Canyon Road from an old Italian man who owns a tourist gift shop on the Plaza. Mort agrees to do odd jobs and keep the compound yard in exchange for the rent. A couple of weeks after he moves in, Niccolo Strada asks Mort if he can work in his store too. He needs a salesperson. For some reason he thinks Mort is good with people. "My instincts are good about what people can do." Mort has never had a permanent job. This is uncharted territory. That evening, after a bowl of mac and cheese topped with diced green chiles, he sits at the small dining table in his new abode looking into the dark courtyard.

He is surprised to think, "What would Suzy have me do?" He goes to bed without an answer. He accepts Mr. Strada's job the next morning. Gradually "Nicco" becomes a mentor and confidant. The first time

Mort and he convene in his cluttered office after closing with a bottle of tequila and a complimentary lime from the little market two doors down, he tells Mort, "People can't decide if I'm Hispanic or Italian. I can be both here in Santa Fe. You can be what you want to be too."

Mort's focus on his new job helps to stabilize his life. He enjoys the process of coercing tourists into buying things made by local craftsmen and artists. He knows something unique about each artist that he can tout to sell their merchandise. He reads each potential buyer coming into the shop. He can craft a story about the artist suitable for what he thinks the potential buyer wants to hear. He is a natural salesman. He turns down several lucrative offers to get back into his line of work transporting "confidential" cargo to an airport locker at a non-towered Denver airport or an upscale art gallery in Aspen.

The old man pays him bonuses when he makes big sales. His financial security doesn't relieve his concerns about being found. Each day that passes, however, he looks over his shoulder less. He lies in bed at night trying to decide if the bag eight feet away in his bedroom closet is a good or bad thing. When he is feeling most insecure, he wonders if he is a thief. Some nights he replays the fateful last seconds with Suzy over and over. She was to leave Battle Mountain with a plan and purpose. Their fateful meeting at the diner changed her plan. It is ironic to him that she was trying to get her life together and she is dead. He had no plan or purpose and he is alive.

Sometimes he sits up to clear his head. She gave him the bag, which was hers. He hears her fading last words, "You will figure out how to handle it." He sits up suddenly one cool fall night after tossing and turning for a torturous hour. He will keep the bag. He falls back to sleep, waking the next morning with a new sense of relief.

Mort learns everything he can about Lander Blue turquoise. He is surprised by how many traders have heard of the mine. He learns how cabochons are made. He recognizes that being a rich man is within his grasp, but he does not feel worthy. His promise to Suzy has changed his life. He has roots starting in a place and a real job for the first time in his life. It feels much better than his previous life.

He seeks out a lapidary named Oscar Three Bears. Oscar lives in an old shack by the Rio Tesuque near Nambe. Oscar is an old man who has worked turquoise all his life. Many of the craftsmen at Nicco's shop are proud to say that Oscar is their mentor. He has been responsible for a lot of the techniques the younger craftsmen use to work the turquoise.

More than a few of these young artisans sell their jewelry under the long Palace of the Governors awning.

Mort takes him his shard from the Lander Blue Mine. He asks Oscar to make a cabochon. Once that is complete, and he can see the stone, he wants Oscar to make a necklace for him. The old man takes about a week to refine the stone. It is eight carats exactly. The old man has never seen turquoise like this. He says that he can feel something special about the small stone. It wants to tell him a story. When Mort returns to see it, the old man holds it up to the light and asks, "Where did you get this?" Mort says, "It's Lander Blue. Northern Nevada. It was given to me by someone very special. It's Suzy's stone."

Mort designs the silver setting and chain. He thinks about every detail. He likes working with the old man. It is the first time he has designed anything. Mort knows some of Oscar's pieces are in the Museum of Indian Arts and Culture by the Plaza, so he thinks he must be good. Oscar makes each loop for the chain. Due to this Lander Blue stone's uniqueness and feel, Oscar feels honored to be the craftsman chosen to make this necklace.

Mort also likes driving to the old man's place. The dirt road running along the river is canopied with giant cottonwoods. There are places where the tamarisk trees line the river edges. They look out of place because of their thick plumy red tops. Every time he makes the drive, Mort feels reassured that he is doing something good.

When the necklace is finished, Mort puts it on in front of the old man. He does not say anything, but he feels the stone warming as it settles on his chest. He thanks the old man whose gray braids swing back and forth as he nods in agreement. As Mort turns to leave, the old man says, "The stone is warm isn't it?" Without waiting for an answer, he goes into his shack and shuts the door.

As his life normalizes in Santa Fe, Mort's concerns about being connected to Suzy's terrible end and the twenty pounds of Lander Blue fade into an occasional bad dream. Each day, however, he struggles with his role as a father. When he was on the road all the time it was easy to rationalize that his sister across town was raising his son. Now that he is working in town, he no longer has that excuse. He hasn't seen Mel for several years.

8 The Second M

In the late fall of 1968, five years prior to meeting Suzy, Mort is surprised to get a phone call one morning from a woman he dated for about two months. The Mort Hamilton luck had run out with this woman. At age thirty, his sex drive too often influenced his decision-making. With this woman, however, Mort decided the steamy part was not worth the crazy part. He ended the relationship. He has not heard from her in eight months, so he thinks he is in the clear.

He is, but not in the way he hopes. She erupts, "I left a package at your sister's. Finding you is like trying to find the fucking wind. You better call her quick. Don't ever call me again or bother me. I have a husband now. We don't want your baby or anything to do with it." Mort hears a loud click as she slams the receiver down.

He stands for a minute staring at the floor of his small apartment. He is living on the south side of Santa Fe. He has been saving money by doing odds and ends for long-time friends that need "confidential" help. He is on the road, in and out of town several times a week. The money is good because these friends are under the radar and pay in cash. He keeps his mouth shut and assumes risk as it is needed. He enjoys his life, or at least he thinks he does.

Mort knows it is early morning, but he grabs a Pabst from his refrigerator anyway. He drinks it slowly. When he is done, he calls his sister. Becky is waiting for his call. As soon as he says "hello" she starts in, "You son of a bitch. Did you talk to that worthless skank you introduced to me?" He tries to say "yes," but she starts in again condescendingly, "What the hell are you going to do?"

Then as if another person occupies her body, Becky says, "He is the cutest thing. He has your eyes and chin. She never gave him a name." Mort is unsure what to say. His sister is scaring him. There is a pause, which is unusual for a conversation with her. She blurts out, "He looks like a Mel." Mort laughs. "A Mel, huh. Two Ms. Thanks, sis. Mel it is."

Becky has been single for about a year. It was Mort who bailed her out of an abusive relationship. After a particularly unsettling evening of alcohol and pills, Mort intervened the next day. He meets her husband as he arrives at his work. Mort reminds the hungover asshole about the people he knows and what he can do. He puts his hands on his shoulders and leans his head in close as others are arriving in the parking lot. "You will file for divorce tomorrow. You will pay three hundred dollars a month child support. You will give my sister everything. You will leave town."

He pauses, releasing him slightly. "This is important. You will cease to exist immediately if you do not do these things in three days. Same goes if you ever quit paying child support." Mort steps back slowly and looks around. "Brush your fucking teeth too." Mort never tells Becky he did this, but she knows. He did it more out of duty to his only family than because he cared about Becky.

Mel didn't know until he was seven that Becky was not his real mother. That day came when he asked why he had to call her "Aunt Becky" when his sister and brother called her "Mom." She told him without hesitation that Mort was his father. She also told him his mother was someone he would never know unless Mort told him. The hard look on her face as she towered over him, accompanied with, "Don't ever ask again," was chiseled in his memory. He never asked again, but from that day forward, Mel did not like Mort.

Every month, without fail, Mort sends money to his sister. It is usually enough money to make Becky want to keep raising his son. Mel knows it is a payment. He wonders if it is the only reason she does it. For sixteen years, Mort pays his sister to raise Mel. He rarely visits and makes a big production out of it when he does. While he is there, he spends most of the time talking with Becky.

Mort never denies that Mel is his son, but Mel never fills the "son" place in his life. Mort gives up trying to muster fatherly feelings toward him. Their shitty relationship is not Mel's fault. It's his. He thinks about telling Mel how he feels about him. He rationalizes that Mel is too young and won't understand. Not that he ever cared what people thought, but he wonders if people will judge him for living in the same town as his biological son but having no relationship with him.

Mort starts volunteering at local events and donating to local charities when he can. His changed work ethic is not only reflected at Nicco's business, but also in these volunteer efforts. He eventually becomes the store manager. He learns about business costs and bookkeeping. The selling and the managing employees come easy to him.

One evening he had a brief fling with Nicco's daughter Nina. She came to town during the second year he was working at the store. They are introduced at the end of a busy day. Mort doesn't think much about it. She does. The next morning, she invited him to join her for drinks that evening at the Shed. He reluctantly accepted, questioning the wisdom of befriending the boss' daughter.

Mort is tired, but Nina is interesting enough. She is tan and in shape. After a couple of margaritas his concerns about mixing business with pleasure disappear. He wakes up early the next morning in a suite on the fifth floor of the La Fonda. He and Nina have a couple of more dinners the next week. Their relationship ends when he explains to her that he does not want her father to know. She is disappointed but understands. Soon thereafter she returns to Florida.

9 Life in Santa Fe

In 1976 Nina reappears to persuade Nicco to move to Florida to let her take care of him due to his declining health. He offers to sell the store to Mort and will finance the balance because he likes him. The deal is contingent on Mort coming up with ten thousand dollars. Nina calls late a couple of nights later. He recognizes her nasal voice. "Hi Mort." He politely says, "Hi." In a businesslike tone Nina says, "Father wants his money in twenty-four hours. He wants to leave town." She pauses. "You can't pass this spot up Mort. I hate to say this, but I need the money. Father said he would give me part of my inheritance when it's sold. I don't want to put it on the market. I want you to have it."

Mort has saved about six thousand dollars. He already knows none of his few friends have any money. He has also accumulated a few pieces of nice jewelry, but they are worth nowhere close to four thousand dollars. There is not time to volunteer for confidential work like he would have in the past when he needed cash. He doesn't understand why he wants the store so badly. About ten o'clock that night he takes Suzy's bag out of the closet for the first time in over three years. He stares at it for an hour. He falls asleep with it on the floor next to him.

He leaves the casita early the next morning and drives downtown. He looks up at the intricate cast stone frieze wrapping the top of the Lensic Theater as he walks to a hole-in-the-wall coffee shop down the street. He has always wondered why the architect chose to adorn the pediment with what look like pissed-off sea dragons. Their stubby seahorse bodies are paired looking in opposite directions, separated by turrets, with pointed tops and leaves. He gets two cups of coffee from the little shop and quickly walks back to his car without looking up.

Mort heads to a two hundred-year-old refurbished standalone adobe building nestled among a dozen aspens. The owner, a successful female art dealer about his age, had the good fortune to inherit early and big. She represents many talented craftsmen. She and Mort smoked cigarettes together one night outside the bar at the La Fonda after a benefit. They hit it off, but for some reason their relationship never grew romantically. Mort figured it out one night when he ran into her and her girlfriend at a liquor store in Albuquerque.

He is at her gallery on Canyon Road when she opens for business. As he is waiting, he recounts the conversation he had with himself earlier this morning. He decides that what he is doing is taking care of the turquoise. He hopes he can conduct this transaction without too many questions. He offers her the cup of coffee as he comes in the door.

She gladly takes it while looking him over. "To what do I owe the pleasure?" A bogus story about the shard's history, accompanied with a brief explanation about how he thought this unique turquoise could be cut into four two-thousand-dollar to three-thousand-dollar cabochons was his presentation. He stresses that each polished stone will be like nothing in her store or that she has seen. He sells hard. He even leans on their friendship. "Think what you can get if you mount them right." He knows she wants to ask where he got this stone.

Fifteen minutes later he walks out with forty hundred-dollar bills. His luck continues. That afternoon Mort buys the coveted store space from his former boss and landlord. He opens it as Hamilton's Southwest Jewelry on the Plaza to commemorate the 200th anniversary of the nation. From the day he opens, his goal is for the store to be an icon that is visited by people from all over the world. His few friends are impressed by his initiative and willingness to assume the work ahead.

After he occupies the space and begins remodeling, Mort installs a walk-in safe in the back of the store. After the safe is completed and the massive door hung, he buys a heavy-duty brown leather duffle bag. He puts the almost-twenty-pound white canvas bag of turquoise in this bag. He secures the handles with a new lock. The bag becomes a fixture in the safe. He is the only one with a key. The bag sits untouched for almost a quarter of a century.

Mort quickly aligns himself with several young local artists and craftsmen. Oscar Three Bears agrees to make one piece of jewelry every quarter. The pieces are sold before he ever starts on them. Mort makes a fortune capitalizing on their emerging skills and creativity. Several of his young artists became world-renowned for their work. Though Mort's past was shady he understands the importance of relationships and the value of trust. Throughout his career he sells his artists exclusively, many times acting as their agent for free. Problems were rare.

During this time Mel kept count of the number of times Mort hugged him. When he thought about it, he would instinctively hold up four fingers on his right hand. He curses Mort. Most times he wonders why he wasn't blessed with a normal father. He asks for a twenty dollar a week allowance when he turns thirteen. He looks Mort straight in the face in one of the few conversations he has with him. "You owe me this." That set the tone for their relationship from that time on. Mort paid an extra hundred dollars each month for Mel's allowance.

As soon as Mel turns sixteen and gets his driver's license, he hitches a ride to Michigan with a friend. He has saved some money running errands for the father of one of his best friends. He has learned not to ask questions and not draw attention to himself. He lies about his age and gets work in a Chevrolet manufacturing plant in Lansing. He is an expert at installing windshields on Impalas.

Mel moves back to Santa Fe with Darlene, his wife of two years, in 1990. He needs a job. Mort grapples with his role as Mel's father, but nevertheless needs help with the business. He will never tell a soul, but after fourteen years he has made more money than he can spend. He decides that the son he had paid someone else to raise could achieve financial security if he learned the business at Hamilton's.

This was exactly what Mel had hoped for. He and Darlene had tired of moving around. He could find short term jobs, but the moving was wearing them out. Darlene longed for a baby. The drumbeat only grew louder each time she saw a newborn. Mel wants permanency. He wants a routine and a guaranteed income. He wants to come home to the same house every evening. A more certain future revives Mel and Darlene's relationship. A romantic Valentine's Day leads to Michael's birth in November.

Once back in Santa Fe, Mel speaks to Becky only if it is at a family event or a chance passing in town. Becky and Mort feel like mere acquaintances to him. The other siblings moved to the east coast and Mel doesn't maintain contact. He attends Becky's funeral when she is killed by a drunk driver late one night as she was returning from one of the pueblo casinos in the area. Mel sits on the same row as Mort at her funeral, but it is on the other side of the church. Mort's relationship with Becky had been framed around paying her to raise Mel. They were not much more than acquaintances either.

Many consider Mort the catch of the town. His good looks, profitable business and his growing notoriety as a turquoise jewelry dealer make him appealing. He is seen around Santa Fe with familiar and unfamiliar women. He never marries. Along the way he confesses to a couple of his companions that his heart was taken in the 1970s by a twist of fate. Fact or myth, true or false, the story fleshes out Mort's reputation as a mystery man.

All things considered, Mort and Mel have a good working relationship. They trust each other as businessmen, because money is their bond. The sight of Mel makes Mort feel guilty almost every day. It doesn't help that Mel's aggressive side erupts on occasion. This usually amplifies Mort's guilt. Both feel the other is greedy. This serves as an invisible check and balance on their relationship and makes working together possible. They get back together out of necessity and largely selfish motives. Both secretly long for a bond that never materializes.

Mel does the ordering and negotiating with the native artists for Hamilton's. That is one thing Mort taught him to do well. That skill makes Mel a major player in the southwest jewelry market. Mel takes over Hamilton's from Mort in 2013. After that, he and Darlene make very little effort to see Mort. They send a commercially made birthday cake to him each year. It is symbolic. Mort takes it as an insult. He grouses about it while he eats the cake.

Mort loved hide and seek as a child. He read every Hardy Boys and Nancy Drew mystery published until he was in his twenties. Many summer evenings in his early teens were spent setting up treasure hunts. Neighborhood kids would yell and whoop as they scavenged the neighborhood on a hunt set up by Mort. As an older man, he practices magic tricks until his hands get so arthritic he can't bend his fingers fast enough. Stopping the magic is hard. He is especially good at making things disappear. He doesn't dwell on it but is ashamed to remember that the skill was used to make a couple of wallets disappear along the way in his early years.

His passion for myths, mysteries, riddles and treasure hunts combines with a crusty, sharp-edged humor. Mort writes mystery stories for the Santa Fe paper. They are submitted under the name "The Old Prospector." He writes one per year for a decade. The stories always involve a turquoise mine located somewhere in the southwest. In his seventies Mort has become a local celebrity. He is also one of the most respected and profitable business owners in Santa Fe. He even does magic tricks for tourists in the Plaza. His friends joke that he focuses on good-looking women he can flirt with. He assures them they are correct.

He is “The Magician” at the Riverside Assisted Living Center downtown where he lives now. He fills evenings for the residents with acts that include audience participation. Sometimes the results are comical rather than magical. Nevertheless, they became topics of hall conversation for days. These events are occasionally made more enjoyable by a bottle of Jim Beam that Mort supplies for his fans.

He uses Suzy’s stone in his last trick. As he bows, indicating this is his last trick for the evening, the necklace appears in his right hand when he straightens. He then puts it back on his neck saying, “I haven’t taken this necklace off for more than an hour since it was made.” He holds the stone out toward the audience. He winks. “This necklace is showing its age like me. Good night.”

10 The Third M

Michael is lying on his back in the center of an unmade king-size bed. He is looking up at the ceiling. The sheets are bunched and pushed to the end of the bed along with a worn patchwork quilt. The pillows are shoved up against the dark wood headboard. He has just finished smoking a bowl of some new sativa that he bought yesterday from his favorite dispensary on Cerrillos Road. He was one of the first recipients of a medical marijuana card in Santa Fe County in 2017. He has constant low-level pain from a fractured ankle he got while mountain biking about two years ago. Though the ankle was his medical reason for the card, he really got it because he likes to smoke pot sometimes, especially since he got back from Afghanistan.

The windows are open to the late spring morning which is still cool. Michael can hear faint street traffic and a lone dog barking. He is in the casita in his parent's compound. He has been living there since he finished his marketing degree online two years ago. His degree landed him a job helping to manage Hamilton's. Part of his compensation is getting to reside in the casita rent free. Completing his marketing degree took over ten years, once he started, much to the chagrin of his parents. Traveling abroad, a brief stint living in France on their dime and two tours in Afghanistan with the Marines delayed his completion. He had also taken advantage of the time in between playing carpenter and taking yoga classes.

Michael has not slept well, which is not uncommon. He received a text from a Marine buddy late yesterday evening that another member of his platoon had committed suicide. He feels fortunate that his problems are hidden for the most part. He has gotten past the fear of it consuming him. He doesn't like to call it post-traumatic-stress syndrome, which is rampant with his buddies. They all fight this battle in different ways.

Michael received a Purple Heart and a Silver Star during his second tour. They are wrapped in Kleenex in the pot drawer. He remembers the cold feeling he got after killing eight Afghan soldiers securing the safety of twenty US medical personnel. They were caught on a road without an escort. He patiently hid until the shits bunched together and were intimidating the personnel in the back of a cargo truck. He had loaded ten extra clips that morning. The extra three hundred bullets allowed him to attack solo. He was efficient at ejecting empty clips and loading full ones. It was as automatic as pulling the trigger. He was exceptionally good on the move. They weren't.

He mowed them down when they dragged the head doctor out of the truck. He killed the last two from ten feet away with his pistol as they tried to pull two of the nurses from their truck. It was the Wimbledon of armed combat right in front of the trapped medical personnel. He remembers their looks of horror and relief at the same time. Horror and relief. That was daily life on the ground in Afghanistan. As he reflects, the sativa begins to take the edge off just enough.

Michael's parents' compound is located off Garcia Street in the old part of Santa Fe. It was built in 1922 during a growth period in the town. It was restored completely by Mel and Darlene who bought it when Michael was eight. The grounds are magnificent because his parents pay a landscaper named Luis a handsome fee each month. Luis works in the yard constantly. The compound has been included in the annual Behind Adobe Walls Santa Fe Home and Garden Club Tour numerous times. It is worth a lot of money because of its proximity to the Plaza.

The background noise coming through the open window is accompanied by the smell of a ponderosa pine riding a light breeze through. The five-foot-tall brown stucco courtyard walls surrounding the entire property help keep most of the noise out. Like with many older houses in the neighborhood, the walls were intended to create a private sanctuary. For Darlene, they mainly provide a boundary to where she could plant things. The brown gravel paths that wind through her almost quarter-acre garden are the only surface areas not planted. The courtyard is lush this time of year. There are high-desert plants blooming in a race to see which can be the most beautiful.

The morning is dragging. Michael is tired of wasting time on Facebook and Twitter. He purposely has only a few friends or followers, depending on the social media choice. He doesn't consider himself very social. He runs with only a handful of people. Except for his few Marine buddies, most are local. He has known them since childhood. He doesn't have a girlfriend at the time, though he has been in two serious relationships. He ended both when he feared they were headed toward marriage.

His parents have been married for thirty years. He is impressed by this but suspects that each of them regrets what they gave up. He wonders sometimes if they wished they had tasted more of life before settling down and having him. When Michael was young, his parents would get into heated arguments in front of him. They would say things about each other that seemed awful. Many comments were about what they thought they had missed in life or what they thought they were not getting from the other one. Though he never tells anyone, these fights are the main reason he has run from marriage thus far.

His mother is drunk one evening when he is sixteen. She tells him that they wanted him, but his existence is owed to Mel giving in to shut her up after they moved to Santa Fe. He is not a good father because he does not know how to be. She blames Becky for being a shitty stand-in mother and Mort for being a no-show even shittier father. Mel never got the family bug from either of them.

Michael remembers her searing slurred words. "I'm sorry, but Mel comes first. You have to live with his resentment if you want to be supported." Michael never feels the same about her for telling him this. He never asks her directly, but he doesn't think she remembers saying it. He doesn't care enough to ask Mel if it is true.

Over time Michael has become indifferent about his relationship with his parents, and it is never mentioned. They exist together, without much else. It seems that no matter how hard he works or how well he does at the store, his father doesn't care. He expects it. Based on what he has seen of Mort's and Mel's sterile interaction, the family is used to putting up with bad personal relationships in order to have successful business relationships. Michael thinks of it as a mental sickness. He tries not to think about the hypocrisy as he takes advantage of his parents.

His phone pings. The text is from his best friend, Willow Gantry. "Wake up dude." Michael texts back, "I am. Are you?" Willow's mother, who was Zuni, died in childbirth, never telling anyone who the father was. Willow was adopted by white parents. Michael and Willow are the same age and started first grade together. The longest they have been apart was when Michael was in Afghanistan.

Michael calls him Will. Everybody thinks it is short for William. Women love it when they find out that Will is short for Willow. His dark skin and thick long black hair, combined with his unique name, have been the catalyst for many short-term relationships usually formed in bars. Michael has jealously witnessed this too many times to count.

They have been roommates off and on. They laugh and say they follow each other around. Before the pandemic they would get together and rail about all the shitty things that they thought the government was doing. The BS usually flowed with the help of a six pack and a couple of joints.

They both know that none of the things they hate really affect them that much. Michael's family has lots of money. Will's family has a successful business that must be worked to make money. Both have tolerable and sometimes fun management jobs with these businesses. Their similar paths include being heirs apparent to family businesses, the jewelry store for Michael and the paint store for Willow.

Today is Michael's day off. He is about to load his pipe again when his phone rings. It is a number from Albuquerque. When he answers, a man's voice says, "This is Officer Sanchez from the New Mexico Highway Patrol. Is this Michael Hamilton, son of Mel and Darlene Hamilton?" He pauses. Michael hoarsely says, "Yes." A short silence, "Mr. Hamilton, your parents rear-ended a semi coming up Bajada Hill early this morning. There was quite an impact. Based on the condition of their Mercedes, it appears your father was going very fast. It probably didn't register with them what happened. I am sorry sir, but they died instantly." He sighs and softly adds, "Sorry for the delay in notifying you. We have some of your parents' items if you want to claim them at our headquarters here in Albuquerque."

Because Michael lives right next door, he saw them leave yesterday morning to shop in Albuquerque and spa it up at the Sandia Resort. After all, they had been back in Santa Fe a full day from another vacation in Paris, Barcelona and Rome conveniently categorized as a Hamilton's shopping trip on their income taxes. He had waved to them, but barely looked up. His mother had texted him their plans.

He has not had a conversation with either of them in three months. They left the store for him to run while they went to Europe, though Mel checks the inventory online so he can see how sales are going. He communicates by email when he sees a problem or has a question. Michael assumes he has done a good enough job to satisfy Mel, so there is no need for communication. As usual, they would contact him by text or phone if necessary. Two days after they return from Europe, they are gone. Michael feels some guilt because he is not sure he knows how to miss them.

11 An Inheritance that Wasn't

That afternoon in consult with Dr. Charlene Fernandez, the Riverside on-call physician who had known Mort since he moved to the facility, Michael decides to postpone telling Mort about the accident until the next day. He knows that within a few days Mort will see the story in the local newspaper anyway. Sadly, the real reason Michael debates not telling Mort is that he suspects he will not care. He finds himself feeling much the same.

The next day he starts thinking about what to say to Mort as soon as his feet hit the fur rug next to his bed. When he arrives for their regular afternoon meeting, he is still not sure what to say. On the bike ride over he struggles with his own efforts to deal with his guilt. He knows any reconciliation of his feelings isn't going to happen today. As he sits down in Mort's room, he tears up. He does not know why. This is not how he wants to start the conversation.

Mort looks at him. "Uh-oh. You are supposed to be the one breaking hearts, not the other way around." Michael takes a moment. "I wish it was that. I don't want to be the person delivering this information Grandfather, but Mel and Darlene died yesterday morning when they ran into a semi on Interstate 25 coming back from Albuquerque. The highway patrol pieced this together. Mel was driving fast. The tanker's lights were out. He just didn't see the truck." Michael stops to breathe. He lowers his voice and quickly says, "They died almost instantly."

Mort looks past him. He closes his eyes. He shoulders droop. He puts his chin on his chest. His clean black polo shirt with the always-buttoned top button bunches under his morning stubble. He breathes deeply three times. He looks up at Michael. Mort's eyes reveal nothing. He settles into his chair. "That was unexpected. What are your plans for today?"

Mel and Darlene had made provision in their will to have a grand funeral if they died together. The family lawyer and funeral home handled everything. Michael picks Mort up about an hour before the service is to begin. They are only ten minutes away from the Scottish Rite Temple, but Michael wants to spend some time with Mort before the service.

Once Mort gets into the worn Jeep Grand Cherokee and fastens his seat belt, Michael slowly makes his way out of the parking lot. They drive by the Temple on their way up the ski basin road. Twenty minutes later they arrive at Aspen Vista. There is no traffic. Neither speaks until they are parked facing the vista view. They are three thousand feet higher now. There is a breeze coming through the open windows. This is one of Michael's favorite places.

They look at each other as they are sitting. Mort lightly pats Michael's leg. "I am sorry this happened." Michael expects him to say something about Mel and Darlene, but Mort says, "I didn't think you would get Hamilton's so quickly. I am sure you will be fine. You can ask me anything you need to know." Michael looks ahead. "I guess I haven't thought about it too much. I'm going to have to learn some things quick." They sit a few more minutes and then head down the mountain to the funeral.

The big room in the middle of the Temple is set up to accommodate the town. The temporary pews are half full when they arrive. Mort is dressed in a crisp black suit without a tie. His white shirt is perfect. His initialed cuff links show when his jacket sleeves pull up. Michael has the exact same outfit on, minus the gold cuff links. They sit in a pew at the front. Both are relieved that they cannot see the attendees behind them, as most folks would be surprised to know what they are thinking and feeling. The matching ornate silver caskets are closed, but head to head and covered with giant white rose wreaths. The giant room quietens as the organist begins playing *Amazing Grace.* Mort and Michael make it through the funeral and burial site ceremonies without showing any emotion.

A week after his parents' funeral Michael gets a call from Burt Cromley, Attorney at Law. Burt is another established Santa Fean who made his mark during a time of growth. He arrived in Santa Fe about the same time as Mel and Darlene. He is Mort's attorney too. He has attended many of the local social and philanthropic functions for the same purpose as Michael's parents; to hob nob with the wealthy and create connections that have endured.

Michael remembers that Burt has a gravelly voice. He thinks he sounds like a mafia character. He recognizes Burt's voice as soon as he hears, "Hi Michael." He continues, "This is Burt Cromley. I need for you to come to my office to review your parents' will." They exchange pleasantries. Burt ends the call. Michael doesn't know what to expect regarding what his parents left him.

Part of him suspects nothing. Part of him cares, part of him doesn't. Contemplating this now, he realizes this is not the first time he has thought about it. Most of the time he ends up thinking about what he deserves based on the relationship they had. No matter what they leave him, it doesn't change his feelings about his parents.

After tossing and turning all night, Michael calls Burt's office and sets up a time to meet after lunch. Oralynn Lowry, Burt's legal assistant, seems nice and efficient on the phone. He arrives at Burt's office early. Oralynn is talking on the phone when he opens the door to the suite. She stops talking, looks up and smiles. Her thin lips don't part, like she is hiding something in her mouth. Someone on the other end of her phone gets an abrupt, "I gotta go." She puts her phone down on her desk and stands.

As she stands, she straightens her skirt. Her dark brown hair is pulled up in a bun on the top of her head. The pile of hair is held with a large silver cross hair pin. Her blouse is loose linen. There is something wrapped around her neck that looks to Michael like it would be hot. She blushes when she steps from around her desk and immediately apologizes for being barefoot. Her skin is very pale, a nice contrast to her dark hair. She does have a bright red heart with a yellow arrow piercing it tattooed on the inside of her left ankle. This is the only thing that looks unique about her.

Michael sits down in one of the stereotypical lawyer office royal blue Queen Anne wingback chairs against the wall. He is directly facing Oralynn now. He feels he needs to make conversation. "How long have you worked for Burt?" She smiles. "About ten years. I completed my court reporter certification, but just didn't like doing it. Mr. C was good enough to offer me this job." Michael adds, "He has been the family lawyer for a long time from what I understand." She goes back to her chair. She looks at him and politely says, "One of the things I like about this job is I get to meet prominent people from Santa Fe like your grandfather and father." Michael wonders for a minute if she thinks he will be a prominent person in Santa Fe someday. They make small talk for a minute more.

He smiles and puts on his Ray-Ban sunglasses. Before he can start daydreaming, Burt comes in the door from lunch smelling like cigar. He apologizes. "I had an opportunity to sit outside for a minute and take a couple of puffs." Michael doesn't mind. They sit down in his office. Once Burt gets past the will format explanation, he sheepishly reveals that Mel and Darlene left him one-hundred thousand dollars. He can have it in a year, if he doesn't do anything to embarrass the family's name publicly. He can live in the casita until the house is sold. It will be put on the market in three months. The past decade of him living on the family dime constitutes the remainder of his inheritance.

Mel and Darlene left their total estate of four million dollars cash, plus the proceeds from selling their compound, to their favorite charity. A building will be built in their name on a small religious university campus. Michael is not surprised. It is a last, somewhat expected, slap to his face. Burt continues reading. "Hamilton's is to be immediately sold to the highest bidder." He tells Michael he has already put the wheels in motion on this.

The selling of the store does surprise Michael. Burt continues. "The highest bidder is a local Arab man named Omar Johnson." Michael knows him. He changed his name from Haatimm Akram twenty years ago when he came from Saudi Arabia to join his American wife in Santa Fe. Though he Americanized his name, he lives by his strongminded and generous original family label.

Michael tries not to be resentful, as it doesn't feel right. He fights his feelings of hypocrisy for taking what he can get, but there is a new reality. His future right now probably includes no job and not much cash flow. In the background is also the fact that he will soon not have a place to live.

Omar has several other stores around the Plaza. By having his children run them he has created a potential lifetime job for each child. Omar manages their businesses enough to make sure they don't screw things up. Michael has always respected him as a businessman and has always liked his gentle, yet firm approach with his children.

Omar is most interested in the real estate, but not so much the jewelry. It is sad to Michael. The location will always be on the Plaza, but the merchandise and clientele built up over the years will change. The connection between owner and craftsman is what created the value of Hamilton's. The merchandise that they were able to find, and the quality of the silverwork and turquoise, were the foundation of the success. The money from the sale of Hamilton's is to go to the Santa Fe Food Bank. Michael is good with this, if he is not to get the store.

As he stands to leave, Michael asks Burt, "When did they prepare this will?" Burt verifies the date on the last page. "About six months ago." Michael looks at the floor realizing it was before they left for Europe. He can't hide the look on his face, so he turns and heads to the door. He opens it and looks back to thank Burt. Burt comes to him with his hand extended. They shake and he earnestly says, "I am sorry for your loss Michael. Hang in there." Michael is looking at the floor as he goes through the lobby. He hears Oralynn say, "Have a good day." He doesn't want to reply, but he looks back. "You too."

In the courtyard outside the side entrance to the parking lot he sits down at a four-top cast iron table. His foot scuffs over a padlock securing a chain to the table base. The shade of the giant elm trees is welcome. He hears the leaves blowing gently. What he received from his parents does not surprise him. The way it makes him feel does. He can't believe how premeditated and vindictive it feels. Did they want to hurt him? The will update was recent, which means there is no doubting what their feelings were about him.

After processing what he just learned and how it is going to change his life, Michael thinks about whether he will tell Mort. The selling of Hamilton's will be a blow. Michael knows Mort thought it would always remain in the family. Once again, he will see it in the paper eventually. That afternoon he tells Mort about the will. Mort is openly pissed about Hamilton's. "That son-of-a-bitch promised me he wouldn't sell the store. He thought he would outlast me." He mumbles under his breath, "That changes some things." Michael hears him, but he has no idea what he is talking about. They talk about the coronavirus. Mort hopes it doesn't infect the facility. Neither knows it, but their face-to-face meetings will have to end in the next three weeks.

12 THE TREASURE HUNT

Four days after Michael tells Mort about his parents' will, Mort takes an early-morning walk over to his house on Acequia Madre. He carries a paper bag which contains a small box wrapped in shrink wrap. He has spent the last four days using his knowledge and riddling skills to put together a treasure hunt for Michael. He is energized by the new challenge. It has been fun thinking about how Michael will process the clues. Mort has no doubt he will figure it out. It gives him pleasure thinking about how much Michael's life will change then.

As he walks, Mort wonders as he has so many times before, what it would have been like if Michael had been his son. Michael thinks like he does. He approaches things like he does. This morning Mort feels a sense of urgency. Mel and Darlene dying has provided a jolt of reality about his own mortality. The virus is getting worse. Mort feels his vulnerability.

He doesn't go into his house. He tries to remember the last time he was there. He can't. He grunts, "I don't care." He doesn't want to rent it. He doesn't want anyone else in it. He would have to go through his stuff then. He smiles. "A price Michael will pay for getting this compound someday." He grabs a shovel from a hook on the back portal. He spends thirty minutes in the old well house grunting and sweating.

Mort emerges with dirt on his knees and sweat stains under his arms. He walks over to a table underneath the gazebo that he built twenty years ago. "Not bad for an old man." He sits looking at his yard and lets the breeze dry him off before he walks back to Riverside. He hurries to his room so no one will see him dirty.

Two days later Mort and his old friend, Busy Johnson, embark on a five-day road trip. Busy is eight years younger than Mort. His real name is Solomon Elijah Johnson. His family was one of a handful of black families in Santa Fe when Mort started Hamilton's. They met volunteering at the Food Bank. They found that their backgrounds were similar. Their interest in helping other people had been sparked by guilt over things they had done in their pasts that they would change or do differently.

Busy's grandmother gave him his nickname. As a young man in his twenties he always had multiple girlfriends. She would smile when he came around and tell his mother how busy he must be. The name stuck. He liked it. His real name was too biblical for him. He was Mort's driver, bodyguard and bagman for two decades during Mort's heyday in Santa Fe. Now he is one of Mort's best friends.

Busy has a new silver 2020 CT-6 Cadillac. He is ready to take it on the road. Mort tells Michael they are going to Las Vegas before they shut it down for the virus. "I can't do anything but watch, but I want to see a beautiful naked woman, by myself, for about an hour, before I die." He winks. "About five hundred dollars-worth of woman."

As they had planned, Busy picks Mort up right at eight o'clock at the entrance to Riverside. Mort is dressed in black slacks and a black polo with Suzy's stone on its chain around his neck. Not bad for an old white guy Busy thinks. He always tells Mort, "Clothes won't change your ugly white face." He is dressed in black slacks and a red polo with a thin gold chain visible. Shiny black belts and shoes complete their ensembles. They both still pride themselves on looking good. They laugh about "why" every time they see each other.

Busy has been married to the same beautiful Latina woman for twenty years. She is a local favorite, still singing at events and bars. Busy jokes, "There is more to the singer than there used to be, but she can still belt it out." Mort likes that Busy's thoughts never stray too far from his wife.

After Mort settles into the front passenger seat, he pulls out two rolls of one-hundred-dollar bills. He looks at Busy. "We are going to have a good time in Vegas my friend." Busy smiles and puts the Cadillac in drive. Mort wonders as they leave the covered entry of Riverside if this is the last road trip he will make. He thinks, "If it is, make the most of it." He loves the tree-lined streets in the old part of Santa Fe. The giant cottonwoods and aspens provide a perfect backdrop for the adobe walls covered with flowers and vines. As a boy, Mort would make up stories about the people who lived behind these walls.

Once they turn west onto Interstate 40, Mort turns down the radio and looks at Busy. "We are going to go Battle Mountain, Nevada, north of Vegas, on this trip too. I can't tell you what I am doing right now. You cannot tell Michael about anything we do except what we do in Vegas. For all he knows we spent the whole time in Vegas. I hope Michael will be able to tell you about this if I die. If you are on your deathbed and still care, I will tell you." Mort smiles at Busy. He looks out the window like "That's it, don't ask me anything else." Busy knows Mort. His cryptic message and his mysterious approach to their trip do not surprise him.

They cross the bridge bypassing Hoover Dam as they arrive in Las Vegas twelve hours later. Mort remembers seeing the giant turbine room underneath the dam as a boy. His father and mother had disguised a gambling trip to Vegas as a family vacation one summer. A gratuitous visit to the dam was included for him. The rest of the time he spent in their room or at the swimming pool. That vacation was memorable too because it was the first time as a boy that he was around lots of scantily clad girls and women in bikinis. He smiles as he remembers that he found it stimulating in a way that he had not experienced before.

Both are tired and ready to get out of the car. A brief stop in Flagstaff for lunch and two gas stops had made for an uneventful trip. They check into their reserved rooms at the Rio. Mort wants to stay there because they have tickets to Penn and Teller the next night. He has been kidding Busy the whole trip about doing the Voodoo Zipline.

They spend the next day eating, gambling a bit, and mainly watching people. They ride the High Roller and talk about how Las Vegas has changed. They take a nap that afternoon before the magic show. Mort has reserved front row tickets. He is a big fan of Penn and Teller. Before his hands got stiff, he could do many of the sleight of hand tricks they do. Toward the end of the show Penn asks for a volunteer from the audience. Without hesitation Mort stands up, and without an invitation, heads for the stage. Both magicians look at him. No one moves to stop him, so he continues.

He is on stage smiling at the audience. They have Mort verify for the audience that all is normal. Penn has him stand still and straight, facing everyone, while he pulls six geese out of thin air from behind him. He quickly goes from Mort's right side to his left side. The audience claps and cheers as the geese wander off backstage where they know a nice treat is waiting for them. Penn thanks him and reaches to shake his hand. Mort reaches toward him and a bouquet of flowers appears. Even Penn is surprised. Mort hands them to him. The audience erupts in applause like it was supposed to be part of the show. Mort shakes his hand, turns and bows quickly. He has just fulfilled a top item on his bucket list.

The closest Mort comes to a naked woman during their visit is a picture on a card that a young tattooed man tries to shove in his hand as they walk on the strip their last evening. They get up the next morning to continue their journey north. After a light breakfast at the hotel and a stop at a Starbucks on the way out, they head west. When they are almost out of town, Busy comments, "Vegas does a nice "Starbuicks" latte." Mort has heard this from Busy since the first Starbucks opened in Santa Fe. He laughs like it's the first time he has heard it. "I needed it." He then continues looking ahead. He is trying to figure out what to tell Busy about their next stop.

About an hour later Mort breaks the silence. "Put the Battle Mountain Diner in the map app. That's where we're headed. We should get there in time for an early supper." He expects Busy to say something or ask a question, but he is quiet. Mort continues, "We will spend the night there and return to Santa Fe in the morning." All Busy says is, "Lots of driving Mort. Must be important."

They arrive at the diner mid-afternoon. There are a few cars in the parking lot. Mort remembers the shade tree. It is gone. Its spot is all asphalt now. Mort looks at Busy. "Forty-seven years ago the bacon cheeseburgers were really good here." Busy nods and notices that Mort is clutching the turquoise piece around his neck. He looks preoccupied. Busy gets out. In his opinion it has been a boring-as-shit drive and he wants out of the car.

Mort stops at the diner door. Busy almost runs into him. Mort puts his hand on his back pocket and pretends like he is reaching for the comb he quit carrying twenty years ago. He pushes the door open and holds it for Busy. Busy follows him to the bar. All the stools are open. Mort picks a specific one and sits down slowly looking at it. Busy sits on the one to his right. Mort turns around facing the tables and booths. It is still the same as he remembers it, except for some new pictures.

They order bacon cheeseburgers and chocolate shakes. They eat quietly and hungrily. Mort does not want to show his emotions, but the memories are bombarding him as he sits there. Forty-seven years ago, he had just finished his burger when Suzy came into the diner and his life. Those next six hours with her had changed him forever. Not only was he smitten with her, but she was the catalyst for his successful career.

Mort pays the bill. He generously tips their waitress this time. Busy goes to the car to turn on the AC. Mort takes his time leaving the diner, thinking about the last time he left. He was going to look at a mine for the first time in his life. He was also doing it with a beautiful woman that he had just met. He smiles. There is no better way to meet a woman than fate. These folks with their dating apps should try it.

Mort and Busy sit in the car quietly until Busy breaks the silence. "That was pretty good." Like a teenager, he belches to accentuate the comment. "I do have Tums by the way. I won't ask how the hell you ended up knowing about this place. Where to?" Mort looks at him. "If my Googling and investigative work is correct, put in the Lander County Hilltop Cemetery." Busy does it. They exit the parking lot and head through town.

The tires ripple in unison as they roll over the old brick main street. About half a mile later, they turn east and immediately start up a hill. They can see the cemetery's white wrought iron arched entry in the distance. They go through the gate onto a gravel road that turns into three smaller roads.

There is a storeroom or utility building in the middle of the cemetery. Mort has Busy park on the front side parallel to it. They are the only ones in the cemetery. As he opens the door to exit, "I know this is silly, but would you mind staying in the car?" Busy shrugs. "Okay." He sinks down into the plush leather seat and leans it back. He turns on the radio. Mort goes to the trunk and opens it. He gets a small black leather bag out and takes it with him. If he is correct, Suzy's grave is next to the grove of pines about a hundred feet from the building. Mort walks slowly that direction making sure no one has come into the cemetery.

He finds her gravestone where he thinks it is. He sees 1973 etched on the simple grey granite marker. He thinks of the crazy night again. The memory seems heavier here as he puts his hand on the top of the rough stone. He tells Suzy that he loves her. He wishes it could have been different. He looks back to make sure Busy can't see him. He takes a tape out of his bag. He measures a couple of directions putting marks on the ground with the heel of his shoe. He looks around one more time and grabs a small spade and a pair of gloves. He puts on the gloves and gets on his hands and knees.

He quickly digs a hole in the ground about eight inches deep. He takes a plastic pill bottle about four inches tall and one and a half inches wide out of the bag. "I have plenty of these," he mumbles. He puts a folded piece of paper in a heavy sandwich bag into the pill container. He puts Clue 2 in the hole and covers it. He stomps the ground a couple of times to make sure the hole is full. He brushes the ground with his hands until he is satisfied that the hole is not visible. He takes the gloves off and puts his tools back in the bag. He looks around one last time.

Mort stands in front of Suzy's marker. Staring at it like it's alive he softly says, "I probably won't be back to see you. I haven't done anything with the bag. It's still hidden." He stands straight. "I am going to give it to my grandson. Hope that is okay." Mort feels silly for an instant. He rubs Suzy's stone. Maybe he wants to believe it, but he thinks the stone is warmer than usual. He feels connected to it. He is relieved. "Okay." He continues, "Thank you. The gift you gave me has turned out to be much bigger than a bag of turquoise. I wish we could have found our lives together." He lifts his sunglasses and wipes his wet eyes quickly. Clue 2 is ready to be found.

He puts the tool bag back in the trunk waking Busy when he shuts it. Mort opens the passenger side door. "Get a good nap? Thank you. I want to stay here for a bit." Mort sits down as Busy fixes his seat. He rolls the windows down and they sit silently. This clue is the reason to come back to Battle Mountain. Mort has thought about this day many times. They sit for thirty minutes. One car comes down the road but turns before it reaches the cemetery. Mort is finally satisfied. "Let's go to the Lost Mine Motel."

After a restless night on a mattress that feels like too many miners had slept on it, Mort finally gets out of bed. He calls Busy. They meet by the dusty Cadillac. Neither is hungry. They start the drive back to Santa Fe. "Take Highway 305 south out of town to Austin." They drive until the Prospectors convenience store comes into view. It has a new front and an awning over the four gas pumps. The old prospector is still in the same place. Mort softly says, "Please take a left after the store and go another half-mile or so east." Mort could remember Suzy saying those words before they left the mine.

Mort is grateful that it is gone when they get to where Suzy's little house was. He does not share with Busy what they are looking for as they drive slowly by. After another quarter mile, "Go ahead and turn around. Let's make some time." Busy finds a wide spot about a hundred yards further on. He turns around. Mort is glad to be back on the highway and headed home. They decide to stop in Kingman, Arizona and spend the night after driving eight hours. Both are glad to get back to Santa Fe before dinner the next day.

That evening Mort calls Michael. "We are back. She was a beauty, that's all I will tell you. Didn't win any money but got to be onstage with Penn and Teller." He tells Michael about his magician dream come true. He affectionately tells Michael good night. His eighty-two-year-old bones are tired. He is relieved. This was the hardest clue. He gets in bed after a hot shower, thinking about their quick trip. He wraps Suzy's stone in his left hand and drifts off to sleep thinking about the next clue.

13 The Rest of the Clues

Two days later Busy picks Mort up about seven o'clock in front of the center. Mort spends the day before resting and preparing Clue 3 and Clue 4. Icy Hot has been his friend. He is ready to go. Mort has Busy drive to the nearest gas station and pays to fill the Cadillac. He hasn't told Busy anything about where they are going other than to plan on an eight-hour day. Once the car is full, they stop by "Starbuicks" and get lattes.

As they leave the drive-thru lane, Mort adjusts his seatbelt. "Go to Gallup if you would. We are going to the Bruce Magnum Trading Company." Busy clears his throat. "Yes Mr. Daisy." He loves to do that to Mort. He knows it is not the way Mort feels, but it puts him on the defensive every time. To Busy's disappointment, Mort does not react to his comment.

Interstate 40 runs straight into Gallup, New Mexico. Mort has driven this road numerous times when it was called Route 66. He and the owner of the trading post they are heading to this morning have lots of history. They made a fine art of turning an afternoon of drinking into a night of drinking. They were regulars at a local bar around the corner from Bruce's store when they were younger men.

After a few minutes of silence Mort says, "Sorry Busy. I am thinking about Mel. We will go by the scene of the accident on the way back, you know." Busy quickly cuts in, "I know Mort." Mort continues resolutely, "It seems my sadness is more for Michael's loss than mine. I didn't even like Mel. Haven't for a long time. Truth is, I deserve the heavy burden after being such a bad father to him." They have talked about this before. Busy is quiet. He feels sorry for Mort. "Whether it's to make amends or not, I love Michael like the son Mel wasn't. I don't want him hurt." Mort is quiet. He shifts in his seat. Busy stomps the Cadillac's accelerator. Their heads press back in their headrests. "Let's get us some

Gallup, Mort."

Gallup is the regional center of the retail and food universe for everyone living in or visiting the area. Weekends are a conglomeration of Navajo, Zuni and Hopi Indians coming into town to shop for the week. The tourists, in and out of town all the time, are drawn to the trading posts. It is a veritable mecca of southwest silver and turquoise jewelry, paintings, pottery, rugs and blankets. As they pass the storefronts, Mort thinks about some of the deals he made and the money they made him. One thing he has always done right was to share the money generously with the artists and craftsmen. Those meaningful deals he got to make are gone. For most everyone involved in the business today, it is about making money.

They pull into a parking spot in front of Magnum's Trading just as it is opening. In the front window is a giant piece of polished turquoise sitting in a black wire stand. Written underneath on a sun-faded white piece of cardboard are the words, "The largest natural lunch box turquoise cabochon on display in New Mexico, American Mine, Old Hachita, New Mexico, 1882." The color of the stone is neither blue nor green. It is as though it could not decide.

A small dark-haired Indian woman is flipping the sign to OPEN on the door to start the day. The street is starting to get busy as Gallup wakes up. Busy waits to open his car door until a truck hauling cattle slowly rumbles by. Mort waits at the entrance with his hand on the door pull. He opens the door for Busy and they both go in.

The small woman looks up and smiles instantly. She comes to Mort and hugs him with her head in his chest. "You big guy. Have they had you locked up in that home in Santa Fe? Bruce will be so glad that he came in with me today. He has felt bad and he worries about this virus thing." She stops and looks at the back of the store as a white-haired thin man walks slowly toward them. He has on a white cowboy hat tilted back just enough that his eyes are visible. The red cowboy shirt he is wearing is pressed, but too big. He extends his hand to Mort but decides instead to hug him. After they embrace, "Bruce and Lulla, this is one of my best friends, Busy Johnson. We came down together this morning."

They move away from the door. They stand next to a counter covered in small blankets. The glass case below is full of turquoise jewelry. Bruce sees Busy looking in the case. "You don't want any of that, it's all stabilized and some barely turquoise. If you are interested, I have some real turquoise in the back. I don't keep it out because the tourists think it's too expensive. Then they say on Yelp or some bullshit the store is too expensive. I wait to see what kind of customer they are before I bring it out."

Mort smiles at Bruce. "Show him what a real piece of turquoise jewelry looks like." Bruce pulls up the right sleeve of his cowboy shirt revealing a twenty-five carat Lander Blue stone set in a gold bracelet. The black matrix covers the slightly irregular oval stone. The bracelet slides around on Bruce's sinewy wrist. Bruce smiles. "It's part of our retirement. It's worth about thirty thousand dollars today, and I have three people waiting for me to die so they can try to get it from Lulla." They all laugh.

Mort excuses himself to go to the lone bathroom at the back of the store. It has been a couple of years since he has been in the store, but not much has changed. Merchandise hides behind other merchandise. Bruce's life has been dedicated to collecting pretty much anything Navajo. His collection is worth several million dollars, so retirement is not really an issue. Mort closes and latches the old white wooden door. The glass in the small window to the alley is cracked. It has a metal bars on the inside, but the window frame is so rotted the metal bars are for show. Mort waits to flush the commode.

As expected, the two inches by two inches hole to the right of the sink (made when someone jerked the soap dispenser from the paneled wall probably fifteen years ago) is still there. Part of the stud is showing. Mort removes a folded taped-up plastic bag containing Clue 3 from his pants pocket. He sticks it in the hole. About two inches above the opening, out of sight, he thumb-tacks it to the stud. He stands back and looks at the hole. Nothing looks different. He hopes the hole stays the same for at least another five years. He flushes the commode and washes his hands with soap from a plastic dispenser sitting on the old porcelain sink.

He rejoins the group. They talk for another fifteen minutes about old times. Mort invites them to lunch. They have some folks from Tucson coming by. They need to stay to meet them. Mort thinks about another Gallup habit. "Is Earl's still as good as it used to be?" Bruce knows what Mort is thinking. "They've redone the building, but the fry-bread tacos still hit the spot." That sounds pretty good to both. Mort and Busy say goodbye and prepare to start the drive back to Santa Fe. A few blocks from Magnum's, they pull into Earl's to get an Indian taco.

Busy turns the radio up as they drive up Bajada Hill on the return to Santa Fe. Loud noise disrupts his thoughts. Maybe it will disrupt Mort's. Neither says anything as they drive over the burned spot in the asphalt. Mort turns his head slightly to the window as they speed over it. He nods off after that. He wakes as they pass the abandoned horse track outside of Santa Fe. He slowly comes to and sits upright in the Cadillac's soft leather seat.

He stares straight ahead. "Thank you Busy. You are a good friend. I want you and that senorita of yours to go on a nice trip." When he gets out at Riverside, he pulls a bank envelope from the front pocket of his wrinkled baggy khakis. He puts it on the passenger seat. He stoops and looks at Busy with a familiar grin on his face. "You all better have a good time. Thank you again. I'll see you soon."

Mort spends the next day going over the clues. Michael will get suspicious if he travels too much. To hide Clue 4, Mort hires an Uber driver. He doesn't want to wear Busy out. He also looks forward to a new experience. He has used Uber twice before to get around when Michael was busy. He likes the business model.

It is early in the morning. The day will heat up, but it is still cool when he leaves. He wears a long-sleeved denim shirt untucked. He thinks it looks good that way with his straw cowboy hat. He wants the protection from the sun because where they are going there is little shade. He is waiting on a bench next to the entrance door clutching his small black bag when his driver arrives.

A spotless black Subaru Outback stops precisely in front of Mort. He sees a middle-aged woman in a baseball cap driving. She is on her phone. She rolls the passenger side window down and looks at him. "You Mort?" He nods yes. She starts back on her phone, motioning for him to get in the back seat. He hesitates. She is not what he expected. She senses his agitation and gets off her phone. "Hey I'm really sorry. Kids. Please get in."

"I'm Madonna." Mort smiles and she knows what he is thinking. She has a head of shocking red hair. She is covered with freckles on her face and arms. She laughs. "You'll have to ask my parents." He gets in and feels better about things. The car is spotless inside too. "So, you want to go to Cerrillos. It's gonna cost probably three hundred and fifty dollars." Mort flashes one of the rolls of hundred-dollar bills left from the Vegas trip. "I understand. I got this. Just be careful."

Mort has not been to this old mine on Turquoise Hill in over forty years. He visited it with a friend after he opened Hamilton's. Native people and Spanish colonists mined turquoise in these hills for over a thousand years. This mine is the one that the famous Tiffany turquoise came from. Tiffany & Company purchased rights to every piece of turquoise pulled from the mines on the Hill in the late 1800s. Though the mines never produced as hoped, the small bit of mined Tiffany turquoise is iconic. He hopes he can find the hole again.

Once they leave the paved road, they drive onto a gravel road that winds through small outcroppings of faded red rock. After about a half mile they get to a rusted gate that has a small faded metal sign hanging from the hinged top left side. The faded turquoise letters "TIFF Ameri" are all that are left on the once white background. Rusted holes created by shotgun pellets over the years make the sign blend into the view even more. To Madonna the gate looks no different than the rest they have passed.

Mort says, "Please pull off in that open area ahead." She slowly pulls off the road. Madonna asks anxiously, "Do you know where we are?" She stares at her cellphone. "There is no service." Her GPS shows no road. As soon as she turns off the ignition and without answering her question Mort asks her, "If you don't mind, can you stay in the car? I will be back in about thirty to forty-five minutes." Madonna looks around at a lot of rocks and a few juniper trees. "Not a problem. I am going to lock the doors when you get out."

Mort starts slowly up an overgrown trail. After about a half mile, he sees the old hole in the side of the bluff. It has not changed since the last time he was there. To the right of the opening is a hand painted NO TRESPASSING sign on a post. There is a falling down shack to the side. The letters Tiff are visible on an old splintered wooden sign partially buried in the dirt.

He sits down on a big rock. He looks around thinking about how fun it must have been to find a vein of this world-renowned turquoise. Mort puts his gloves on. He takes the spade from his black bag. He is on his knees digging a hole beneath the sign as two curious crows fly over. Clue 4 is already in the pill container sealed in a sandwich bag. He places it in the small hole and covers it. He brushes the ground slowly. He stands and again uses his foot to compact the replaced dirt. He grimaces, then smiles, and puts his hand on his low back as he straightens. He is thankful this is the last hole to dig. He walks slowly back to the car.

The cool air from the AC is welcome. As Mort fastens his seatbelt,

"You know the way out of here?" Madonna does. She is already headed onto the road leading back to Santa Fe. The dust behind them looks like smoke is following them. As if he senses what Madonna is thinking, "I'll give you some money to wash your car." Mort falls asleep until they reach Santa Fe. He arrives back at Riverside before his afternoon visit with Michael.

The next morning Mort is tired and feels drained. He stays in bed and falls back to sleep. After a quick mid-morning shower and a cup of black coffee from the dining room, he musters the strength to make the fifteen-minute walk to his house to place Clue 5. He is relieved that the treasure hunt is set up. During the walk back, he stops to rest at a concrete picnic table by the river.

He covers his face with his hands waiting for his head to clear. He is having trouble breathing. He is obsessing. This is unusual for him. He thinks about what will happen if a clue gets disturbed or becomes unfindable. What if Michael is unsuccessful? On top of everything he thinks about how he couldn't smell the coffee he had before his walk this morning. He is relieved that he left the letter with Cromley.

14 The Assistant and the Investigator / Session 1

Cromley has been gone for about thirty minutes when Cozy comes into the office. It is almost closing time. Oralynn is surprised, but pleased. She and Cozy can be alone. She fantasizes about that sometimes. He is about ten years older than she is. He seems authoritarian and sure of himself. She is the exact opposite. He comes through the door smiling and looking at her. "Hey good looking. I was in the neighborhood and thought I'd come by and see what you were up to." He was in the parking lot on his phone when he saw Cromley leave. He knows Oralynn is by herself. That is the reason he comes up.

He thinks she is nice. Some of her comments like, "My dad is a hard person to like" or "My mom really puts up with a lot from my dad," lead him to believe all is not perfect with her family. She still seems thankful for them. He envies this. She seems naïve, but he doesn't know her that well. He is unsure if she has had a relationship with anyone before. He would swear that the last time they talked in person she was flirting with him. He thought this afternoon he might find out.

Lester "Cozy" MacFarland is that kind of guy. At the Albuquerque Police Department he had worked his way up to Investigator. During his ascent in the department Cozy was not the only nickname he had earned. He was also known as "The Storyteller." He was often creative with the facts when his methods for dealing with suspects approached unacceptable. His reports were often different from those of his partners or witnesses. He was trusted by his peers up to certain point, but he was not liked by any.

As with most everything in his life, Cozy pushed until the threat of breaking was imminent. He was asked to retire after twenty years. Getting a pension for his service was better than the internal review he would face. His chief told him that he was going to take him out, that he would make sure Cozy wasn't a menace to anyone again. Currently

Cozy's only work is as an investigator with Cromley's law firm.

He got the nickname Cozy because as a young beat cop he would threaten anyone on his beat if they were not paying proper homage or if he thought they were doing something wrong. Not illegal, but wrong by his standards. He told several wife abusers, "I'm gonna cozy up in your business if you don't cut that shit out." If they didn't, they received some of Cozy's love. His willingness to cozy up earns him his nickname and is problematic his entire law enforcement career.

Cozy is married to Cromley's sister. Her large breasts were the attraction when he met her five years ago. He found after their marriage that the appeal of her breasts was overshadowed by her bigger mouth. She talks constantly. She knows everything about everything. If she doesn't, she is on her fucking phone looking for it. Slipper Cromley is making his life miserable. He hates her stupid first name. "The Slipper this. The Slipper that." He hates her friends for calling her The Slipper.

He remembers her venomous tirade the last time he was home. He walked in the kitchen door and was lambasted. "I have had it with your bullshit. I'm tired of the bad attitude. You are rough. What's wrong with you? You used to be great in bed. Now you just throw me around. I think it's time to get shed of your ass. Consider yourself kicked out asshole!" That was it. He despises her so much that he can't force himself to argue his case. She is the ride. She knows it. He knows it. If the marriage ends, his only job with the law firm will probably end too. At age fifty-three, Cozy McFarland is disappointed and feels he deserves more.

When Oralynn sees Cozy she immediately perks up. It has been a long day at her desk. She hopes that she looks presentable. There is no time to check. She remembers the last time he was in the office she had been flirty. She had pretended that her blouse had come undone momentarily revealing her skimpy pushup bra and lots of cleavage. She is surprised and embarrassed that she did something so brazen. She wonders if he remembers.

Oralynn has dated a few men over the years, but none remained interested. One undesirable suitor from her Sunday school group told her, "You should want to have sex with me, what's wrong with you?" Part of it is that she comes from a very Catholic family. She leaves work a couple of afternoons each week to light candles at the Cathedral Basilica of St. Francis of Assisi down the street, but Cromley doesn't mind. He knows it means a lot to her to be able to do this. Sometimes he asks her when she returns, "Did you light one for me?" This is their inside joke and always makes her smile and blush.

Her Hispanic mother holds it together when her white father's behavior needs realigning. As a young woman, Oralynn was badgered and verbally abused by her father. Her mother still is. The difference is her father is afraid of her mother. Oralynn has been seeing a therapist off and on for about a year, fighting to overcome the bad feelings she has about herself and him. She struggles with self-esteem issues. Being willfully passive helps mask her dissatisfaction with herself. This evening she is feeling a need, however.

She stayed up late last night finishing the last book of the Harlequin "Love Is the Law" series. She had trouble going to sleep. She imagines Cozy is the rogue detective that saves the troubled vulnerable woman in the story. She wants to be the woman in that story. Her unsatisfied yearnings are barely below the surface right now. She stands and smiles at Cozy. "Please come in. You want something to drink?"

Cozy rubs the stubble on his chin. "Water would be great." Oralynn goes into the kitchenette across from her office and gets a bottle from the refrigerator. She hands it to him. "Excuse me for a minute." Oralynn hurriedly goes into the bathroom adjacent to the kitchenette. She checks herself in the mirror. She is anxious with excitement. She unbuttons the top two buttons of her blouse. Cozy is seated at her desk when she comes back in the room. "Nice view from here." She thinks he means the view from the window. He swivels from the desk. "I was talking about you."

She pretends she doesn't hear. She sits on the corner of the desk facing him. She feels like she should say something. "It was kind of a weird day." Before she can continue, Cozy rolls the chair in front of her and puts his hands on her thighs. She flinches at first, but then relaxes. She shifts her legs slightly as if trying to decide what to do. Cozy slips his hand under her skirt between her legs. "I've wanted to touch you here."

Oralynn is facing him. He senses she is embarrassed. She abruptly says, "Wait." She pulls her skirt down and heads for the suite door. Cozy thinks she is trying to leave. He starts apologizing, "I didn't mean to offend you." Instead, she locks the door and turns sheepishly back to him.

They both smile and head for the kitchenette. Cozy lifts her onto the counter facing him. He undoes his pants and they drop to the floor around his feet. Oralynn is breathing heavily already. Her fantasy is happening. He pulls her to him. "You ready for me?" She is not used to a partner who talks. He rhythmically pushes into her. She grips him tightly. She thinks about kissing him.

Cozy senses her submission which excites him more. He works slowly until Oralynn is panting and weak. He caresses her breasts which are now on the outside of her pushup bra. He holds her tightly now as he starts coming. They hold each other until both are not moving anymore. Cozy is breathing heavily. He leans backward against the wall. She slowly slides off the counter. Her skirt and blouse are one band of clothes about two inches above her waist. Cozy's pants are tangled around his shoes. She comes over to him against the wall and kisses him on the cheek. They both laugh nervously. He doesn't return the kiss.

15 Mort's End

It is still dark. Michael slowly rolls to the edge of his bed and swings his feet to the cool wood floor. His stiff legs only heighten his restlessness. Santa Fe, like the nation, is coming out of the Covid-19 pandemic shutdown. The New Mexico governor ordered all non-essential businesses to close temporarily and to hang on until it was safe to reopen. Hamilton's has been closed for about a month. The shutdown has affected about half of Hamilton's business. The online portion is doing better. The employees who were laid off are on unemployment but getting increasingly uneasy about their futures.

Michael feels shutting down is necessary, but he knows people who are really hurting because of no work or no customers. He tries not to watch the news too much. He finds it depressing. He thinks the country's leadership is failing. It is 2020 and he feels like the country is being taken back to the mid-1950s. He knows the Governor and thinks she has done a good job. Though the virus has crushed the local economy, he feels that the Governor's actions are the reason the virus has flatlined in the county.

Michael worries that he can infect his grandfather. He has hibernated for the largest part of the last two months. Because of the circumstances, he has not minded. He visits Mort almost every day. He usually runs or bikes the mile to the center. About a month after his parents' wreck, the reality of the pandemic sets in. He can no longer see Mort in person. No more physical contact. All his life hugging Mort was a part of their relationship. Michael would smell English Leather on Mort's neck every time. Mort continued using the aftershave after the company quit making the cologne. That smell triggers a fond memory for Michael.

Michael texts to let Mort know he is at Riverside when he arrives to visit. He loves that an eighty-two-year-old geezer can use a smartphone and most apps as well as he can. Mort sits in a reclining chair that he pushes around to face the window. He prides himself that his legs are still sturdy and strong. The weekly chair yoga class keeps him surprisingly flexible. The gray recliner is his TV chair until Michael comes around. He sits on one side of the big living room window of his ground-level room. Michael sits on the other side of the window in a lawn chair. He folds and stashes the chair behind a bush near the window every time he leaves.

They usually talk on their phones to each other for about an hour. They can see each other's facial expressions and eyes. The handwaving and loud talking, even if on a phone, is a family trait, especially if they start talking politics. Sometimes they sit quietly looking at each other, not for a lack of words, but knowing they can talk if they want. That is enough.

Michael loves Mort. He feels a kinship with him than he could never imagine with his father. It isn't just their shared love of puzzles, riddles, mysteries, clues, treasure hunts, and aliens that creates that bond. Mort always supported what Michael was doing if it was even close to responsibly grabbing life. Even if it was jumping into the unknown. They talked about the unknown when he told Mort he joined the Marines. The first thing Mort told him was that he would worry about him every day. This was not a sentiment expressed by his father.

Mort had a disqualifying hearing problem that was discovered when he registered for the Viet Nam draft. He continued to try and enlist after being denied. He didn't necessarily agree with the war, nor did he understand it, but he felt he should serve the country. Michael loves this story. He feels that his service was for Mort too. Mel would have done anything to get out of serving. He expected others to serve.

From what Michael understands, Mort may have grabbed too much life in his younger days. He doesn't care. He is still not sure how his Father came to be. Mort never mentions Mel's mother. From what he understands, Mel never had a relationship with her. Michael will never know his grandmother.

About two and a half weeks after the window visits start, Mort's allergies really start acting up. He answers his phone, but Michael can't understand him. Mort can barely keep his head up when Michael arrives. Michael immediately calls the front desk and asks them to hurry and have someone come to his room. About thirty seconds later he watches as two staff nurses enter. He recognizes one of them. Her name is Rosa. She is attractive and well educated. He knows Mort likes her. She is wearing a red mask that matches her red pants.

Mort finally looks up. He is clutching his chest and trying to breathe. She puts her hand on his shoulder. Michael can read her lips. "Try to relax Mort. We got this." The young man with Rosa leaves the room. Michael can see her dial a number. The serious-looking young man returns with a green bottle of oxygen in a stand. He wheels it next to Mort.

Hurriedly he rips the plastic wrapper off an oxygen mask and hooks it to the tank. He puts it gently over Mort's nose and mouth. He snugs the straps and holds his thumb up in front of Mort's face. Mort seems to relax. He sees Michael and waves limply. The color starts coming back into his face. After a few minutes Michael hears a siren in the distance. As it gets closer, he knows it's coming for Mort.

Michael goes around to the canopied entrance where the ambulance parks. After about five minutes, two EMS personnel wheel Mort out the door in a wheelchair. Mort sees Michael and smiles weakly again. Not being able to hug his grandfather at that moment causes him to tear up. He can only imagine how lonely he must feel, though he would never show it. It is the virus. Michael knows it. What started as allergies was the fucking virus now. It seemed unnecessary to Michael. It pisses him off.

The facility has an outbreak and they are having trouble containing it. Like many family members of the sealed-off residents, Michael helplessly watches the slow spread. He knows several of the infected residents are now being taken to Presbyterian General on the south side of town. They are characters he will always remember as part of his grandfather's crew. He has witnessed them go after each other unmercifully, but no better friends exist. Some are in critical condition. Michael talks to anxious family members in the waiting room when Mort is checked into his room. They are battling the same frustrations and helplessness that he is.

Mort is confirmed as case number eight at Santa Fe's best assisted living facility. Since the first case was reported there, Michael had been afraid this was going to happen. Mort is in good health but susceptible because of his age. Now he is a data point in the Coronavirus Daily Update issued from the Governor's office. Four days after his hospital admission, Mort can't breathe on his own. He is transferred to ICU and put on a ventilator.

The night prior to his transfer to ICU, Mort calls Michael after midnight. Michael accidentally leaves his phone on vibrate so he doesn't hear the call. Mort leaves a message. Michael hears the message early the next morning. He is alarmed and thinks about going to the hospital. He decides to wait and see if Mort calls back in the next hour. He listens to the message again.

He decides to shower. He grabs his phone and heads to the bathroom. He remembers his chair in the bushes at the center. He had winked at the grizzled old custodian as he was hiding it before he left the last time. The man smiled and continued sweeping the sidewalk. Michael wonders if he has removed the chair.

Michael shaves this morning for the first time in a week. He doesn't have a heavy beard, but it looks scraggly after a couple of days. He is coming into his small kitchen from the bathroom when his phone rings. He looks at the number. It is not Mort's, but it is a Santa Fe number. He answers. A high-pitched woman's voice says, "Is this Michael Hamilton?" He hesitates for a moment thinking it is a solicitor and then answers, "It is." She starts slowly and deliberately, "I am sorry to be calling you with this news, but Mr. Mort passed about an hour ago." Mort had succumbed to the coronavirus. Michael will never talk with him again.

Michael places his phone on the counter. Stunned, he leans against a stool in the small kitchen. He stands barely feeling his feet on the floor. He turns and straddles the stool, now facing the counter. He can see his parents' house through the window over the white porcelain kitchen sink. The sun is too bright. The aspens near the house are the only protection on this side. Their shadows on the flagstone sitting area between the casita and house are lifeless. The portal over the back entry to their house is dark and is the only possible spot to hide from the sun in the yard.

The kitchen counter is the center of Michael's universe in the casita. The little social activity he has occurs around it. Michael pulls the stool closer to the counter and sits. He puts his feet on the stool's scuffed bottom cross pieces. The stool is the perfect height for him to rest his elbows on the counter and cradle his head. This is the drunk talking position, the next morning hangover position, or in this case, the grieving position. He closes his eyes and lowers his head into his hands. Tears well up in his eyes long enough to blur his vision and then he catches himself. He stops. Soon the tears come again. Michael can see his parents leaving that morning. He can see Mort through the window for the last time.

With his parents, what he felt wasn't sorrow as much as guilt. All the relationship difficulties came to an unexpected end. There is nothing he can do to change anything now. With Mort, it isn't just the loss of his grandfather, but also the loss of his other best friend. Mort was the one person he felt was always in his corner. Michael ends up using a folded dish towel to muffle his sobbing. He has a lot of sorrow with no place to put it right now. He sits for an hour trying not to think. His right leg falls asleep. The numbness forces him finally to get up. He thinks about what to do.

The night before he dies, Mort wakes in a start. He gasps. He doesn't know what time it is. He is on an "iron lung" as he calls it when the tube is out of his throat. The air forced into his lungs by the rhythmic up and down of the respirator pump is all that makes him feel alive. The sound reinforces the alive feeling, but it has become annoying. Mort wonders what it would be like to not hear it.

He remembers that he never told Michael about the box he put in the well house. All day he has felt like he may not have another chance. He is exhausted. His mind is heavy and without many thoughts. He calls a nurse. Upon arrival she sees he is anxious as he tries to breathe. He wants something.

To settle him down she puts her hands on his shoulders. She tells him with her eyes that she will take the tube out, "I know how much it bothers you." Mort understands. She slowly extracts it. She places it on a sterile pad on the side of his bed. He doesn't try to talk. His throat is on fire. He sits up as much as he can and takes a sip of water from a glass on the rolling nightstand next to his bed.

Weakly he asks the nurse, "Please get my phone." She takes it out of the nightstand drawer. She turns it on. "I'll dial it for you." Mort recites Michael's number. He smiles weakly that he remembers. She hands it to him. His eyes are dull. His face is drawn as he breathes on his own.

She leaves the room to give him privacy. Six rings. No pickup. In a dry strained voice, "Find the box with the clue buried under my well house." Mort is about to say something else, but there is beeping in the background. Two seconds go by, then swooshing heavy footsteps.

A nurse agitatedly, "Mr. Hamilton your pulse is erratic. Your lungs are working too hard. You need to..." That is the end of the message.

16 Mysterious Instructions

Mort dropped by Cromley's office unannounced about four weeks before he died. He does not feel well. His allergies are acting up. Cromley remembers Oralynn offering him a glass of water. He is sweating. He is complaining that they are going to stop face-to-face visits at the facility. How is he going to see Michael? Without explaining, Mort asks Oralynn to take down what he says. She looks at Cromley who nods. "Just a second." She grabs a pad from his desk and turns toward Mort.

When he is done, he hands Cromley a sealed envelope. Cromley can tell it has several pages folded in it. Mort turns his back to Oralynn and moves closer to him. "If you don't hear from Michael that he has found the box within seven days after my death, you call him and remind him to find it." This makes no sense to Cromley, but he figures there is more explanation in the letter Mort just gave him. Oralynn is writing. "You have my revised will." Cromley nods looking at Oralynn. She instinctively starts to the files. "I'll check." She returns smiling. "The one dated less than a month ago. Yes, we do."

At this point Mort thinks he will be around for several more years. He will have time to start Michael on the treasure hunt of his life. He is so proud of himself for designing and implementing it. This is the final episode to be added to the myth of Mort, but it will happen after he is gone.

He also instructs Cromley to open the letter he just handed him exactly twenty-four days after Michael informs him that he has found the box. Read my will then too. As Mort walks out of his office Cromley shakes his head and looks at Oralynn. "That damn Mort. What a piece of work. Who knows what he is up to?"

He gives the envelope to Oralynn. "Go ahead and put that in Mort's folder in the Hamilton file." She takes it. "I'll put the notes from our conversation in too." He walks back in his office and she hears him sit down hard. Cromley doesn't even know about it, but she has a procedure for sealed items going into files. She places a ruler across the back of the envelope. Using it as a guide, she lightly scribes a two-inch straight line with her fingernail, catching the sealed flap and envelope.

In normal light you can't see it. If you hold it up to the light, it is visible as a slight crease. In a world where she feels powerless most of the time, the idea that she is doing something that no one except her knows about makes her smile. She deposits the letter and quietly shuts the old metal file drawer.

As instructed during the unplanned meeting with Mort, Cromley calls Michael two days after Mort's death. He remembers Mort saying, "Have him come in that second day, so you can tell him some things." Oralynn hears Cromley talking to Michael and remembers her notes about what to tell him. She stops working on the letter she is writing. She hurriedly gets the notes out of Mort's file and takes them to Cromley. She knows there will be questions now, further keeping her from what she is trying to get done.

Later that day, Michael sits in front of Cromley's desk. He reads Oralynn's notes from the conversation with Mort. "I want to be cremated. I want Michael to throw a party for all my geezer friends that are still alive. Good booze and good food. Host it in my backyard. I want each one of them to touch my urn and say something about me as part of the gathering. It doesn't have to be nice. Invite Omar, the new owner of my store. After the gathering, I want Michael to spread my ashes as he sees fit."

He doesn't say where. Cromley has no explanation for the open-ended statement. Michael assumes Mort wants them spread around Santa Fe, but with Mort he isn't sure. The last sentence that Cromley reads, "Michael keeps Suzy's stone." There is no mention of any will or anything else. Cromley doesn't tell Michael that Mort gave him other instructions. He does have a will, but it is not to be opened for twenty-four days, just like the mysterious letter.

Michael thinks about burying the necklace with Mort's ashes, but he decides to keep it like Mort wanted him to. It seems like the right thing to do. He puts it on that next morning while hanging at the casita. Shortly he finds himself sitting on the end of his bed blindly staring into the courtyard through the east window of the casita. He is daydreaming. It isn't a dream though. It is a feeling. It isn't about an event or anybody.

It is a feeling of sadness, while at the same time thankfulness. He puts his hand on Suzy's stone and it is warm. The black matrix looks alive. He takes the necklace off. He puts it in the back of the pot drawer wrapped in an old red handkerchief.

17 Session 2

"You want to see me again?" is what Oralynn hears when she picks up after the customary two rings. The deep voice is unmistakable. She is looking at Cromley at his desk as she speaks. Quietly she says, "If you can wait an hour till Mr. C leaves, I can get the kitchenette cleaned up." She smiles and wonders if he gets it. She hangs up before he says anything else.

As predicted, Cromley begins gathering his stuff to leave about forty-five minutes later. He makes three trips out of his office to talk to Oralynn before he finally goes out the door. As he passes the third time she says, "I'm going to finish this filing before I go." There are papers spread all over her desk. He is preoccupied. He nods as he passes her desk on the way to the door.

As soon as the door closes, she deftly gathers the papers that she intentionally and carefully spread on her desk to make it appear that she was filing. She is like a slick card dealer picking up a deck of cards spread on a table. She stacks them on top of a filing cabinet behind her.

She goes to the window to make sure Cromley is gone. The sun is lowering and there are shadows of the tree limbs on the parking lot. The leaves splinter the sunshine onto the brick patio. Her only production the last hour was fantasizing about what she was going to do with Cozy. She is unsure how she feels about her behavior.

As soon as she sits back down at her desk Cozy comes in the door. She is nervous. She fights showing it. She smiles and stays seated at her desk until he is in the door. He motions to the knob. "You want me to lock it?" She looks at him and decides right then. "Yes," is all she says. He does and walks toward her. She gets up from her desk and heads to the kitchenette. Knowing what to expect, session two lasts longer. Oralynn is giggling when they are done. Cozy pulls her into him one last time.

After a quiet couple of minutes their hearts are beating normally again. Oralynn weakly finds the floor with her feet. She struggles to pull her blouse back onto her shoulders. She straightens her skirt. "How's your day been going?" Cozy breathes heavily, "It's been pretty shitty up until now. It's much better though. Nothing really going on other than looking for some more work."

Oralynn wants to talk about something as they get dressed but realizes she doesn't know anything about Cozy other than he is an unhappily married retired cop and interested in fucking her. She remembers Mort coming in and how that mysterious story might interest him. "You know the Hamilton family? Hamilton's on the Plaza, the jewelry store? The owner and his wife died in a wreck recently." Cozy nods while he fastens his belt and straightens his pants.

"Old Mort came in a couple of weeks ago babbling some mysterious instructions about finding a box or something. It was for his grandson Michael. Sounded like a treasure or something that was worth a lot of money. It made no sense. I put a letter about it in their file. It seemed important, but really off the wall." Cozy listens intently while staring at the window.

He sits down in one of the chairs facing her desk as she finishes straightening her hair and removing the lipstick smeared on her chin. Cozy watches her retrieve a key from the middle drawer of her desk. She quickly puts the stack of files in a cabinet and locks it. To herself, "They will have to wait till tomorrow." She puts the key back in the drawer. As she closes the drawer, she looks at Cozy sweetly. "I wish we could go get a drink somewhere like normal people."

Cozy doesn't look her in the face. "I have work to do. I need to use the conference room to spread out some papers." Oralynn knows he came in with nothing. She is unsure what he is trying to do. Ignoring what he said, "Does it bother you that you are married, and we do what we do?" Cozy doesn't bite. "I really need to work." After a second of awkward silence he looks straight into her eyes. "This is about sex. If you are looking for more than that, it's not here." Oralynn sees a hardness in his eyes that she has not seen before. She is embarrassed. She hides her face as she turns to grab her purse from under her desk. She walks past him without a word.

From the window, Cozy watches her get into her car and drive out of the parking lot. He locks the office suite door again. He made a bet three days ago that he can't cover. Slipper is on his ass about paying his share of the bills. He lied about staying behind to do work. Now the goal is to see if there is something about a treasure in old Mort's file. He is crossing a line that he has never crossed before.

He takes the key from the desk drawer. He finds the Hamilton file. There are three folders. One each for Mort, Mel and Michael. He finds a letter in Mort's folder and mutters, "This must be it."

Cozy takes the letter into the kitchenette. Knowing Cromley drinks tea, he finds the stainless tea pot and fills it with water. After ten minutes, steam is billowing out of the opening. He has experience with this. He opened some of Slipper's mail this way to find out if her parents left her money when they died. Holding the envelope by the corners he runs it though the steam for about twenty seconds. He lays it flat on the counter. He takes a knife out of his pocket and carefully runs it underneath the flap. The flap releases perfectly.

There are two blank pages with a handwritten letter in between. The letter mentions Lander Blue treasure, you will be a rich man, millions of dollars, set for life. There is a riddle at the very end that makes no sense. He goes to the copy machine to make a copy of the letter. As is customary, the machine is turned off for the day. He takes a picture of the letter with his phone. He meticulously reassembles the three pieces of paper and puts them back in the envelope. He carefully flattens the dry envelope flap on Oralynn's desk. He places a blank tablet he takes from a stack on another file cabinet on it. He presses down hard for thirty seconds while telling himself to be patient.

He quickly takes the letter back to the still-steaming pot and runs the glue flap through the steam for another twenty seconds. "Now the hard part." He lays the envelope flat and slowly folds the flap back into place. He looks closely to see if it matches and lightly runs his finger along the edge of the flap to reseal it. He mutters, "Close enough for this outfit." He takes the tablet and presses on the envelope again. He then puts it between the pages in the middle of the tablet. He puts it in the small kitchenette freezer for about two minutes. He takes it out and looks at it. "No one will know, especially that punch Oralynn."

Satisfied, he turns off the burner. He empties the tea pot and places it upside down in the strainer. He puts the cold tablet back in the stack where he got it. He puts the cold letter back in Mort's file. He puts the Hamilton file back in the cabinet. He locks it thinking about what he has just done. He just moved his personal bar a bit lower. Desperation is a great rationalizer. He puts the key back in the drawer just like he found it. Details. His curiosity is high. It makes him feel better. Maybe this is the break he has been looking for. He decides to learn more about Michael Hamilton, possibly surveil him. Cozy wonders what would happen if he could get his hands on this treasure or whatever it is.

18 The Box in the Well House

As evening sets in Michael realizes he hasn't eaten all day. The visit with Cromley took the starch out of him. He wonders what Mort has done with his house and his assets. He feels guilty for thinking about it, but he expected to hear more about that today. He realizes that about this time every afternoon he is used to returning home from visiting Mort. He places an order at Back Road Pizza. Their homemade sausage and smoked bacon pizza is the best in town.

He goes to his desk and opens the pot drawer. He loads his pipe and steps out onto his little portal. As is the custom, he sits down in a red Coleman camping chair. It faces the back of the compound. The sprinkler system is misting the plants against the back wall. He can feel the cool mist when the wind blows hard enough. He takes a few puffs and immediately feels better. He is hungry now.

On his way to pick up the pizza, he decides to go by Mort's house on Acequia Madre. It is also a compound, without the casita. It has not been occupied since Mort decided to move into the facility two years ago. Mort was emphatic about not wanting to rent it. It isn't neglected, but it is getting there. The stucco is cracking around most of the windows, but the adobe block walls underneath the plaster are still sturdy and intact. Michael feels guilty that he has not done more to help maintain it. He rationalizes that he has not had time. Mort hadn't seemed to care.

He pulls in the entrance. The gravel drive has purple and white hollyhocks growing into the edges. He parks and walks up the brown flagstone path to the front door. He reaches into his empty pocket for the key. As he starts back to his car to get it, he remembers Mort's midnight message.

"How could I have forgotten," he mutters to himself. As a follow-up he mutters even louder, "One reason was it made no fucking sense." He walks around to the well house. The well has been disconnected since the house was added to the city water system in 1960. Calling it a well house is generous. The wood siding is so dry that he could peel off big pieces with no effort.

He walks to the doorless entry. He peers into the ten feet by ten feet space. A hole in the roof at the very back allows a sliver of sunshine through. He hears a rustling in the accumulated leaves he can see against the back wall. He quickly decides to come back better prepared with a flashlight, long pants and boots, instead of the flipflops he is wearing now.

Michael continues walking around the house. The backyard is far from manicured, but it is beautiful. He counts ten different-colored rose bushes in full bloom. The stand of five aspen trees to the left of the sitting area is full of glistening leaves quaking in the light breeze. He remembers sitting by the fire pit in the middle of the sitting area when he was in his twenties sipping expensive whiskey with Mort. He would buy the bottle. Michael thought he was so grown up when he did that. This memory brings back a flood of others. All good. He has just lost the most important person in his life and he feels it most strongly in this place.

The path around the other end of the house is overgrown with Apache Plume. The hairy pink blooms reach out to grab him as he walks through. He slowly makes it back to his Jeep. Thirty minutes later he is back home taking his first bite of hot pizza. For the first time in days he smiles and chuckles. He needs to decide if he is going to look for the box. Surely Mort wasn't jerking his chain, but what the hell. He thinks about all the tricks he has seen Mort play on his friends and unsuspecting tourists over the years.

After three pieces of pizza he stops and closes the box. He likes cold pizza for breakfast. He puts it into his near-empty refrigerator. The pizza can keep the lone six pack of Pacifico company for the night. He goes back to the pot drawer for the last smoke of the day.

The next morning Michael calls Will. He feels bad because he didn't have a chance to say anything to him at Mel's and Darlene's funeral. The phone rings five times. He doesn't leave a message. He gets a text almost immediately, "Good to hear from you. Give me five." Michael fixes another cup of coffee. He feels a sense of comfort before he even connects with Will. "Man, it's good to hear from you. Been wondering what you were up to. Started to call so many times." Michael says, "I missed you too, you little fucker." Will chuckles and then pauses.

"You do know you can still go fuck yourself." Michael, "I feel like I have."

Michael asks, "How's the paint business?" Will replies, "That's what I was doing. Selling paint. Lots of builder business." After another pause, Michael says, "I need to talk with you. Can you drop by after work? I have a six pack and some new stash."

Will arrives at Michael's casita about six that evening. His tucked-in black Sherwin-Williams polo has red and white paint splotches near his waistline in the front. The pressed creases down each leg of his khaki dockers are still visible. He is more buffed than Michael, though both are in good shape. Neither goes to the gym much, but their running, hiking and biking conditions them. Michael meets Will at the door before Will can clang the cast iron loop serving as a doorbell. They hug like best friends should.

Michael grabs another red Coleman camping chair near the back door. He puts it on the other side of a small round-top wood table next to the other camp chair. Both chairs face the shadowy courtyard wall. Will sits down and sighs. "I've been on my feet since six-thirty this morning. I'm feeling it." Without comment, Michael goes back inside without shutting the door. He grabs the Pacifico from the refrigerator and the Dave and Buster's opener he won over a decade ago on a visit to Dallas. He sets the beer and opener on the table between them. They both stare into the yard without saying anything. Michael lights a joint and takes a small hit. He hands it to Will.

Michael looks over at Will after they have each had a couple of more puffs. "It's good to see you dude. Sorry I haven't been in touch." Will keeps staring ahead. "Shit man I know you needed some space. Your world is upside down. In two months, the Hamilton clan is down to just you. I'm sorry. I can't imagine." He trails off, "I'm just sorry." Michael tells him about his parents' will. He thinks he will be okay for a while. He has over twenty-thousand dollars in his savings. Will is surprised about the sale of Hamilton's. "Are you cool with that?" After a second Michael slowly says, "I don't know. At this point I guess I have to be."

After opening a second beer for each of them, Michael starts to talk about Mort. He eventually gets around to the strange message Mort left before he died. Without hesitating, Will says, "Let's go over to his house in the morning and look for the box. I'll go in late." Michael replies, "You don't think Mort is fucking with me? He was in rough shape that last night. The lead nurse said he was really agitated. She told me he would try to take the respirator tube out. He was saying my name and Suzy's name over and over."

They sit in silence in the dark. About half the joint is sitting unlit in the ashtray. Will opens his third beer. He is slumped down in the chair with his legs straight out. The heels of his worn hiking boots are planted on the concrete and his toes are pointed straight up. Michael breaks the silence. "Okay, let's meet at The Pantry at eight in the morning and I'll buy you breakfast. Then let's go to Mort's and waste some time. Wear your boots." Michael immediately feels better. Will's opinion matters to him. Will knew Mort and he doesn't think it's crazy, not yet anyway. For the first time in a while Michael feels he has something to look forward to. It may be a waste of time, but they will find out in the morning.

They arrive the next morning at the restaurant on Cerrillos Road at the same time, about five minutes early. They congratulate themselves on being punctual. The locals are leaving. A few tourists are starting to arrive. Most are talking loudly as they come in the door. They both have a plate of eggs over easy, hash browns and adovada. Steamed corn tortillas assume the role of toast. They talk about Mort's house and what might happen to it. Each has a second cup of coffee as they sit and watch more people arrive. The conversation changes to the virus. They talk about having to wear masks and how weird that has been. They are glad having to do that is over.

A young clean-cut Hispanic waiter with a pompadour puts their check on the table as he grabs their empty plates. As they are getting ready to leave a tanned middle-aged guy with a mean look on his face starts ragging on his waitress two tables over. The young woman is embarrassed and tries to walk away from the table. The bully gets up and blocks her way momentarily. The man scowls at Michael and Will before he heads to the door.

"Don't be a dick," Michael says under his breath. He pays the check at the register and they walk to the parking lot. The dick is getting into a black Tahoe. As he passes them, Michael sees an adobe-colored Albuquerque Police Department parking sticker in the upper right corner of the windshield. The dick is a cop.

When they are parked at Mort's, Michael goes to the back of his jeep and grabs a couple of pairs of old worn leather gloves. He hands a pair to Will, "I'm not sure what we are going to be getting into. I came by yesterday evening and the well house is leaves and spider webs inside. Something started rustling around at the back and scared the shit out of me." He looks up and smiles at Will. They both put the gloves on as they walk to the back.

They smell the roses as they round the side of the house. The gazebo on the other side of the fire pit is surrounded by chamisa. Their green feathered branches hide the bottoms of the two furthest posts. The metal table and four chairs in the middle are dull and faded. Leaves and assorted twigs are wedged in the arms and between their curving frames and the seats. Michael notices that one of the chairs is not turned to the table like the rest. It looks like it has been moved to look back at the house.

Will looks inside the well house door. It is light enough to see inside. He steps back waiting for Michael to look. "So, you don't know if it's under the slab or inside this rubble pile." Michael once again repeats the message "Find the box with the clue buried under my well house." It is engraved in his brain by now. "That's all I know." Will walks around the building looking for any evidence of digging or for anything disturbed. Michael is looking in the doorway when Will completes his circle. "I see nothing disturbed, no digging, at least recently."

Michael pulls off a couple of more pieces of wood siding. They crumble into smaller pieces and fall on the ground. The light spills into the space offering a new comfort zone for entry. Will grabs a dried elm branch about five feet long laying nearby on the ground. The overgrown grass reluctantly gives it up.

He steps through the doorway. He uses the branch to get rid of some of the years-worth of built-up cobwebs in the corners. They fall to the concrete slab in stringy dusty clumps. He notices that there aren't any cobwebs hanging in the middle of the space. He pokes the branch into the pile of dried leaves against the back wall. A pack rat sticks his head out of his hiding place. He scurries into the yard through one of the many available escape routes.

Other than the leaves, the well house is cleared. The pump was junked a long time ago. The cast iron well head pipe coming up through the center of the slab is capped. The band around it is rusted and hard to see due to the caked dirt. An electrical wire coming through the wall is rolled around a stick and stowed in the corner. In the middle of the slab against the protruding pipe is a piece of weathered plywood lying flat. It had been cut badly leaving the edge frayed and jagged.

Michael bends over and gingerly lifts a corner. When nothing tries to escape or attack, he continues lifting. He sees the rim of dust on the slab outlining the plywood edges. He notices that the way the plywood is lying does not quite align with the dust outline. He leans the plywood against the back wall. The cutout in the slab for the water pipe is about two feet by two feet. The hole is full of dried apache plume blooms. Michael and Will look at each other. Michael quickly kneels and starts clearing out the dried blooms. The light breeze blows them around the floor.

The square hole is full of dirt. Michael scoops out a handful with his hand. It is red and crumbly. He asks Will if he will go back to the jeep and get a shovel that he retrieved this morning from his parents' garden shed. While Will is gone he catches his breath. He is excited. Will comes back with the shovel. Michael gets out of the way as Will removes the first scoop full. The dirt is loose and comes out easily. Will keeps removing the dirt. He is about a foot down when the shovel hits something solid. Will looks at Michael. "Holy shit."

Michael is down on his knees digging with his hands. He feels the edge of something solid. He gets his hand underneath its edge and wiggles it out of the dirt. It is a white wooden box about four inches by ten inches covered in shrink wrap. Michael turns the box over and finds the end of the wrap. He starts removing it. The box is not heavy. He shakes it gently. Something moves around slightly. He unravels about three feet of the wrap. Mort had done a good job of sealing it. The box appears old, but sturdy and clean.

Mort the trickster was serious. Michael holds the box with both arms extended. They both look at it. They step back from the hole and outside into the bright light. Both are squinting. They walk hurriedly to the gazebo table. Michael puts the box down and removes his gloves. He puts his left hand around the end of the box. With his right hand he reaches for the rusted hasp holding it shut.

19 In the Box

Will excitedly says, "Stop. Let me take a picture." He pulls out his phone and takes two shots of the box sitting on the table. He tells Michael to stand up and hold the box in front of him. They are both grinning, but neither really knows why. Will takes Michael's picture holding the box out in front of him. He turns and takes a selfie of himself with the well house in the background. They each pull a chair out from the table. The dust and the trapped debris don't matter as they both sit down and pull their chairs up to the table.

Michael says, "What the fuck?" while looking at the box. He gently turns the rusted top catch to where it aligns with the slot. He pulls the hasp handle up ready to open the box. They hear a car horn out on the street and two women talking as they walk by the courtyard fence. Michael feels a weird sense already that there is a need to be secretive about this.

He opens the box. It is lined with thick turquoise-colored velvet. Inside there is a Crown Royal bag and a neatly folded newspaper clipping. There is also an envelope with Michael's name on the front in blue ink in Mort's handwriting. Will is just watching now. It's Michael's show from here on. Michael retrieves the envelope first. He wants to grab the bag and see what is in it, but he restrains himself hoping he will soon have a clue about what this means. He starts to open the envelope. He stops and looks at Will. "Let's go to my place and do this."

Will stands. "I don't want to leave, but I need to change and get some lunch before I go to work. You need to sort this out on your own too bro. This is so cool." He pushes Michael lightly on the right shoulder. As he walks off with his back to Michael, "Let's talk later. Gotta know more about this." Michael loudly says, "I don't want to see any of this shit on Facebook either."

In a minute he hears Will's Land Rover Discovery start. He sits for minute more. He puts the box under his arm as his phone pings. The sound startles him. Four photos of the box are attached to a text from Will. He scrolls through them and slowly stands. He looks around quickly and heads for his Jeep. His phone pings again with three more pictures and a thumbs up emoji.

Michael is too excited to think about lunch. He drives straight back to the casita. The drive is automatic. He pulls his Jeep into his parents' garage. He thinks briefly about the empty space. His mother's blue Mercedes has not been started since the accident. He thinks he should drive it, but he really doesn't want to. He goes through the back door of the garage into the back courtyard. No one knows he is there. He unlocks the door to the casita, enters and locks it behind him.

He grabs a LaCroix from the refrigerator. The bite of the first sip causes him to wince and choke slightly. He takes a white hand towel from a drawer by the sink and spreads it on his dining room table. He sets the box on it. He takes another sip and sets the drink on the counter. He sits down in a chair and pulls it up to the table. It looks like a place setting where the main course is a white box. He aligns the hasp and opens the box. He once again curbs the urge to see what is in the bag and takes the letter out. He remembers an old wooden handled letter opener Mort gave him. He gets it from the pot drawer and slits the top of the envelope open.

Mort's handwritten letter starts, "I knew you would find the box. At one time I thought this story would end with me. It would be an unsolved mystery. I made a promise to the woman in the newspaper clipping that I would take care of her treasure. She trusted me to know when the time was right to do something with it. Selfishly, I wanted this prize to be an eternal bond between the two of us. That was good enough for me. You are reading this letter because I decided after your parents died to create something special for you."

The next sentence encapsulates Mort's disdain for Mel. "I didn't want Mel to have this. I decided he got enough from me." Damn, Michael thinks. He pauses as this soaks in. "You hold the key to solving this treasure hunt. If you succeed you will be wealthy." That is all. Michael is impressed by how steady Mort's handwriting looks. It is better than his.

No further explanation. The next paragraph starts, "Within the next twenty-four hours you should let Burt Cromley know that you have found the box. He is expecting a visit. This will start the clock. You need to find the treasure twenty-four days from tomorrow." Michael stops reading and looks up. He reads the paragraph again. Once again, not enough explanation. He mutters to himself, "Why is there a time limit?"

Written in uniform capital letters at the bottom of the page were the words "LOOK AT THE NEWSPAPER CLIPPING." The clipping is laying under the Crown bag. Michael gently picks up the bag and removes the clipping. The clipping is folded symmetrically and sharply. Michael unfolds it. The creases are yellowed and dry. It is brittle. The first thing he sees is a black and white photo of the top half of a beautiful woman in coveralls standing in front of what looks like a hole in a dirt embankment.

She is standing in front of a sign hung on logs placed upright. Michael can't read what the sign says. The photo next to hers is a picture of a man wearing a Hawaiian shirt sitting in a golf cart. Even in grainy black and white, his shirt contrasts with his white slacks. He has a big smile on his face and a gold chain around his neck. Beneath the side-by-side photos the headline reads "Mysterious Domestic Dispute Leads to Deaths."

Some of the article print is hard to read because the ink has bled through as a result of the clipping being folded for so long. Michael starts reading the article from the 1973 *Las Vegas Review-Journal*. The first mention of the woman's name doesn't surprise him. It is Suzy. The article talks about her owning a turquoise mine called the Lander Blue. The man was a local loan shark who liked to play golf.

From the article it appears they shot and killed one another in an argument. The brother of the husband is to inherit the mine. He is quoted as saying that one of them had stolen a bunch of turquoise from the mine. He had not located it, but it was worth a lot of money and he was looking for it.

Michael sits for a minute holding the article with both hands as though he is still reading it. He looks at the woman's face. He sees how beautiful she was. The man looked like a lounge lizard. He immediately wondered what she was doing with him, though he was identified as her husband, Cal. Michael lays the article on the bare table out of the way. He reaches for the Crown bag.

Inside that bag are four smaller turquoise-colored velvet bags. The drawstrings are tight on each. He picks up one and takes out a large turquoise cabochon. He recognizes the color and matrix immediately. It looks like Suzy's stone. From two other bags he removes two more cabochons about the same size as the first one. He smiles and exhales through his mouth. He places the three cabochons in a row on the white towel. The contrast with the white background looks like three dark blue holes had formed on the towel.

In the fourth bag is a folded piece of paper. It is another handwritten note from Mort. It starts with a statement that made Michael feel like he was coming in at the middle of a story, "I was there. I stole nothing. I acted on Suzy's request." He looks up at the window and then starts reading again, "I took two shards from the treasure you seek. A lapidary named Oscar Three Bears near Nambe made these three cabochons many years ago from one. The other was sold so I could open Hamilton's." Once again, a mysterious series of statements from Mort. Then, "Good luck with Clue 1. Four more clues to follow."

Below this paragraph printed in uniform lettering is Clue 1.

Wake up little Suzy: *A line from the Everly Brothers song Wake Up Little Susie, because of Suzy.*
Know you weren't a floozy: *A personal statement from Mort.*
The corner of your stone: *Go to her grave headstone.*
To the trees is known: *Go to the side to the pine grove.*
Nearest the front: *Go to the front corner.*
Marks the start of the hunt: *Measure the first distance from that front corner.*
Perpendicular lines meet: *Measure two lines to form a ninety-degree angle.*
Measure in feet: *Measure in feet.*
Slept the same as trouble deep: *4:00 o'clock is the time when they wake up in the song. Measure four feet one way.*
Mama's time is the other feet: *10:00 o'clock is when Susie told her Mama she would be in. Measure ten feet the other way.*
Wake up little Suzy: *The same line from the song as the beginning.*

Michael reads Clue 1 for a second time. Reading it slower while he moved his lips didn't help. He sets the letter on the table. He is exhausted. He looks at the empty box, the three perfect Lander Blue cabochons, the ominous newspaper article and the letter. He smiles, because he knows Mort must have really enjoyed setting up this farewell treasure hunt. This is so Mort.

Michael finally gets out of bed at eleven that night after tossing and turning for an hour. He keeps thinking about the clue. He had spent most of the afternoon researching Lander Blue turquoise, Suzy and Cal, and lots of other useless Internet information about mining and stolen turquoise. He is fascinated by the different mines in New Mexico, Arizona and Nevada. He figures out very quickly that the cabochons Mort put in the box are a small inheritance by themselves, if they are real. He thinks about calling Will, but it is too late.

The casita is cool. Moonlight is coming through the kitchen window. Without turning on a light, he goes to the pot drawer and loads a bowl. His Birkenstocks are waiting at the back door. When he opens the door, he hears the aspen leaves rustling in the light breeze. He sits with his legs out listening. He thinks about sitting with Mort on his back portal when he was a teenager. Mort was never judgmental. After a few puffs he puts the pipe down. A lone car goes by with the windows down. The radio is too loud. He goes back inside.

The next morning at eight Michael calls Cromley's office and asks to see him that morning. Oralynn remembers him from his visit two days earlier. "Mr. Cromley can see you about ten-thirty if that is good for you. He has about thirty minutes." Michael replies, "Perfect. Thank you. See you then." He showers and makes a peanut butter and jelly sandwich. He reads Mort's letter again while he sits at the kitchen bar.

His phone rings. It's Will. "Morning dude. Are you rich?" Michael chuckles. "Not yet, but the prospects are better today than they were yesterday. Come over this evening. I'll get a pizza and some beer." Will replies, "It will be after six, if that's okay?" Without a pause, "See you after that. Don't get any paint on your pretty shirt. Bye, dude."

The visit to Cromley's office was not as fruitful as Michael had hoped. Oralynn smiles as he walks into the suite. "Hi." She quickly returns to the papers on her desk. Cromley comes to the doorway of his office before he can sit down. "Hi Michael. Once again, sorry about Mort. You have had a rough couple of months. I sure am sorry." Michael steps closer to Cromley. "Thank you. Mort told me to come tell you that I found the box. Supposedly a clock starts. Is it true I now have twenty-four days to find a treasure?"

He is trying to read Cromley's face. "You know anything about this?" Cromley laughs and quickly apologizes. "That damn Mort. He came in here about a month ago unannounced. He told me to make sure you found the box. I didn't know what the hell he was talking about." Mort had also told Cromley not to mention the other instructions. He doesn't. Cromley and Oralynn look at each other, both knowing that the other is thinking about that mysterious letter in the file.

Michael leaves Cromley's office disappointed. He is still overwhelmed with questions. The treasure hunt must be real if Mort went to all this trouble. Why twenty-four days? He knows there are five clues. The first one is on his dining table waiting for him to figure it out. After lunch he examines the cabochons again and puts them back in their small bags. He puts one in the pot drawer and the other two back in the Crown bag. He copies the letter, the newspaper article and Clue 1 using his printer. He gathers the original items in a red rope binder and secures it.

For the first time in his life he rents a safe deposit box at his bank. It feels weird. He never felt like he had anything worth securing this way. When he is alone in the room, he opens the top of the long gold box sitting on the fabric-lined island in the middle of the room. He puts the refolded newspaper article in first and the two cabochons on top of it. He lays the envelope with Mort's handwritten letter on top. He folds the lid back and secures it. He slides it back in the only empty slot in the room. He puts the two keys in his pocket. As he walks by the young woman who helped him, he thanks her. He breathes a sigh of relief as he leaves the bank.

20 There Really Is a Turquoise Museum

Back at the casita, Michael parks his Jeep in the garage again. He quickly eats another peanut butter and jelly sandwich. He takes a break from the clue and lays down on his bed in his clothes. Three hours later, he wakes with a start. He thinks he has missed Will. He looks at his phone and flops back down with a thud. He has plenty of time to get the pizza and be back before Will arrives. On his way to get the pizza, he stops by an office supply store and buys a large 2020 wall calendar.

Michael texts Will, "My car is in the garage." He doesn't want Will to think he is not there. Will is a few minutes late. Both are hungry. While Will is in the bathroom, Michael places a garden salad at each setting. Will sits down and looks at Michael. "Where's the pizza?" Michael earnestly explains, "This is it. You need to eat healthier." Will looks disappointed, then pissed. Michael bursts out laughing. He takes the pizza out of the oven, flips the box open and puts it right in front of Will. "Bastard," Will says as he takes two pieces. Michael shows him the cabochon. He then reads to him from the copies of the newspaper clipping and the letter. He tells him what he thinks he has figured out.

Years of playing games and trying to outsmart Mort had prepared Michael in a way that surprises him. He is filled with excitement as he talks with Will. "Mort would not design a hunt that I couldn't figure out. He just wouldn't." He has realized to his relief that his financial well-being was probably not an immediate concern as the cabochons alone were worth sixty thousand to seventy thousand dollars. Michael and Will sit at the dining room table and start dissecting what is in the box.

As Michael holds the newspaper clipping copy in both hands again he says, "I'm not sure exactly what the connection with Suzy is, but she is key. She had a turquoise mine called the Lander Blue. She and her husband shot it out and killed each other. My guess is that Mort was there when it happened." Michael stops. He picks up the copy of the letter and reads the sentence, "I was there. I stole nothing. I acted on her request."

For the first time he focuses on the comment by Cal's brother about the missing turquoise. He slowly reads aloud from the newspaper. He looks at Will. "Maybe this is what Mort is talking about? Maybe this is the treasure?"

Michael lays his new calendar on the table. He writes START on Tuesday, July 13, 2020. They talk about the twenty-four-day deadline for finding the treasure. It seems daunting. There are so many unknowns. Michael looks at the newspaper clipping again. He looks at the letter again. They start to discuss Clue 1. As is tradition, Michael loads up the pipe and they move to the back portal. They both settle into their chairs. The compound is dark. The moon is covered by clouds. Will starts to relax. "This is cool Michael. What if this is true and you become rich?"

"Don't jinx it dude." Michael smiles. They come back inside. "Have you heard the song Wake Up Little Susie? I never liked it. I looked at the lyrics on YouTube this afternoon. I think that's what Mort used for the clue." Michael starts singing the song badly off key. He stops as he pulls up the lyrics on the desktop computer. They sit down at the dining table and look at the clue again.

Wake up little Suzy.
Know you weren't a floozy.
The corner of your stone,
To the trees is known.
Nearest the front,
Marks the start of the hunt.
Perpendicular lines meet,
Measure in feet.
Slept the same as trouble deep.
Mama's time is the other feet.
Wake up little Suzy.

"The corner of your stone." Michael leans back in his chair. "I think he is talking about Suzy's grave. The newspaper clipping mentions the Lander County Hilltop Cemetery. It is in Battle Mountain, Nevada. It's about a fifteen-hour drive. I think the second clue is in this cemetery."

Michael continues, "Looks like there is a grove of trees in the cemetery according to Google Earth. Sounds like the front corner of her grave marker nearest the trees is where to measure from. Slept the same as trouble deep is from the song. They slept till four in the morning in the stupid song. It's a distance. Unsure which way to measure though." As if he is talking to himself, "Mama's time is the other feet is from the song too. Looks like the other dimension is ten feet maybe. That's when Susie tells her mother they will be home." He smiles at Will. "We gotta go and check it out."

Michael knows what Will is thinking. "It's fifteen hours. It's a long-ass drive through some pretty barren land." It doesn't take long for Will to reply. "What if I did go? I could help drive. I can't leave until Thursday after work though. You thinking about doing it all in one leg?" He stops to see if Michael has any reaction. Seeing none he enthusiastically continues, "We could drive it like we used to when we didn't have a lot of time and just wanted to get there."

Michael reacts now. "Would you mind driving some? It's some dull driving for sure. I'd just as soon get there. Probably leave a couple of hours after you get off work. Drive all night in shifts. Take naps." This sounds familiar to both. "We get to Battle Mountain for a late lunch. We have the whole afternoon to explore and see if I am right about the clue. If we need the next morning we can stay. Maybe spend Saturday night in Vegas on the way back. Really would like for you to come with me." He is grinning at Will. "Be nice to have another half brain on the case."

Michael looks away and then back at him. "I will even pretend to like you." Will has heard this a hundred times. He pushes Michael playfully. "Okay asshole. Let's take my car." Will leaves soon after their plans are made. "Pick you up Thursday evening. I am going to take casual stuff. Let me know if anything changes. I think I can make it happen at work. Bring the bikes?"

Michael sits down at the computer. He continues thinking about the clue. He feels like they have a loose grasp on it. The distances are still confusing, but he hopes once they are at her grave, they can figure out what they mean. In his online research, Michael had discovered that there is a turquoise museum in Albuquerque. One of the first images he sees on their website is an elegantly detailed silver squash blossom.

At the bottom, hanging in an intricately stamped setting is a piece of Lander Blue about two-thirds the size of the cabochon in his desk drawer. The rest of the necklace is comprised of twelve silver pods of eight Lander Blue stones each. The caption reads, "Fit for a queen. The most carat weight of Lander Blue in a piece of Navajo jewelry." It is owned by the museum curator. The stones look just like the stones Mort put in the box.

Michael thinks about how little interest he had in learning about turquoise while working at Hamilton's. He was personnel and accounting. He rarely worked with clients or craftsmen. He has a couple of silver rings with stones from the Tyrone and Cerrillos mines. They both are about twelve carats. He knows that the Navajo silver craftsman, Benny Red Feather, is renowned for his work. Mort considered him one of his best. Benny chose his turquoise stones for their quality. On the inside of each ring Benny stamps his trademark three vertical feathers with a line connecting the quill bottoms on one side. He stamps the circle of life on the other side.

Michael looks for anything about missing turquoise from the Lander Blue mine. He finds it mentioned in a couple of rock hound blogs, but nothing official. Several sources mention that only one-hundred-eight pounds were taken from the mine in Lander County, Nevada. The mine has been abandoned for almost fifty years. His eyes are tired. He shuts everything down and goes to bed. He decides to drive to the museum in the morning and see if the curator knows anything about missing Lander Blue turquoise.

The next morning Michael takes the cabochon from the pot drawer and puts it in his pants pocket. He checks the museum address and double-checks the notice on their website to make sure they have reopened from the pandemic. The traffic is light. He arrives at the museum as it is opening. From the street all he can see above the granite-clad eight-foot fence are three metal roofed turrets with ornate wrought iron rails around their tops. After looking at pictures online, Michael already thinks it looks like a commercial version of the Addams Family house.

Adding to the compound's uniqueness are giant out-of-place blue spruce trees surrounding the building. He takes the first left after he passes the museum. He enters a small parking area and parks in one of several empty spaces. As he goes through a heavy black wrought-iron gate he smiles. "Morticia and Gomez, here I come."

The entry to the museum goes through the gift shop. He asks a woman behind the counter if he can meet the curator. She smiles. "May I ask why?" He replies, "I have something personal I want to discuss with him." The nice woman smiles. "He is quite busy and..." She stops. Michael is holding the cabochon in his extended right hand. He holds it closer to her. "I want to talk to him about this." She is visibly surprised. He sees from her face that she recognizes the Lander Blue turquoise.

She introduces herself, quickly extending her hand. "I'm Elizabeth Doring. I'm Butch's wife. He is the curator. He is not in right now, but will be in about thirty minutes if you want to tour the museum? I know he will want to talk with you." Michael smiles. "I hoped to tour it, so that will be great. How much is it?" She moves toward him and quietly says, "This is on the museum. Please go on in." As he starts walking off Elizabeth adds, "Sorry, I didn't catch your name."

He stops and returns to her and extends his hand. "Michael Hamilton." They shake hands briefly. Michael follows the arrows out the door of the gift shop and through the courtyard to the museum entrance. He opens one of the big wooden doors expecting to hear the theme to the Addams family.

He is immediately drawn to the exhibit which shows how a raw piece of turquoise is turned into a finished stone. He has never seen raw turquoise. As he is looking at the display, Michael hears a voice behind him. "Just by some wild coincidence are you related to Mort Hamilton from Santa Fe?" He turns. An impeccably groomed and dressed man is about four feet from him. His hand is extended.

Michael introduces himself as Mort's grandson. "I hope that is a good thing being his grandson." Butch chuckles. His eyes sparkle. "I haven't seen Mort in a decade at least, but we dealt a lot of turquoise and used some of the same artists. He was a character." It's quickly apparent that Butch liked Mort and recognized his expertise. He motions to Michael to follow him to a small table coincidentally located next to the Lander Blue Mine display. As they sit Butch eagerly says, "Liz thinks you might have quite the stone with you."

Before he takes out the cabochon Michael puts his arms on the table and looks at Butch. "I am sorry to say, Mort passed away unexpectedly recently from the virus." Butch puts his hand on Michael's right arm and softly laments, "I can't believe it. He was only in his early eighties. I am so sorry." They sit for a minute quietly, as if they are enjoying the light coming in from a nearby window.

To continue the conversation, Michael takes the cabochon from his pocket and shows it to Butch. Butch immediately takes it gently in his hands. He stands and walks over to a window and holds it up to the light. He studies it, turning it very slowly. "It is perfect Lander Blue. Twenty-eight carats at least. Rare. It is truly blue gold." He comes back to Michael and hands him the stone. He is looking at Michael curiously as he sits back down. "This stone is priceless. It's worth more than gold." His voice is excited. "If you don't mind my asking, where did you get this?"

Michael had pondered his answer to this question since he left Santa Fe. "The family had it." He knew that was not the answer Butch wanted, but he had his attention. Butch continues, "I am aware of most Lander Blue that exists. Especially the larger stones. Do you know where," he lowers his voice, "the family got it?" His tone is more forceful. He is excited. "I am very curious about its origin."

Michael doesn't want to bring up the treasure hunt. He decides to ignore his question and pursue the reason he came, "Do you know anything about a missing twenty pounds of Lander Blue turquoise? I have become quite interested in this unique turquoise now that I have this piece. I have seen references on a couple of rock hound blogs about how only eighty-eight pounds of a hundred and eight pounds mined are accounted for?" He gives Butch a chance to process his question. "Is this true? Do you know anything about it?"

Butch is ready to strut his stuff. "It's a mystery for sure. I have seen the mine logs that show the mine production. It's now a legend that has existed since the mine shut down fifty years ago. Collectors hope it will be found, but I stopped speculating about it long ago."

Michael pushes Butch. "So, the missing twenty pounds of turquoise could exist?" Butch stares at him. Michael knows he is thinking about the cabochon and its relationship to the question he just asked. "Do you know any of the theories related to why it is missing?"

As if Butch had seen the newspaper clipping in the well house box, "There was a weird domestic dispute that ended badly for the husband and wife who owned the mine I believe. It was before my time. I think that is when the story started about the missing turquoise. Every piece of Lander Blue turquoise over ten carats is accounted for. Whether it exists or not, I don't know, but based on the mine records, there should be another twenty pounds worth a lot of money somewhere."

As Michael stands to leave, Butch stands too. He looks directly at Michael. "I head an exclusive turquoise collectors club. I am sure someone would be interested in this stone or any other Lander Blue that you have, especially if it is like this. I could set up a bidding war with a couple of emails and a picture of this beauty."

Michael feels the cabochon in his pocket. He doesn't acknowledge what Butch said, "It was a pleasure to meet you. Thank you for your time. I'm sure I will see you again." He is too absorbed in what he has learned from Butch to notice the burned area on the highway on his way back to Santa Fe.

21 First Trip

Will is to pick Michael up at eight o'clock in the evening. Michael has checked the weather in Battle Mountain. Dry and hot with more dry and hot. Looking at the online *Santa Fe New Mexican* to kill time, he sees that the virus that took Mort has subsided in New Mexico. Things are getting back to normal. He doesn't want to think about the wasted lives, especially his grandfather's.

Will pulls up in his clean Land Rover ten minutes early. His bike is locked on the back. They put Michael's worn Ghost in front of it and lock it in. "I'll take the first leg. Got us some Starbuicks." Will had heard Mort call it that before. It seemed appropriate to use the term to refer to their coffee as they start the search for Mort's Clue 2. They have each driven two four-hour legs by the time they get to Austin, Nevada late the next morning. The drive is uneventful. Both have napped along the way. They are in pretty good shape.

Michael pulls into a convenience store. He stands next to the Rover thinking about how nice it is not to be moving. He is waiting for Will to use the restroom. He remembers seeing a sign in Ely, Nevada a couple of hours ago when they stopped for gas. "The only supermarket for the next hundred and fifty-three miles if you are going west. Stop in at the Liberty Pit Market." When he pays the station cashier for the gas the kid is talkative. "You are lucky to get gas. The tanker came this morning. Today is the first time we have had gas in two weeks." Michael remembers thinking, "What a shithole part of the world."

An old woman with a colorful scarf poorly wrapped around her gray hair walks by carrying a twelve-pack of Keystone beer. She opens the door to a beat-up rusted red Toyota truck parked in the adjoining space. She smiles at Michael. She sees the clean Rover and the bikes.

"Where are you headed?" she asks in a friendly voice. Michael doesn't like engaging with strangers, but he replies, "Battle Mountain." She smiles. "I was born there." She continues, "We were designated the

Armpit of America for our lack of character and charm in two thousand one." She smiles again. "They said we are nasty people. As you can tell we are." Michael sarcastically replies while smiling, "You are really making me want to go there."

"We have an annual Festival of the Pit coming up," she yells as she gets in the Toyota. "Get it?" The door hinges creak loudly as she gets in. The old truck belches smoke when it starts. The old woman waves as she passes him on her way out of the parking lot. Michael chuckles out loud. Will comes back and gets into the driver's seat. Michael tells him the story of the woman with the Keystone beer. "We're going to the armpit of the world. It may be a close shave during a hairy experience." Once Will gets the joke, they laugh about it the rest of the trip.

The sun is hot and bright as they drive the last leg to Battle Mountain. The land is flat with little vegetation. It is baked. There are mountains in the distance all around. Towering thunderheads cling to them. Occasionally they see an expanse of weirdly shaped rock formations and then nothing. Michael tells Will, "I read that people come to this area to disappear. By the looks of this land I wonder where they go?" They laugh. Battle Mountain is visible five miles out. They drive in on the main street. The Rover's tires rumble as they roll over the bricks. They pass the Battle Mountain Diner and keep going west. Four blocks later, they have seen the sights. They turn around and head back to the diner.

The lunch rush is over. There are a few tables of locals drinking coffee and shooting the breeze. A couple look up, but resume talking quickly. The greasy diner smell is unmistakable. It sticks to everything that enters. The counter is empty. Michael is sure the locals take them for adventure-seeking young men passing through. They sit on the middle two stools. They both immediately spin around taking in the diner. They look at each other and laugh. It is like they choreographed it. Michael looks around to see if anyone saw them.

Down at the end of the bar where it turns into the wall is a slim young woman. She is watching them as she fills and wipes salt and pepper shakers. When she sees Michael look her way she smiles. She has a loose-fitting red linen shirt tucked into 501s. Her long brown hair is pulled up messily on her head. She walks down the bar grabbing a French fry from a hidden plate. By the time she reaches them it is gone. "Could I help you dancing gentlemen?" Will chimes in, "If you are talking about the stool twirl, we do that all the time." They all laugh.

She gets a couple of menus and holds them to her chest, "Do you want something to drink?" Both reply at the same time, "Coke please." When she reaches to set the plastic laminated menus down, her right sleeve draws up revealing a silver bracelet with a large Lander Blue stone. Michael is stunned when he sees it. Without thinking he says, "Is that a Lander Blue stone in your bracelet?" She has started walking away. She stops. "Do you know what Lander Blue is?"

She goes to get their Cokes. She returns and sets the drinks on Miller Lite cardboard coasters. There are so many water rings in the copper countertop that Michael wonders why bother. He is pleased that there is a lot of ice. He inserts the straw and drains the glass in front of the young woman with a loud slurp at the end. He looks up and apologizes to her, "We've been driving all night and I need the sugar and caffeine."

The young woman clutches the edge of the bar. Her hands are tan. Her fingernails are manicured and red like her blouse. There is a circle of life tattoo on the top of the fourth finger of her right hand. "Where are you two from?" Will replies looking at Michael, "Santa Fe. Guess you live around here?" She replies, "My father lived here."

Michael asks again, "Not meaning to pry, but is that a Lander Blue stone?" The woman looks at him hard, "Yes. I got it from a family member. How do you know about Lander Blue?" Knowing he had to answer Michael says, "My grandfather left me some and I have learned about it. We are exploring the area. Lots of turquoise mines near Battle Mountain."

She asks them what they want to eat. They both order a cheeseburger with fries. She grabs Michael's empty glass and leaves them without another word. She goes to the narrow chest-high window into the kitchen. They hear her give the cook their order. When she brings the Coke she says, "I had a family member a long time ago who had the Lander Blue mine." Michael is alert. He leans toward her. "This is too much. Was her name Suzy Hapgood?" The waitress pauses. She is staring at the entry door. "Okay, this is weird. How do you know this?"

Michael introduces himself, "I'm Michael Hamilton. This is Willow Gantry. He doesn't look like much, but he is my best friend. We are here seeing the area. Maybe do some bike riding." There is an awkward silence while she tries to decide if she will introduce herself. "I'm Rita. Rita Owens. Suzy was married to my grandfather's brother." Before she can continue Michael interjects, "His name was Cal." She nods, still trying to figure out how they know about her family. A group of four workmen come in and sit down at the bar. Rita starts toward the new group. She looks back at them. "Your burgers will be out in a minute."

When she brings their food Michael softly says, "I know you are busy, and this is very presumptuous. Could we visit some more when you get off work? I know you don't know us, but I really would like to talk to you about the mine." Rita walks away. "Let me think about it." After taking the workmen's orders and turning them in, she walks by. "My curiosity is too much. Meet me in the courtyard of the Blue Gem Tavern at four-thirty."

They finish their burgers. Rita is busy now. Workers getting off work and eating before they go home to their trailers or manufactured houses fill the stools. Michael leaves a twenty-dollar tip. As they are walking out, he catches Rita's eye. He mouths, 'Thank you. See you in a bit." She smiles again. There is something mysterious about her that he finds attractive already. He is looking forward to seeing her again and they hadn't left their first meeting.

They walk to the Rover, both thinking about Rita. Michael can tell Will is attracted to her too. He is trying to figure out how to approach her about the missing twenty pounds of turquoise. They open the Rover's doors. The heat blasts out. Will starts the air conditioner sarcastically saying, "Really nice here in the armpit. At least the burger was pretty damn tasty." After some of the heat is pushed out, they get in the car and head back onto the main street.

They drive to the Rainbow's End Motor Court, where Michael had made reservations. The old motor court is shaped like a U. There is a liquor store on one end. There are two other cars in the lot. Continuing with the sarcasm Will smirks, "Bet the tourists are still out seeing the pit's sights." They pull right up in front of their room. As they unload their gear they decide not to nap. They get back in the Rover and drive until they find the Lander County Hilltop Cemetery.

As they stare at the stark cemetery, Michael muses, "There's no grass. Bro, I don't want to be buried where there's no grass." The tombstones, the faded plastic flowers, the tattered barely discernible mini-US flags stand out on an otherwise gray surface. Michael excitedly says, "Let's go. We can check it out early in the morning. Head back to Vegas for tomorrow night." They arrive at the Blue Gem Tavern about fifteen minutes early.

The bar's courtyard is accessed through an opening between two large rocks. The rocks have visible veins of turquoise running through them. Two large cottonwood trees shade the brown gravel surface which contains four-top tables. They find a table and sit down on either side. Michael sits looking west at looming Long Peak. The sun will be going down behind it in about three hours. They order Pacificos and look around. There are a couple of bikers sitting at one of the tables. Despite the heat, they have matching Dark Rider emblazoned leather jackets on. They have their heads together talking softly.

A light breeze comes up as Rita enters the courtyard. Her hair is braided. She has changed from hiking boots into black Birkenstocks. Her red toenails match her fingernails. Michael and Will look at each other and smile. Both realize she is going to choose a side of the table to sit on. This was not the first time that a woman would choose between the two of them after a brief meeting. Will usually has the upper hand because of his dark skin and smile. Michael is more serious, but also has a look that women find attractive, especially with his shirt off. The Marines chiseled him, not just mentally.

She walks straight to Michael's side of the table and sits down. Like she is alerting them, "One of the perks of working at the diner is you smell edible until you can shower." They all laugh politely. Michael looks at her. "I like that smell." A woman about Rita's age brings a ginger ale with ice and a big lime wedge and sets it down in front of her. She departs without saying a word. Rita doesn't even acknowledge that she didn't order the drink, or that the waitress brought it without being asked. She is looking at Michael. "My curiosity got the best of me. So why are you here again?" As if ordered, he replies, "Like I said, my grandfather left me some Lander Blue cabochons. Will and I came to the area to learn more about it."

He pulls the small felt bag from his pocket and shows her the twenty-eight-carat cabochon matching the one in her bracelet. She takes it in her hand and holds it up to the light. Michael remembers Butch, the Turquoise Museum curator, doing the same thing. She hands it back to him and stares at him curiously. "So, what do you all do?" Will answers, "I run a family-owned paint business and Michael ran a family native American jewelry business." Michael adds, "We've known each other since childhood and have still managed to stay friends." Rita focuses on the Willow part this time and looks at him. He smiles and explains it. "The only time our bromance was in question was when this stupid shit spent four years on the ground in Afghanistan." His tone becomes serious and with real admiration. "He is my hero!" Michael is looking at the mountain range to the west.

He doesn't acknowledge what Will says and looks at Rita smiling, "So what's up with the Battle Mountain armpit designation?" She laughs out loud. "How do you know about that?" He tells her about the old woman at the convenience store. Nodding her head, "I think I agree. I came here because of my father. My family has been in the area for several generations. Most of them worked for the Vegas mob." She quickly adds, "My father was a truck driver. I'm not sure why he stayed here. He was not like the others."

"My grandfather Roscoe inherited the Lander Blue mine when Suzy and Cal permanently ended their relationship. He was a known asshole too. He had it for two years." Michael asks Rita, "Have you ever seen the mine?" Rita replies, "It's been a while. It's been shut down for a long time." Before she can finish Michael adds, "About forty years."

"My grandfather dealt with a lot of turquoise." Michael presses on, embellishing the story. "He loved Lander Blue. He told me a story about twenty pounds that disappeared after it was taken out of the mine." He looks at Rita thinking, "She's gonna think I'm crazy." She does. She has a WTF look on her face. "How would you know anything about that?" Michael shrugs. "It's just what my grandfather told me about the mine."

Rita starts talking about Battle Mountain without answering the question. Like a good wingman Will interrupts, "I gotta ask. Are you married? A boyfriend?" She retorts quickly, "What does it matter?" Will smiles and looks away sheepishly. "We just want to know if we need to be afraid of anybody other than you." She smiles and looks at Michael. "Not right now." Will's phone rings. He looks at it and mumbles "Shit" under his breath. He gets up from the table as he listens. A serious look comes over his face. Michael recognizes that something is wrong.

Will comes slowly back to the table. He looks at Rita. "Sorry Rita." He looks at Michael. "My fill-in manager had a car accident about an hour ago. He is in intensive care." Michael knows what is coming. "The store is short-handed. There's a big order for one of our main customers. I knew this shit would happen. My parents are gone too." Will is visibly agitated. "I am sorry, bro. No one knows how to set the mixes on the new computerized paint mixer. The salesman from Albuquerque is on vacation too. Shit." He paces away. "There's no one to call."

Years of friendship became apparent. "Hang on Will. We got this."

Michael turns to Rita. He starts slow. He is looking at the ground. "I really enjoyed meeting you. It feels like more than coincidence. I think my grandfather met your great aunt." Michael was unsure if she heard the last sentences. The bikers start their bikes on the other side of the courtyard wall drowning out any conversation. He thinks maybe it's best if she doesn't hear, "Would you mind if I stayed in touch? I probably will be back this way when I can dump his lame ass." He hugs Will with one arm.

Michael is relieved when Rita speaks. "I think there is more to your story. You are not hurting my eyes either, at least yet," she mischievously taunts him. "Since you started it, do you have a wife or girlfriend?" She is looking at Michael. "Will's the only friend I have, much less a girlfriend." He looks straight at her. "I sure don't." She shyly smiles, looks at Will and then back at Michael. She takes a napkin and writes her number on it. Michael sticks out his hand to shake hers. She hands him the napkin. He takes it and stuffs it in his front pants pocket. He extends his hand again. She realizes he wants to shake her hand. She likes this. She thinks this might be the first time it has happened since she has been in Battle Mountain. To her it's a subtle sign that a man views a woman as being an equal.

She shakes his hand and then Will's. Michael is standing. "I got your unordered soda. Thanks again for visiting with us. See you soon." She smiles one last time and turns to go. Both stare as she walks away. They hear a throat clearing. Their waitress is standing next to Michael with the check. Rita exits the courtyard before either turn. When their waitress returns Michael asks, "You know Rita?" She replies looking around, "Yep. She probably is the smartest person in Lander County." He starts to ask another question. "Got to go. You want change?" Michael gets it. "No. Thank you." She is already at another table.

They checkout of the Rainbow as they now call it. They gas up and get on the road. Will starts apologizing again. "It's not your fault, other than your poor planning." Michael stops and waits for effect. "You have done so much stuff for me. Let it go. Besides, there is something about Rita. I will come back soon. Having the lay of the land helps. Don't you think it's weird that we ran into Suzy's great niece?" Michael lowers his voice. "What if we are in an episode of the Twilight Zone and the Lander Blue is pulling everybody together for some unknown reason?"

"Speaking of the zone." Michael reaches into his shirt pocket and pulls out a store-bought joint. They drive all night arriving about an hour after Will's lone employee opened the shop. Michael drives most of the way so Will can sleep. He would have to stay awake for forty-eight-hour periods sometimes in Afghanistan. When they were shorthanded on patrol and they needed multiple guards, there was no choice. He didn't have the constant fear to motivate him this trip, but he manages just fine.

He drops Will at his store and takes the Rover to his casita. He parks and moves his Jeep out of the garage so he can park the Rover next to his mother's Mercedes. He shuts the garage door and heads through the courtyard to his bed.

22 A Girl with History

Rita leaves Will and Michael feeling cautiously happy, but mainly curious. Nice guys. Pretty normal. Must have money. The story about being interested in Lander Blue combined with how much Michael knew about her family was disconcerting. Though it was not a secret, there were not many people who knew of the missing twenty pounds of turquoise. Those who do know consider it an almost fifty-year-old myth. The family gave up trying to find it. She gets a text from her best friend in Battle Mountain, the waitress at the Gem. "Who were those guys?" There are two thumbs up emojis. Rita texts back, "Tell you when we catch up."

Michael has an assuredness about him that she likes. He looks like a rich hippie type. She thought for a minute, maybe frat boy meets hippie meets army guy. On the ground in Afghanistan for four years. Not your typical frat boy or hippie. She takes off her red linen shirt and bra, dropping them to the floor by her pants. She goes into the bathroom adjoining her room in the trailer. The shower water is cool. She moved into her dad's trailer house when he died. He owned it and the half acre it was on. Now she does. She misses her dad. "Thanks, Pop, for the trailer."

Battle Mountain was her dad's home base. He was a truck driver up until three years ago. At age fifty-two he was diagnosed with stage two lung cancer. He was a smoker, so no one was surprised. Though the radiation had stopped the spread, he had part of his right lung removed. He no longer could drive because of coughing spasms that were almost uncontrollable. Breathing oxygen for a couple of minutes usually helped. Each time Rita witnessed an episode she feared if it would be his last.

Rita was away at the University of Texas, two years into a finance degree, when her mother died. Her father never remarried and never showed any interest in being with another woman. This was atypical of an Owens man. Womanizing seemed to be a part of the genetic heritage.

Rita moved back to Battle Mountain from Texas to help her father after she completed an internship. She was one of two graduate students chosen from Nevada to participate in the University of Texas MBA program. At twenty-six, she was a post-grad rising star. The virus hit and all of that went out the window. Her dad had helped her with school, but she has accrued student loans that have to be paid. She is a hard worker and does not consider herself to be above the job at the diner.

Dwight Owens died about a month ago. Rita's grieving was short because he was so much better off. She thought that the virus would be the culprit, but he passed in his sleep from the cancer. She is settling his small estate and planning her next move. She works at the diner for the cash flow. Being an investment adviser requires clients with money to invest. Battle Mountain has none.

The shower water splashes on a small red rose outlined in black on her tanned left shoulder. It is simple, perfectly done. The owner of Atomic Tattoo in Austin did it himself. He and Rita had taken a graduate negotiation class together and became friends. She finishes her shower and dries only her hair. Her unexpected encounter with the Santa Feans this afternoon occupies her thoughts. She wants to sit, smoke a cigarette and think some more.

Despite her dad's cancer, Rita is a closet smoker. Still wet, she puts on a light robe and goes out the back door of the trailer onto a small wooden deck. A large faded green umbrella covers a table with two chairs. She sits down in one of the chairs. She watches lightning rip through a thunderhead to the east. She lights an American Spirit, tossing the two-week-old turquoise pack on the table.

She finds Willow and his name endearing. She smiles thinking about the shit that Michael gave him about being a paint salesman. It is obvious that there is a strong bond between the two. They protect each other. She wishes she had a friend like that.

She looks at the bracelet on her wrist. She knows she could always sell Suzy's bracelet to make money. She had been offered over twenty-five thousand dollars for it. She slides it off her wrist and holds it. She smiles. "Not today. A sister of yours made a visit to Battle Mountain to see you." Her phone pings. There is a text from the only man she has dated since she returned. Now he has become a nuisance. "I need to talk to you."

She has been trying to get him to leave her alone for about two months now. She was at a low spot when they met. Normally men in uniform did not turn her head, but she needed something and thought he might be it. It took her a while to take to the idea. His possessiveness was obvious immediately. He drove her away after only a couple of weeks. They had a difficult breakup after she told him that she did not want to see him again.

Not running into each other was an impossibility in Battle Mountain. As expected, Deputy Sherriff Hugo Benson could not handle it. He refused to believe it is possible for a woman to have a male friend without it being sexual. Rita regrets ever having anything to do with Hugo. She doesn't respond. She is tired of him to the point of not really caring what he thinks or says.

Her phone rings. It is Hugo. She stuns her phone. It rings the full six times. He leaves a message saying that he is hurt that she has not returned his calls or texts. She has heard it before. "I'm gonna have to get a restraining order to keep this asshole away if he doesn't die of natural causes." She puts the cigarette out. She leans back in the chair, stretching her legs. She wonders if Michael will call her. He said he was coming back. Whatever he is up to it must be important for him to drive fifteen hours back to Battle Mountain. She closes her eyes and hopes he does.

23 Session 3

It has been several days since Oralynn has heard from Cozy. She is conflicted about the way he treated her after their last liaison. He hurt her feelings. She is so used to ignoring her feelings that she still wants him to like her. He is still a mix of her father and the gallant lover from one of her smut novels. She thinks she can overlook that he is married, but that is nagging at her too. She still wonders why the tea pot was in the dish drainer when she came in the morning after he stayed late to work on whatever. Maybe he drank tea, but she doubts it. She is crazy today. She no longer trusts him, but she still wants him.

To compound her anxiousness, she has discovered something else. Yesterday she put a note about Mort's will in his file. Cromley remembered that Mort wanted it opened after the designated twenty-four days. Out of habit she takes out the letter out and looks at the back flap. Her nail crease does not align. She lays the envelope flat on her desk in the light. It's off about an eighth of an inch. She quickly puts the envelope back in Mort's file. Because of her, Cozy is the only other person that knows about the letter and Mort's mysterious requests. The wave of guilt that sweeps over her is almost unbearable.

Guilt and lust. By lunch she can't stand it anymore. She calls Cozy's cell when Cromley leaves for lunch. Surprisingly he picks up. He is very nice, throwing her off guard. She stammers briefly. "Can you come by the office this afternoon after closing?" Cozy lied. "I only have a short time. I'm busy." Oralynn somewhat whiney, "Will you be nice to me?" There is a pause. "I'm going. May be later when I can get there." Cozy hangs up. Oralynn is even more frustrated after the exchange. Under her breath, "It's gonna be a long afternoon."

She stresses all afternoon. Sex or not? She finally flips a coin. Sex wins, but by the time Cozy arrives she has changed her mind several times. The sun is going down when he comes in the door smiling. That was enough. They have sex. It is rougher than before. At one point he pins her against the kitchenette wall after picking her up off the counter. She makes him release her. She puts her feet on the floor. She gets back on the counter and they finish, perspiring and breathing hard.

They dress quietly not looking at each other. Oralynn looks at him. "Something has been bothering me. Did you tamper with anything in the Hamilton file the last time you were here?" Cozy doesn't say anything. She continues, "You are the only other person who knew about Mort's letter. Did you open it?" Cozy looks hard at her. She is reminding him of Slipper as he replies with a line from arguments with her "Why would I do that?" As with Slipper most times, his answer does not satisfy Oralynn. "You did it didn't you?"

She backs away from him a couple of steps. "So fucking what," he angrily blurts out. Without giving her a chance to reply, "How did you know? The letter had a riddle about what the son had done with Mort when he was ten. It made no sense. It did mention finding a treasure worth millions of dollars."

Cozy is pacing. "Don't be stupid. What do you care?" Oralynn is mad at him and herself. "I need to tell Mr. Cromley. You can't get away with doing this." He steps toward her. "You better not." He grabs her and holds her in front of him. His face is about six inches from hers. She feels his fingers sinking into her biceps. It will leave bruises to explain. She starts crying. "I may not be anything to you, but I'm not going to be a victim. You don't get to do this. You have taken advantage of me."

Oralynn starts kicking and flailing her arms. She tries to kick Cozy in the crotch, her foot glancing off his thigh. He smacks her in the face. They tussle until it is out of hand. At point blank range he punches her right in the face with his clenched fist. She falls and hits her head on the corner of the desk. She is immediately lifeless. Cozy can't believe it. He feels for a pulse. Nothing. Instantaneous second-degree murder. He looks around the office. No sign of a struggle. There is nothing to clean up. He takes a few breaths to calm himself.

He places her in her chair for the last time. He stares at her while he thinks about how to handle this. His police instincts kick in for the wrong reasons. Fingerprints are not a problem. He's a regular here. If he leaves her here it will be easy to trace his DNA because they had sex. He has been responsible for deaths no one cared about, but he had never had to dispose of a body. He is not in the mood to dig a hole or carry a dead weight load for a long way. Diablo Canyon requires too much walking to get away from where the hikers go. Everyplace he thinks about has too many hikers. Burying the body is required unless he can get to a remote area. "There's no way I can lug her far on foot."

He's got it. He gets her purse and removes her car keys. He looks out the window to the parking lot below. It is dark now. He wonders if they will test her body to see if she had sex before her death. If he is lucky, it will be several days before her body is recovered at this place. Cozy hopes it won't matter by then.

He goes through the courtyard to the parking lot. There is no one around. He moves his car to a spot on a side street a block away. He returns to her car. He looks around as he puts on a thin pair of leather gloves that he always carries. He gets in and adjusts the seat. He remembers the setting. She has a cross hanging from the rear-view mirror. He instinctively touches it as he starts her car. He drives her car into the parking spot closest to the courtyard. He can't believe this is happening.

Being outside in the cool night air calms him. He stops in the courtyard and looks around again at his path to Oralynn's car. "Slow down. Hurrying unnecessarily is how you miss things." Once he is back in the office, he calls a young man who always owes him a favor. "Teddy, it's Cozy. Listen to me. No fucking questions. Pick me up at the Gorge Bridge parking area at ten o'clock." There is no response. Then, "Hey, I got a girl at my place and it's going good. I can't leave." Cozy laughs meanly. "I don't have time for this shit. You do it or you won't have to worry about it ever going good with a girl again. Worse, your mother is gonna know me better than you want her to. See you in three hours at the bridge parking lot." He knows Teddy will do it, even without the threat to his mother.

He puts Oralynn's left arm over his shoulder. His right arm grabs her waist. He starts helping her to her car like she is drunk. After he exits the courtyard it is too much. He picks her up and carries her. He sits her down roughly in the passenger seat. He secures the seatbelt so she will be sitting up. A tiny stream of blood is coming from a gash on her forehead. Cozy is puffing and sweating by the time he gets in. He wonders if he will be able to dispose of her body like he has planned.

As he drives north, he ruminates about the times he used to frame suspects. Some watched him do it. Nothing to be proud of, but just like the task he is performing now, it is necessary. "Me or them." He stops in Pojoaque to put gas in her car. Running out of gas is not an option and the warning light is on. He pulls to the end pump, away from the only other car at the pumps.

Oralynn's head is on her chest. She is slumped against the door. He hopes no one is looking as he goes around to her side and opens the door slightly. He gently straightens her. He knows the risk, but he quickly pays with cash inside the store. He jumps when the pump makes a loud click as it automatically stops at fifteen dollars. The station's flickering canopy lights are giving him a headache. He is glad to get back in the car and on the road again.

He and Oralynn are headed for the Rio Grande Gorge Bridge ten miles northwest of Taos. This is his best choice for body disposal this evening. He has read in the paper that most jumpers come from somewhere else. Usually they don't leave notes or explanations. This bridge has been the choice of over one-hundred-forty suicide jumpers in the last twenty-five years. Locals are numb to the deaths, except someone must eventually go into the gorge and retrieve the bodies. Sometimes they land in the river. Most times they land in the rocks. This makes retrieval even more complicated. There are no lights or guards. It is perfect.

The night is cloudy. The traffic thins as he leaves Espanola. By the time he sees the bridge, the moon has escaped the clouds and is illuminating the steel structure. Another good thing about this place is you can see someone coming for ten minutes before they arrive. He stops at the end of the bridge near the parking area. He lays Oralynn flat on the ground down the slope out of sight. He doesn't want to carry her body from the parking area. He then drives to the parking area. There is an old GMC truck parked in the lot. Cozy hopes the driver does not show up, because that will complicate things.

He backs her car into a spot at the far edge. He locks it. Whoever identifies it will at least have to go to the back of it to see the license plate. He keeps looking to make sure no cars are coming. There is no place to hide once they are on the bridge. They will be two loving tourists clutching each other tightly as they stroll to the middle of a bouncy steel bridge six-hundred-fifty feet in the air on a moonlit night. He picks up her body and holds her erect. He puts her car keys in her skirt pocket. She is starting to get cold and he doesn't want to touch her.

He is thinking as they start out, the drive to the bridge was the only time he was ever with Oralynn outside of Cromley's office. Sadly, he thinks she kind of got her wish to be out with him. The thought doesn't last long as he sees lights coming from the direction of Taos in the distance. He must now hurry. He carries her body over his shoulder the last hundred feet. He is sweating and gasping for breath when he arrives at the observation deck at the bridge midpoint.

He breathes loudly for thirty seconds as he watches the car get closer. With no choice but to continue, he musters the strength to heave Oralynn's body over the five-foot-high chain link guard rail. The gorge is a dark void under the gigantic night sky. He watches her fall until he can't see anything anymore. He looks up at the sky. Thousands of twinkling stars just saw what he did.

Chicano hip-hop blares to these same stars as a lowrider speeds by with the windows down about two minutes later. Cozy is almost to the end of the bridge. He looks straight ahead as they pass. He is glad he thought to grab his M1911 from his car. The scabbard is clipped to his belt under his untucked shirt. This will be a matter of "Do they want to fuck with someone or not?" Cozy keeps watching the lowrider to make sure no brake lights come on. They don't. He is sweating again by the time he reaches the parking lot.

He knows the chances of being identified are slim, but he is pissed that he has been seen on the bridge. He sits at a concrete table out of the lone parking lot light. A couple of cars pass while he is waiting for Teddy. The breeze feels good, but the quiet is eerily bothersome. Cozy is tired. At about 9:45, he sees headlights coming from the east. A young frizzy-haired driver slowly pulls into the parking lot. Cozy has kept Teddy from being jailed for drug possession several times. He is his stooge now. As the stooge slowly rolls up, the window comes down. "Hey, fuck you Cozy. Hey, this wipes the slate clean." Cozy gets into his car. "No it doesn't you little asshole. I'll tell you when the slate is clean. Get me back to Santa Fe."

The road through the gut of Taos is deserted. During the day it is a constantly flowing artery of motorcycles, cars and semis. Cozy thinks about stopping at the old Adobe Bar in the Taos Inn for a drink. Its iconic neon sign is a beacon to the only open bar in town. He mumbles, "Wish I had my flask." Teddy ignores his comment. "Hey, what the fuck are you doing at the bridge?" Cozy is ready for that question. "This deal came up suddenly. I had to ride with someone else there. We met a drug smuggler. After the meet I was to be left there. That's all you need to know." Teddy is quiet the rest of the drive.

By midmorning the next day Cromley is on the phone with Oralynn's mother. He has work she needs to do, but he is more worried that something has happened to her. This is not like her at all. She never misses work without calling and without having a good reason. Her mother is worried too, because she isn't answering her cell. They have gone by her house and things look normal, other than her car is not there.

24 Session 3 Fallout

Cromley has a feeling of dread all morning. Oralynn has worked for him for ten years. He calls her the brains of the outfit. He does the lawyering part. She runs the organization and is the face of the office. People like her. He likes her. He calls her mother again at lunch. No word. He calls mid-afternoon. She starts in frantic Spanish and then switches to English. "I called the Santa Fe Police and the Sherriff's office. They can't do anything until my darling girl is missing forty-eight hours. Can you do anything Senor Cromley?"

He calls the Sheriff's office after he hangs up with Oralynn's mother. He knows until an APB is issued there is no real search. The dispatcher tells him that anyone on patrol or moving around in the area is already looking for her car. An APB is issued the next morning. The police contact him by phone when he is about to leave the office. A female officer introduces herself and asks, "Her mother mentioned that Oralynn fights depression and issues with her self-esteem. Do you know anything about this?" Cromley thinks about his answer. "Yes, I know about these things." Without prompting he continues, "It seemed she had turned the corner. We talked last week as we were getting ready to leave for the day. Her work with the therapist has really helped. She could laugh at herself." Cromley stops as tears fill his eyes. "She could use more self-confidence, but she is such a good person."

When asked, Cromley replies that he doesn't think she has a boyfriend. "I doubt it. She has not mentioned anyone. She usually tells me that stuff." Next question. "Does anyone else work out of your office?" Cromley thinks of Slipper and gets a harder look on his face. "The only other person is a Private Investigator, Lester MacFarland. He's a retired cop from Albuquerque. He is in and out some on an as-needed basis."

The night Cozy returns from the bridge he rents a room at the Desert Scene Motel on Cerrillos Road. He is unsure how long he will stay there. His outlook darkens as the reality of what he did sinks in. He spends the next day drinking heavily and the day after that getting over it. He feels that weird adrenaline rush he gets from using raw power over weaker people. He is afraid to contact Slipper because of the dark thoughts he has about her. He has felt his world shrinking around him like this before.

When he sleeps, Cozy dreams about walking with Oralynn's body to the middle of the bridge. Her dead weight almost drags him down with each step. It is almost impossible to get her body over the chain link barrier. Once over, she is visible only for a short time twisting in the wind as she disappears into the dark of the gorge. When her body finds the bottom there is a thud. He knows that this sound never makes its way out of the gorge darkness to the bridge, but he hears it loudly in his dream.

As soon as the APB is released a Taos County Sherriff's Deputy finds her car in the Gorge Bridge parking area. Her purse and phone are in the front passenger seat. Coincidentally that morning someone had called to report what might be a body in the rocks below the bridge. Barely visible, the body is lodged between two giant boulders about twenty feet from the river.

Three days later the bridge has an added tourist attraction. It takes the three-person retrieval crew five hours to descend the nearly sixty-five stories to Oralynn's body. Standing at the river's edge and looking up at the bridge meant half the job was almost done. Traversing the obstacle course of sharp rocks, cactus, rattlesnakes and precipitous drop-offs had cost two rescuers their lives four jumpers ago. The difficulty of bringing a body bag up is complicated by a steep trail at spots only wide enough for one person to travel.

The team is back up top seven hours later. It had taken an hour to take photographs and complete the delicate task of working her body loose from the rocks' grip. The rescuers were glad when her body was finally in the heavy canvas body bag. The sun is going down. They are sweaty and exhausted. Oralynn's body is identified at the Taos hospital about two hours later. The photo sent to her sister only showed her face. From experience, the Sheriff knew the family did not need to see anything else.

The coroner's report said she had been dead about five days. That was consistent with the first day she missed work. Cromley is beside himself. His heart is broken. "She did not do this. She did not do this. I know she did not do this." If the coroner is right, she jumped at night.

Sadness consumes him as he thinks about how lonely she must have been walking to the middle of that bridge in the dark. He sits down in her chair at her desk. He puts his head in his hands and sobs.

He closes the office for the remainder of the week. Like most people close to someone who commits suicide, he feels he should have done more. Though the autopsy results are not complete, because of her past and perceived instability, her death is ruled a suicide. The newspaper talks about her work with the church and how people loved her. Her mother is quoted in the article, "My girl was not perfect, but she did not commit suicide. She knew suicide is a sin. She did not want to go to hell. She didn't live her life like that." The reporter talks about how Oralynn's mother's heart is broken thinking her daughter is bound to spend eternity in hell. Old Catholics reading the article feel sorrow not only for the loss of a daughter, but for the burden her poor mother must now carry.

25 SECOND TRIP / PART 1

It has been two days since Michael and Will left Battle Mountain. Rita is still curious about them, but her life is too convoluted to give it more than a cursory thought every now and then. She works all weekend at the diner. Sunday evening, she gets a text from Michael. "Enjoyed meeting you. Would like to buy you another ginger ale with lime when I come back." She is surprised because she is relieved. She thinks "What the hell? I need a smoke." She adjourns to her back porch to watch the evening lightning show.

The old umbrella fringe is fluttering in the light breeze. Rita thinks about what a mistake Hugo was. The uniform thing was so uncharacteristic of her. Apparently, a uniform was a big part of Michael's life too, but he seems different. She thinks about how old fashioned his handshake was. She smiles. She really likes that. She laughs about how she is obsessing about Michael and not focusing on the mysterious questions he asked. The thunderheads tonight are nothing more than a backdrop for the lightning. Rita replies to Michael in about an hour, "Nice meeting you too. I might upgrade to wine." About thirty minutes later she receives a thumbs up emoji from him.

The next morning Michael parks his Jeep in the garage. He has decided to take his mother's Mercedes to Battle Mountain. It will be good to drive it. Comfort is his primary consideration. "I look good driving it too," he muses. He stops in Flagstaff for the night. He doesn't want to be dull from the driving this time. He arrives in Battle Mountain mid-afternoon Wednesday. He has texted Rita asking her to supper. "Restaurant of your choice." He smiles when he sends it.

They agree to meet at the Blue Gem. When he sees her, he realizes that his self-manufactured buildup and anticipation is worth it. Her hair is down. This time she wears a form-fitting red top that also acts as a short skirt. She is perfectly proportioned. No baggy 501s this time. Lululemon black tights did her muscular legs justice. Michael had actually paid more attention to his look than usual. He sports a black polo untucked over-worn 505s. He is still breaking in his new Birkenstocks. He even shaved after a short nap. They both smile when they see each other.

He has the first sexual thought he has had in over three months. He realizes that he has not been around a woman for that long. He stands when Rita gets to the table. There is a goblet of the Gem's finest Nevada Chardonnay and a glass of ginger ale with lime. Rita sits down. "How considerate." Michael sits down. "I hope you like Chardonnay." She smiles. "Actually, this is one of their best wines. I'll take it." They sit looking at each other for a few seconds. Michael looks in her eyes. "I was looking forward to seeing you again." More silence. "I found you on LinkedIn, but no social media pages." Rita looks at the ground thinking about Hugo's bullying on social media before she deleted all her accounts, but she says, "Not much going on in my life right now to post."

To change the subject, Rita comes back, "I looked at your Facebook page. You and Will have lots of history." Almost braggingly, "He's always been my best friend. Since we were little, it's been my grandfather and him. He is one of the reasons I stay in Santa Fe." Michael wants to get this out, "I guess you're wondering why I asked you the questions about the Lander Blue?" Without hesitation Rita says, "Yes." Michael tells her about the iconic family store in Santa Fe. He tells her about Mort and how he just died from the virus. He looks down at the ground. "And the really shitty part is my parents died in a car wreck two months before that." He pauses, takes a breath and looks up. "I really only miss my grandfather."

Michael is quiet. Rita is quiet too. She is content to wait for him to speak. They both end up staring at the chalkboard behind the outdoor bar. A hand-drawn roadrunner is staring stupidly with a big blue gem in its mouth. A hand-drawn coyote is sitting in a recliner with a drink to the roadrunner's left. There is a word cloud above the coyote's head. "Who needs a blue gem? I have a Blue Gem drink. Try one!"

They both look back at each other at the same time without saying anything. Michael starts talking again, "He left me three cabochons like the one I showed you. The curator at the Turquoise Museum in Albuquerque told me about the missing twenty pounds of turquoise. I am curious about it." He looks around the courtyard. "And I'm curious about you too." Rita is not quite sure what to say. She is still skeptical, but this story does make more sense. The quick trip turnaround is still unexplained.

The conversation turns to her. She tells him about getting her MBA and her fantastic internship. "It's coincidental that my dad passed away about a month ago. My grandfather passed away two years ago. It's just me now." After a second Michael says, "I haven't thought about it that way, but I guess I'm like that too." They sit absorbed in their own thoughts.

Eventually Michael's eyes are steady on hers again. "How did you end up in the armpit?" He is so serious, she smiles. "I came back to help my dad. He had lung cancer. He suffered, so it was good when he passed." Softly Michael says, "I'm sorry. You must have had a good relationship with your father." She nods yes. He doesn't wait for her to say anything. "I can't say that. My parents' passing was weird. My relationship with them was only through our store. When I went to Afghanistan, part of the reason was to get away from them." He takes a sip of his beer. "One of the dumbest things I ever thought." He looks at the courtyard entrance. "My parents died so suddenly, it's like they are still on one of their long vacations."

It's Rita's turn to be sympathetic. "I'm sorry. Lots on your plate lately, but I don't want to get drug down. I don't know you that well." She has no makeup on. Her dark eyebrows and brown eyes pop out of her tan face. She knows Michael is looking at her. She playfully says, "Stop. You are embarrassing me." He immediately responds mischievously, "That is my intent." Rita acts annoyed, but she likes the back and forth. "You wanna know about the Lander Blue Mine?" Michael picks up his Pacifico and leans forward on his elbows toward her. "Part of the reason I'm here." It hangs for a minute as he takes another swig.

Rita leans forward on her elbows. "You know Cal and Suzy shot each other. Cal was a loan shark who liked the shark part of the business as much as the money part. He was not a well-liked man. He and his brother, my grandfather Roscoe, were known bad asses in Lander County." She takes a sip of wine. She wants a cigarette. Michael politely asks, "Is the wine okay?" Another mark in the plus column for him. She likes the attentiveness. She is starting to remember what it's like to be around people with manners, people who listen.

She continues, "Yes, thank you. I remember my grandfather. I can picture him coming through the door of my dad's house. The sun would be completely blocked when he stood in the doorway. Slivers of light had to fight to get through when he stopped to wipe his feet. I would look up at him and ask him if he was a giant."

Michael is gazing at her with no expression on his face. Rita stops. "Am I boring you? Too much info?" He snaps to quickly. "No, no, please go ahead. I can listen and enjoy looking at you at the same time." Rita acts like she doesn't hear him and continues, "Roscoe got the mine when Cal and Suzy shot each other. Roscoe sold the mine after five years. He ended up extracting about thirty pounds. My dad did most of the mining in his spare time." Michael stops her. "So to clarify, Suzy mined about thirty pounds while she was alive. The missing twenty pounds is from what she mined?"

Rita provides the answer he is looking for. "Yes. Roscoe looked for it for a long time, but he never found it." In the same breath, "Why are you so interested in the twenty pounds? Is there a connection between the cabochons you have and it?" Michael has been dreading this question. "Can I tell you tomorrow?" Rita ignores his mysterious answer and sounds hopeful. "Does that mean you are going to be around?" Michael takes this as a good sign. "If I survive tonight at the Rainbow's End."

She laughs out loud. They have talked for almost two hours. She stands, stretching her arms above her head. "I need to run errands in the morning before my shift at the diner. You want to meet here at four-thirty tomorrow afternoon and see the Lander Blue Mine?" Without hesitation Michael replies, "Let's touch base at lunch?" Rita cautions him, "I'll be busy at lunch. I won't be able to talk much." Michael stands. "I would imagine. This is about the chicken fried steak." She is pleased. He walks her to her car.

26 Second Trip / Part 2

Michael gets up early the next morning. The sun is just coming up when he goes to the motel lobby to get a cup of coffee. He heads to the cemetery wondering whether many people visit cemeteries first thing in the morning. According to Google Earth there is a small building in the middle of the cemetery. He parks near it, as he planned. There is a shopping cart full of belongings against the chain link fence. The owner is camping underneath one of the big cottonwood trees at the edge of the cemetery. He appears to be asleep. Michael doesn't really care, but he keeps an eye on him. He retrieves a collapsible army issue shovel, gloves and a worn twenty-five-foot retractable metal measuring tape from the trunk. He anticipates digging.

He has the clue printed on a note card in his shirt pocket for reference. Even though he doubts anyone is watching, he holds the shovel against his leg as he walks toward the pine grove. He finds Suzy's headstone near the grove. He looks at the sleeping "shopping cart" camper. No movement. The grey granite headstone base is slightly darker than the soil beneath it. He thinks fleetingly again about being buried where no grass grows. He focuses. "Well, here's the front corner nearest the trees." He has guessed that the ten-foot distance is from the stone base. He hopes the four-foot direction is offset in the direction of the trees.

He takes his tape and marks the ten-foot distance using the shovel tip. He measures four feet perpendicular to this line. He marks this spot. He quickly digs a hole about a foot deep. Nothing. "Shit." The camper is looking at him but hasn't moved. Michael measures four feet the other way. He digs about six inches down and hits the top of the yellow plastic pill bottle. He gets on his knees and digs the rest of the soil away with his hands. He has Clue 2. He quickly puts the dirt back in both holes compacting it with his feet. He folds the shovel and lays it on the ground next to the headstone base. He waves to the camper. There is no wave back.

He opens the pill container and removes a piece of folded paper from a small plastic bag. He reads Clue 2 for the first time. As expected, it is going to take some figuring out. He folds the clue and puts it back in the bag. He puts the bag back in the container. He wonders if Mort used pill containers for any of the other clues. He puts the container in his pants pocket.

Michael has Mort's necklace in the other pocket. He takes it out. He holds it by the chain looking at it. He places Suzy's stone on her headstone, settling the chain around it. The silver setting and chain blend into the headstone. The early morning sun makes the small dark blue stone vivid against the grey granite. Staring at it, he picks up the necklace by the stone.

The stone is warm. He attributes it to the sun. Michael realizes after taking a sweeping last look around the cemetery that the stone is still warm in his pocket. As he feels it he thinks about the supposed mystical properties of turquoise. He thinks about all that he has read about connectivity with a piece of turquoise as he walks back to his car. What if this little Lander Blue stone somehow linked Suzy, Mort and now him? He smiles to himself, not thinking about Mort or Suzy, but Rita. "I'm good with that." The stone is cool by the time he reaches the car. He decides to put the necklace on. He feels the best that he has in two months.

Michael goes back to his room at the Rainbow and lays down on the bed. Within minutes he is out. He sleeps with no dreams for a couple of hours. He awakes thinking about Rita and food. He washes his face and brushes his teeth again. His look is a blue linen shirt and shorts. He arrives at the diner as the lunch crowd is thinning. He goes directly to his stool at the counter. Rita has her back to him when he sits down. She sees him in the mirror and smiles. She goes to the other end of the bar. Her arms are bare and muscular. He sees part of the rose tattoo on her shoulder when she reaches out to the bar. The Lander Blue bracelet is the only jewelry she has on.

He smiles when she makes it to him. "Good afternoon. Hopefully the lunch crowd was kind and generous." She curls her lips in a small smile. "We can say they were kind." Directly facing him, "I was wondering if you were going to sleep all day or if the Rainbow got you." As was her intent, he takes her in. For a moment neither speaks. An older waitress walks behind her briskly. As she goes by, she hits Rita with her hip without saying a word. She looks at Michael, smiles and is gone. Rita breaks the silence. "Millie's a character."

Michael, still excited about his find in the cemetery that morning, "I was productive this morning, and I had a nap. I'm ready to see the mine. How about you?" He finishes mashed potatoes and a chicken fried steak, both swimming in white peppered gravy. His appetite surprises him. They agree to meet at the Blue Gem again and go to the mine in one vehicle from there. Rita finishes the conversation, "Let's eat there when we get back. Wear hiking boots. It's a bit of a walk. Bring some water too." She is looking back over her shoulder at Michael flirtingly. With that, she turns to a new customer at the other end of the bar.

Michael parks next to her dusty 2017 Volvo S60 in the Gem's parking lot. Once the dust settles, they meet at the end of her car. "The road's pretty rough in spots, don't want to hurt your Mercedes." Michael shyly replies, "I look good driving it, but it's my mother's car. They are the ones with the money, not me." He thinks to himself, not yet anyway. "I live in a casita rent free in my parents' Santa Fe compound. They let me do it in exchange for working at the store. I drive a ten-year old Jeep that has hauled Will's and my asses everywhere."

This information clarifies why she thought he had an affiliation with money. She likes his honesty. "The Jeep fits you better. I mean that in a good way. I bought this Volvo when I thought I was going to be making money off other peoples' money. Now I pay for it with what I make waitressing with an MBA. That's okay. It's temporary." They head south out of Battle Mountain. He asks Rita what her plans are for the future. She replies and asks him, "What are yours?" Neither knows. They find it coincidental that neither of them has a plan. They agree that their lives are works in progress. She catches him staring at her as she is driving. She likes it. He's so quiet sometimes. She likes that she doesn't always know what he is thinking.

They turn at a faded sign for the Copper Basin Mine. Rita is driving slowly as they veer off the paved road onto a dirt road. She turns left down what was once a worn two-tire path. Forty years of weeds and cactus are hitting against the bottom of the Volvo. She stops in a small overgrown area that was used for parking a long time ago. They get out and stand looking around. "I learned a lot about Lander Blue during a curious phase after I got the bracelet. I asked my dad to show me the mine. He brought me here. He showed me another pretty cool thing too." She heads around a rock outcropping and starts up.

Michael can see that they are walking on an overgrown trail. He stops several times tó take in the view as they go up. Soon they stop in front of four weathered vertical logs. They are half concealing an opening into the cliff face. Someone has carved "Sammy + Wendy" in a heart on one of the logs. Rita peers in the opening. "This is the Lander Blue Mine. Probably the most famous turquoise mine in the world. I like being here, because of what it is. I wish I had some of the turquoise my family mined. Guess I am lucky to have great aunt Suzy's bracelet."

There is still enough light to see temporary shoring tossed against the sides of the cave about ten feet in. The dust and cobwebs almost camouflage it. Rita steps aside and Michael peers into the hole. "Do you think there is any more turquoise here?" Rita has the answer. "The current owners spent a year and about ten feet and found nothing. The closest mine to here, the Stormy Mountain, played out about the same. All the mines in this area are different, but I think this one is spent too." The sun is going down and as usual, thunderheads are forming to the east and west.

She grabs him by the hand, "Come on. We can catch the sunset." He is surprised at first, but then clutches her hand. He releases it as she starts up another overgrown trail. It strangely felt like the first time he held a woman's hand. They end up sitting on a rock ledge looking at a seventy-five-mile vista, complete with thunderheads. The constant air to ground lightning bolts liven the scene. They sit silently watching the show for about ten minutes. Michael turns to Rita as the sun disappears. "Thank you for showing me the mine and especially for bringing me up here. This is one of the best sunsets I have ever seen." She feels the same. She doesn't say so but scoots closer to him.

After another minute she stands up and starts back down the trail. She looks back and holds out her hand. He takes it. She gently squeezes his and then she is off. This girl can get around. She doesn't stop till they are back at her Volvo. On the drive back, they decide to get a pizza and go to her trailer. They swing by the Gem to pick up Michael's car. After they pick up the pizza, they stop at the one open convenience store and Michael gets a six-pack of Pacifico. She waits while he runs into the store. Five minutes later they are at her trailer.

After they are in, she sets the pizza down on the counter. She grabs the beer and puts one on the counter for him. She puts the rest in the fridge. She looks at him, embarrassed, "I know you are hungry, but I have this habit that I hope you don't mind. I want to do it now." She opens a drawer in the kitchen and pulls out the pack of American Spirits. With his beer, she heads to the back porch without waiting for his reply.

Michael smiles. "Just a minute." He heads to the Mercedes. He comes out the back door in a couple of minutes. "As long as we are trying to drive each other away." He holds up a joint. They laugh. Michael, "We good?" Rita, "We good." They both light up. He takes a swallow of his beer. Michael offers her the joint, but she declines. "I tried it a long time ago. Just didn't like it. In Austin, if pot bothered you it was not your place. It doesn't bother me. I just don't do it."

She pauses, then asks, "You don't get crazy, do you?" He thinks this is a reasonable question, but he answers flippantly anyway, "Sometimes, but it's usually alcohol induced." He takes a puff, "I find it takes the edge off." The lightning dances through the thunderheads. The towering individual clouds are only visible when the light flashes behind them. "Mostly I find it helps when I get stressed or real tired. That has happened a lot lately. When I got back from Afghanistan." He stops abruptly. "You ready for some pizza?"

They go inside and sit at her small dining table. She doesn't forget his abrupt change of subject. She has not known anyone personally who served in the Middle East. She wonders how much to pursue it with him. She gets a beer for herself and another for him. They talk about politics for the first time. Michael comes right out, "I'm a libtard." Rita is surprised, but pleased. A giant hurdle jumped. Political differences became a giant barrier to her relationship with Hugo. "I am too."

There are two pieces of pizza left and the beer is gone when they finally slow down. Michael pushes back from the table slowly. "I should let you get to bed." Rita is feeling her two beers. "I am tired." Matter of factly she says, "If you want to crash on the couch that's okay." Her face immediately flushes. "There's something about you." She comes over and pecks him on the cheek. She heads to her bedroom without looking back. As he is wondering what to do, she comes back with a pillow, sheet and a blanket like it's decided. "Lock the front door and turn off the porch light." She goes to her room and shuts the door.

She hears Michael preparing the couch. A couple of minutes later she hears the front door lock. She sits on her bed thinking, "I have known this guy a week, kind of, and I invite him to sleep on my couch. I don't do that." Michael is lying on the couch in his clothes smiling, replaying the best evening he has had in a long time. Seeing a mine for the first time, a vista view sunset, a joint, beer, pizza and best of all, Rita. He starts dozing off under the blanket when he hears something outside against the trailer. He sits up and listens. Nothing more. He slips his sandals on. He flips on the front porch light and goes out the front door.

He quickly starts toward the back of the house. He sees a guy in a uniform getting into a sheriff's car parked up the alley from Rita's trailer. He smells gasoline. He continues around the house. The corner of the trailer has been soaked with gasoline. The can is on its side about ten feet away. He must have come outside right before it was lit. "What the hell?" He goes back inside. Rita is up and in the living room. She is wearing a long white tee shirt. "You okay?" is the first thing she asks when he comes back in the door.

He tells her what he saw. He sees her face harden. Her mouth tightens. She tells him about Hugo. "He's not the sheriff, but close." She starts apologizing, "I know he has seen you in town. I know he saw your car. God, I can't believe he would do something like this." She is visibly shaken. Michael gets a glass of water for each of them and gently sets the glasses on the table. They sit.

Michael is calm, but Rita can tell he is getting pissed. "This is not safe. He could come back and finish the job. Call the sheriff." Rita looks at the table. "I have. He's an asshole like Hugo. He won't do anything to his golden boy." He can hear the anger in her voice. "The real problem is Hugo thinks I jilted him because I'm too uppity. He can't let it go because I fucking am." She quickly puts on some shorts and a shirt. She gathers up a few toiletries and a change of clothes. They take both cars and go to Michael's room at the Rainbow.

They enter his room. It looks like no one has been there. Before she says anything Michael bluntly says, "I think there's enough bed to share, but if you are not comfortable with that, I can sleep in the chair." Michael is feeling the pizza and wants some Tums, so they get in his car and head back to the convenience store. He decides to fill the Mercedes. As they are leaving the pumps, they see Hugo beating the shit out of a young black woman he has cornered between the convenience store wall and a dumpster.

Michael's instinct is to jump out and intervene. He heads the Mercedes toward them and stops about twenty feet away. Rita has her phone out videoing Hugo grabbing the woman and throwing her down on the pavement. He kicks her in the stomach. He stares directly into the headlights, and her camera, surprised. He bends toward the woman's face and says something. He quickly leaves. Michael dials 911. Once again, he sees Hugo's taillights as he leaves the scene of another misdeed.

The woman is struggling to get up from the ground. Rita sees Michael's face turn to stone. His eyes are somewhere else, "I'm gonna catch that motherfucker and beat the shit out of him." He is starting to get out of the car as an ambulance enters the parking lot. Rita puts her hand on his leg. It's taut like a spring ready to explode. "You can't do that in this town. I have a better idea."

27 Back in Santa Fe

The EMS attendants spot the woman on the ground at the end of the building and go straight to her. Michael and Rita let them check out the woman before approaching them. She is sitting. Her forehead is bleeding. She has a dark shoe scuff mark on the front of her light-colored shirt where Hugo grazed her with his boot. She doesn't acknowledge them when they walk up. She is telling the kneeling EMT attendant, "I don't want to press charges. Won't do any good in this shithole." She looks away from everybody. Without saying a word, Michael and Rita leave.

They go back to the motel. Michael is visibly agitated. He wonders out loud if Hugo will mess with their cars parked outside the room. Rita shows him the video. It is unmistakable who is doing the beating. She proposes threatening Hugo with posting the video on Facebook if he doesn't leave her alone. Michael still wants to confront him. They agree they will wait until morning to decide whether he beats the shit out of Hugo, or she sends him an email about posting the video on Facebook if he doesn't leave her alone.

After looking at their phones they turn out their lights about fifteen minutes later. Rita softly says, "Thank you." They each politely tell the other good night. Michael thinks about how a good day can change quickly. Rita is asleep facing him and breathing heavily almost immediately. He thinks that he can't leave her with this shit going on. He thinks about what that means. Does it mean getting into a relationship? "Pretty fucking presumptuous to think about that," as he thinks about her coming back to Santa Fe with him. She could hang out and help him find the turquoise until she felt safe to return to Battle Mountain. He realizes for the first time that he is willing to take this risk to continue seeing her. This is crazy.

He gets up and looks out the window. Everything looks normal. He lies back down. He wakes when he hears Rita in the bathroom.

Slivers of light are coming in around the lone window curtain. The air conditioning unit is running full blast already. He can smell a brewed pot of motel coffee. She comes out of the bathroom with a towel wrapped around her hair. She is dressed in jeans and a black tee shirt. Her face is shiny. He sits up for a minute. He smiles at her and grabs his bag of toiletries. He excuses himself to the bathroom.

When they are both finished dressing, he asks her to consider something. He apologizes ahead of time if she thinks he is out of line. He blurts out, "Why don't you come back to Santa Fe with me. You can stay in my parents' house. You can drive the Mercedes. You can leave your car here or in the garage there." He pauses. She doesn't say anything. He continues, "All the northern New Mex food you can eat and all the tequila, or whatever you want, to drink." Smiling and looking directly at her, "I don't mean this as a threat, but I will also give you most of my attention."

She looks at Michael like she is weighing the good and bad. He asks, "Are you weighing the cost to benefit Ms. MBA?" She smiles. "You don't think that's too weird. We don't really know each other." She wistfully and overly dramatically says, "However, we did spend an uneventful night together, so I guess I can trust you at some level." He looks at her without changing expression. "That's on you." He breaks into a big smile. She does too. She has been working hard and saving her money. She doesn't want to admit it, but Hugo's craziness has really unnerved her this time. "I'll take my car so if I need to flee I can." Michael nods his head. "Fair enough, but you won't. Let's go." They gather their stuff and put it in their respective vehicles.

He follows her to a small coffee shop in a strip mall near the main street. They each get coffee and a breakfast sandwich. They sit on the front patio watching Battle Mountain come to life. Lots of semis taking the back roads today. She calls the diner and talks to Millie. She tells her about what Hugo did. She is leaving town for a few days and going to Santa Fe. There is a pause and Rita smiles. Michael hears, "None of your business. I'll talk to you in a couple of days." She then calls her friend at the Blue Gem and tells her the same story. This time he hears, "Yes, I'm going back with him." She is embarrassed when she realizes he is looking at her.

They continue to her trailer. It is still standing and not a pile of smoldering embers. She goes inside and he walks around to the targeted corner. The gas can is still laying on the ground. He picks it up and puts it under the back deck. The gasoline has dried. He imagines the siding would combust if there was a lightning strike within a mile. He continues around the trailer to the front. He goes in to find Rita sitting at her dining table.

He slowly walks to her. "Did you change your mind?" Rita looks up with no expression. "No. Did you?" Michael quickly replies, "No." He puts his hand on her shoulder. "Hang in there." Rita softly mutters, "I'm thinking about what I am going to need if I am going to live off the fat of the land in Santa Fe." She smiles and mouths, "Thank you."

After she loads her Volvo, she sits at the table again and calls the sheriff. She leaves a message, "This is Rita Owens. There was suspicious activity at my trailer last night." Her voice is pointed and terse, "You better make damn sure my trailer doesn't mysteriously burn up while I'm gone. Ask your fair-haired boy about it. I'll let you know when I'm back." She looks up relieved. "Think I got it." They get up. She looks around the trailer. Michael goes out first. She closes the trailer door, gives it a yank and locks it.

As anticipated, the drive back is long, boring and tiring. About five hours into the trip they take a three-hour nap in the Mercedes at a roadside stop. They stop in Flagstaff for gas and a meal after that. They arrive early morning in Santa Fe. The town is deserted as they drive to Michael's parents' compound. Rita immediately falls in love with everything behind their courtyard walls. She goes into every room of their house before she picks the guest room in the back. It is dark. It has its own bathroom with a tub. She is undressed and between the linen sheets on the bed before Michael gets into the casita. He is exhausted. He is smiling and holding Suzy's stone on his chest when he falls asleep.

About eleven o'clock he hears a knock on the casita door. He wakes, knowing it's Rita. He puts on his shorts. He goes to the door. She is in shorts and the black tee shirt. No bra. He invites her in. She looks around the casita. She doesn't hesitate. "You hungry?" Michael wipes his eyes. "I didn't grocery shop before I left. I can toast some bread and make one of my favorite meals, peanut butter and jelly sandwiches." She starts to his kitchen. "What kind of jelly?" They are eating their sandwiches at the counter in five minutes.

She sees Michael for the first time without a shirt. He is tan and muscular. He has four, one-inch to three-inch scars randomly located on his back. Below his right shoulder is a 45-degree angle scar about four inches long. All nicely healed. She doesn't say anything about it. She also sees the only tattoo he has. A small black rose outline on his back. She notices how low it appears. It's almost out of place. "I have a rose too." He finishes his bite. "I know. You have the circle of life on your finger too." Rita seizes the opening. "You first. Why did you get your rose?"

Michael doesn't address her question. "You wanna smoke?" She nods okay, wondering if he is going to answer her question. They go to the back portal. After sitting and looking at the backyard for a few minutes Rita breaks the silence, "This place is so unique. There is plant life." Michael agrees politely. Rita turns to him. "You okay? If you want to go back to bed, I won't mind." He sits up in his chair. "I'm just considering whether I should tell you my rose story."

Silence. "If I tell you about some of my Marine stuff, will you not judge me?" Rita senses this is hard for him. "I guess. I expect you to tell me the truth. That's my baseline." Michael slowly acknowledges her comment. "As long as it's a two-way street." More silence. Their eyes meet and without a word there is agreement. Michael starts his rose tattoo story.

"Three platoon buddies and I survived a vicious all-day shootout when we were ambushed in a residential area. Four of our guys died that afternoon when it was most intense. The little fuckers stormed the building we were holed-up in." He stops for a second. He wanders off topic. "One of the three other guys that got this tattoo committed suicide recently. He couldn't get over it." He gets back on topic. "We got drunk and got black roses tattooed on our backs in line with our hearts. We wanted something beautiful, something that had nothing to do with war. We really wanted to commemorate the fact that we survived that day. It is almost strange to think about being that scared now."

"The two black guys I ran with got their roses colored in with red so you could see them better." He stares straight ahead. "Neither of them had ever had a tattoo either. Melon, one of them..." He pauses as if anticipating a comment. "Yes, I know it's not politically correct, but that's what he told me to call him the first time I met him. Lot of miles with him. He is a high school football coach who is into meditation. He was a prankster and so full of shit. I love him. He convinced us that a black rose means the loss of a loved one. It represents the beauty of the rose along with the darkness of death. We all bought in."

Michael looks at her, then into the yard again. She puts her cigarette out. Somberly, "My rose story is nothing like that. I just thought the rose is beautiful. I had a friend who was the best tattoo guy around. The circle of life was done when my dad died. I wanted to see it every day to remind me to be thankful." They sit for a few more minutes. Michael is nodding off. She pats his arm. "I'm going to take a nap now that I've been up a couple of hours. Thank you for the sandwich."

Later that afternoon they walk downtown. Michael shows her where Hamilton's used to be. "I guess I don't miss it. I like not being around the memories and the family bullshit." Rita thinks about how different her feelings are about her father. They sit on a bench in the Plaza and watch the tourists. They are quiet as they walk down Palace Avenue toward Cathedral Park. He takes her arm and turns her into a courtyard as they walk down a covered walkway.

He takes her to the back of the courtyard and shows her a modest bronze plaque on the wall. "Scientists coming into town were dropped off here. They would pick them up and take them to Los Alamos to work on the nuclear bomb. Pretty strange." They sit in the park until they are both hungry. They commandeer two bar stools at The Shed and join the locals drinking margaritas and eating carne adovada.

The next morning Michael goes into the house early to find Rita doing yoga on the floor in the sitting room which looks out at the courtyard. He quietly moves an armchair to create more space. Without saying a word, he gets on the rug beside her and joins her routine. He follows every pose until she finishes. They are both lying on the floor looking up at the ceiling. "I would have worn a bra had I known you were coming in." She has her arms across her chest. "Obviously you know something about yoga. Your form was better than mine several times." She rolls over facing him.. Her arm is no longer covering her chest. He isn't looking at her, but he wants to reach out and touch her.

28 Michael Plus Rita

A clock chimes softly nine times in the background. Still looking at the ceiling, Michael nonchalantly says, "Nice Lululemons." He rolls over and looks at her. "You sure are beautiful." He reaches out and gently touches her cheek. She flushes and softens. "Oh my." Rita feels it. She reaches out and touches his cheek. She scoots closer to him. Their faces are about six inches apart. Michael is looking into her eyes, "I sure am glad you came to Santa Fe." She scoots another couple of inches closer to him. They are within kissing distance.

Surprisingly, he rolls back onto his back. Rita is confused. He quickly apologizes, "I am sorry. It's not you." He rolls back over looking at her. "Please know it's not you. God it's not you." She is up on her elbows looking at him. "What is it then? I was feeling pretty good about things." He sits up in easy pose. He is staring at her. "I have wanted to be with you since the first time I saw you in the diner." He taps his chest a couple of times with his fist. "It's me. Since I came back from Afghanistan, I have dreams. I fight depression and anger at the same time. I'm not crazy. I fight to stay balanced is what Melon says. It's better each day, but I fight it. If we have a relationship you need to know this."

Rita softens. She seizes the opportunity. "So what are the scars on your back?" Michael looks down. He is silent. She encourages him. "You know we talked about telling the truth." She adds, looking at his sad eyes, "If we are to have a relationship. Just saying." She sits up and easy poses facing him, as if expecting him to speak. He does. "One afternoon I was with a group of hospital staff. We got stopped by a group of Taliban assholes." He stops and looks out the window. "I was the only grunt with them. They started molesting a couple of the nurses. I took out the eight assholes and got the group back to their hospital. In the process, I got a cheap shotgun blast to the back from about thirty feet. Those are the little scars. The bigger scar on my right shoulder came from a piece of shrapnel that went through my vest the day before I got my rose tattoo. My right shoulder hurt so bad I didn't feel the tattoo on the other one."

She puts her hand on his knee. "That's a lot to carry around. I'm sorry." Michael is embarrassed, but says, "I want you to like me. You are the first person except Mort, Will and a few of my Marine buddies that I have ever talked to about this." She smiles softly. "So, you are saying I am special." She turns serious. "Why do you think you are gambling any more than I am? I decided to trust you after one night at the Rainbow's Butt End. You slept on a bed with me and didn't try to molest me." He realizes what she just said and laughs out loud.

"Okay, the problem is I have dreams sometimes about those few minutes. I wake up, not real often, but sometimes abruptly. I sweat. When I do, I scare the shit out of myself. I fight my anger and fears when I get stressed. I don't like it. I don't want you to be part of that." He adds in a softer voice, "That is assuming we have a relationship." Rita responds, "I'm not sure about the relationship, but I am definitely checking out the possibilities." She eases even closer to him. She turns facing the window like he is. They sit without talking, just looking out the window watching a squirrel greedily gather pinon nuts and take them to a hole at the back-courtyard wall.

They don't talk about it anymore. They take showers and go to breakfast at The Pantry. When they return Rita asks Michael for the M&DHAMI network login and password. She logs onto the Internet with her laptop. She sends her threat email, with the video attached, to Hugo. Michael can hear her cussing under her breath while she writes the email. She looks small as she sits at his parents' dining table. After she hits send, she turns around. "Who knows what the stupid shit will do, but I am sure I will find out." He confidently says, "We will find out. He shouldn't bother you here anyway." Both are yawning as Rita says, "I'm going to go lie down. You want to come? I'd like to continue what we started this morning."

She turns with her hand out. They laugh as they pretend like she is dragging him. When they enter her room, Michael stops her. He clutches her softly to him. He puts his lips on hers for the first time. He closes his eyes. When he opens his, hers are closed. They separate and start taking their clothes off without talking. She is naked first. He slows taking his underwear off when he sees her. Her muscular body is perfectly proportioned. Her breasts are larger than he thought. He wonders how he will measure up to her expectations as his underwear falls to the floor.

Michael gently gets on top of her. He rests on his elbows laying between her legs. He is erect, but wants to take her in, "Are you okay?" She puts her arms around him pulling him down on her. She is pleased that he is affectionate and not in a rush. "I am better than I've been in a long time." She reaches down and massages him. She gently pulls him toward her perfectly shaved and wet crotch. They both clutch each other as they engage. He gently kisses each of her nipples. When they are fully engaged, they start rocking gently. After a minute of this Michael puts his head on her chest. She holds him tightly. "Roll over." Without disengaging, she is sitting on top of him. He is holding her up by her hands. She closes her eyes and starts rocking gently.

She slows and bends over and kisses him. It's his turn. He puts his arms around her and pulls her to him. That lasts only a short time. They rhythmically start rocking together. Both are sweating. She sits up and starts coming, pulling herself down on him by putting her hands under his buttocks. He stares at her arched chest. He starts coming like he never has before. Their hands are locked. He holds her up until he is spent. Rita moans and settles softly on his chest. He opens his eyes. Her face is next to his. He feels her heart beating. They stay like that for about five minutes, smiling to themselves and wondering what this means.

After a short nap they walk downtown and meander along the line of vendors at the Palace of the Governors. Rita's Lander Blue bracelet captures the attention of several of the artists. They sit in Cathedral Park again and watch tourists wander around. As they walk in front of the Cathedral, they stop to admire the statue of Kateri Tekakwitha, also known as the Lily of the Mohawks. Michael folds his arms and takes a scholarly stance. "She was the first native American to be recognized as a Saint by the Catholic Church."

He looks at Rita seriously. "Questions?" Hearing none, he takes her by the arm, and they walk across the street and into the lobby of La Fonda. Michael remembers meeting Mort at the little French coffee shop there before he left for Afghanistan. He has been going through this lobby since he was a child. He tells Rita, "This is a special place. It's the living room of Santa Fe."

Michael shows her Gerald Cassidy's Los Matachines Dancer hanging prominently on one of the lobby columns. They stand and stare like they are in a museum. Quietly Michael says, "Mort took me to the

Taos Pueblo when I turned sixteen to watch the Christmas dance. This guy is from that dance." The dancer is holding a multi-colored wooden palma. The ribbons coming from his miter-shaped cupil suggest motion. Michael takes a couple of steps to Rita's right. "I always end up trying to get the light right so I can see his face." Rita takes the same steps and turns with her back rubbing against him saying, "I didn't think he had a face."

They toast each other with margaritas at the Bell Tower and watch the sunset. After the sun disappears, Michael leans back in his chair. "I like your sunset better. That was a special place. Thank you again for sharing it." Rita reaches out and grips his left hand firmly with her soft muscular right hand.

He softly squeezes her hand back. At that moment he decides to tell her about the treasure hunt. He remembers thinking about this moment before they left the Rainbow. He has wondered several times what her life might have been like if her grandfather had gotten the turquoise instead of Mort.

He had also considered telling her about the treasure hunt the morning they unexpectedly did the yoga together. This was before they went to bed together. He knew when he asked her to come back to Santa Fe with him that the time would come when he would have to decide if he was going to include her in the hunt. The time is here. He smiles in relief. For now, he decides to go with the moment, however. Being with Rita is easy. Meeting her was fate. May his good luck continue. He feels Suzy's stone on his chest. He has worn it since he left the cemetery in Battle Mountain. Michael orders two more margaritas.

29 A Detective Comes

It has been a week since Cozy read Mort's letter. Two days since Oralynn's demise and his disposal of her body in the gorge. Detective Cecil Soledad of the Santa Fe Police Department left him a voice message that morning, "An APB has been issued for Oralynn Lowry. I am working on locating her. I got your name from Burt Cromley, who said you work for him as an investigator. I imagine you knew Ms. Lowry. I understand you are a former Albuquerque cop. If you know anything about where she might be, I would appreciate a call."

After a pause, "Please give me a call anyway." Cozy has not called Detective Soledad back. The paper didn't say it was a suicide, but heavily implied it. Cozy has a brief thought about how Oralynn's mother must feel. He was glad that he did not have kids, especially with Slipper.

Cozy's feelings of guilt come and go. He drinks when he feels guilty. As he eases into the bottle, his brain replays what happened. Should he have done something else? Oralynn was not a person that the world was better without. Not like pimps and drug scum. This morning he is thinking that when she hit her head, he should have called the police and told them what happened. Once again, he chose the dark path. He is now on it and he knows he can't get off. His life has been a series of dark paths.

At least his bad dreams have stopped since he moved out of the Desert Scene into the apartment. He doesn't want a third cup of coffee after his shower, but his head still hurts. The Jim Beam he stole from Slipper's residence yesterday was still talking to him. Her laptop was on the cluttered table in his dirty kitchen in his small apartment on the south side of Santa Fe. Slipper must be aware the laptop is gone by now, but he has not heard from her. He doesn't care if she knows.

The dark spot he has in his heart for her grows darker every day. Between bites of cereal he mumbles, "Get it back bitch." He was so physical with her the last time they were together that he expected to get a call from Cromley or a visit from someone with a restraining order.

He wishes it would have been Slipper instead of Oralynn. It makes him feel better thinking this.

He has been trying to get in touch with Teddy. The kid is smart. Cozy knows Teddy did not believe his story about the drug deal where he was to be left at the bridge. Teddy knew not to ask questions, however. It's a long shot that he would connect Oralynn's death with picking him up at the bridge. He thinks about paying Teddy a visit to remind him who he is "cozy" with. He will call Teddy's mom later. He has found that a threat to his mother usually loosens Teddy's dialing fingers.

Several years ago, when he was still on the force, Cozy realized how helpful the Internet is. While it allows access to a mountain of useless information, it also contains social platforms and hidden conspiracy niches that are priceless for predicting and tracking people. He has been amazed at how stupid young people can be when it comes to posting shit about themselves.

He first searches for Lander Blue. His eyes clear as he reads about the blue gem. If Mort is talking about Lander Blue treasure, it is worth a lot of money. He never knew there was a turquoise museum in Albuquerque. His chair creaks as he straightens. He reads a blog about a legend involving a missing twenty pounds of Lander Blue. He wonders if there is any connection to Mort's treasure.

He Googles Mort. Lots of hits. Started Hamilton's. Known as a turquoise trader and agent for local native craftsmen. He died almost a week before Oralynn. Cozy is starting to feel better. There are lots of holes in Mort's letter, but there may be something here. He Googles Michael, who describes himself as a recovering Marine. He likes the outdoors. His Facebook posts look normal. Nothing too revealing. Lots of pics with a guy named Willow Gantry. He puts Michael's address into his phone. He also enters Mort's address. Both addresses are near downtown in the very old and expensive part of Santa Fe.

He is unexpectedly enthusiastic. He showers and shaves with a purpose for the first time in several days. About an hour later he is cruising Michael's neighborhood which is within walking distance of the Plaza. He had already figured out that he is living in his deceased parents' compound. Cozy put together that the kid lost his parents and grandfather in the span of two months. He probably lives in the casita. He drives by Mort's house. That afternoon he drives by both again. No changes. He drives by in the evening. No lights at either house.

That evening, Cozy parks the Tahoe down the street from Mel and

Darlene's compound. He hops over the courtyard wall at an inside corner hidden by several aspens. He is now in the high-risk zone. He slowly prowls around Michael's parents' compound. He surmises everybody is out of town. He can't find anything open or openable on the house or the casita. He sits in a chair on the back portal listening to the faint sounds of Santa Fe as tourists hit the restaurants and bars. He wishes that he and Slipper had bought something like this back when real estate was cheap.

There are cars parked in the driveway when he drives by the compound the next morning. About nine o'clock that night, Cozy strolls into the compound. Michael's Jeep is parked in the front drive. Cozy's intention is to put a SpyTech LM3 real time GPS tracker on the bottom of the Jeep. He has used this tracker before on junkies' cars when he was trying to find drug dealers. It's easy to set up and track using an app on his cell phone.

He slides under the Jeep and places the magnetized case on a lip of the frame just under the front passenger side. He feels the two high-powered magnets snugly attach the case. He walks a hundred yards from Michael's Jeep, into some trees, and activates the app on his phone. The one inch by two and a half-inch black box, known only to him, was now a red dot on Garcia Street two blocks from Canyon Road. Cozy walks back to his car hoping this will be over soon. The battery in the tracker lasts about three weeks. This seems like a very long time to him.

By Saturday morning, it has been four days since the tracker has moved. Cozy figures the Jeep is in the garage at the compound. There have been no lights or other activity he has seen. On his way to the liquor store that evening, he cruises by. There are lights on in the house and in the casita. The next day the Jeep is on the move in the afternoon. At dark, the Jeep is near La Fonda. He decides to go back to the compound and snoop around some more.

He doesn't take the time to try and pick the lock. He waits until a car goes by. His brass knuckles effortlessly break the glass pane nearest the doorknob and deadbolt in the casita door. His gloved hand releases the deadbolt and turns the doorknob. The casita is dark. He flips on a pen light and starts opening drawers not knowing what he is looking for. He looks at a calendar on the dining table. He goes over to the desk and pulls the pot drawer out. He sees headlights reflecting off the courtyard gate. It's a car stopped on the street before the turn in. Cozy turns his light off. "Fuck it, not worth it." He lets his eyes adjust for a second.

He quietly leaves the casita, not bothering to close the back door. He runs to the courtyard fence and hops onto the sidewalk by the aspens. He steadies himself as he pulls up his hood. Cozy looks around. He sees no one. He quickly walks to the Tahoe and gets in. He waits a few minutes to see if anything happens. It was close, but not that close. He heads to Tiny's for a beer and some country swing.

Will is driving by Michael's house when he sees a dim light in his casita. He is unsure what to do. He pulls over on the street and watches. He sees the light go off. He calls Michael and tells him what he sees. Michael and Rita have just finished eating. "Can you hang there until we get there?" They can hear Will breathing heavier. "Sure. I'm pulling into the drive. I'll wait in the Rover until you get here."

Michael calls the police as they head back to the compound. The pleasant feeling induced by the two margaritas they each had with supper disappears. He can tell Rita is tired. He leads the way through the front door of the casita. He switches a light on. They immediately see the open back door and glass on the floor. They quickly figure out that it was broken from the outside. He sees the open pot drawer and panics.

The cabochon and folder are in that drawer. He looks inside. Nothing is disturbed. It looks like a foiled burglary. He puts the cabochon in his pants pocket. He puts the folder in the house on the dining room table to be stowed in a safer place with the cabochon when things settle down. About twenty minutes after they get back, an unmarked police car pulls slowly into the drive. They are standing in the courtyard waiting.

The officer parks the car and looks around at the compound before he gets out. Once he gets out, he comes to them with his hand out. "Is one of you Michael Hamilton?" Michael steps forward with his hand out. "Sure, I am. This is my..." Michael stops just a second and continues. "This is my girlfriend Rita Owens and my best friend Willow Gantry." They each shake his hand. Michael looks at Rita. She smiles tiredly but her eyes are twinkling. In polished English, the six-foot-tall Hispanic-looking man with a bushy head of premature gray hair introduces himself, "I'm Detective Cecil Soledad." His suit still looks fresh as he just reported for his shift when the call came in.

Michael tells him what they have seen inside the casita. Detective Soledad makes a quick tour of the house and it appears to be okay. They follow him into the now well-lit casita. As they are walking through the door the detective says, "I represent generations of Santa Feans. My family has enough police officers in it to field a football team." He stops and turns to look at them. "There are even a couple of Texas Highway Patrol in the mix, both women." He chuckles. "I was sent because there are no patrolmen available. We are concerned about a rash of recent break-ins in your neighborhood. Our Chief wants someone to respond quickly, so you got me."

He avoids the glass on the floor as he goes through the back door. He looks around outside. He walks to the courtyard wall. "Looks like a burglary attempt. Easy to jump a wall and be here. We can take some prints in the morning, but it's probably not worth the trouble." He looks back at the wall. "I think it's a group of kids that come into town for the night. Break in a couple of places and leave. Someone else hocks the stuff. Will happened along at the right time. Guess they didn't get anything?" He looks at Michael who shakes his head no. "Not that I can tell. I'll let you know if I determine something's missing."

Cecil Soledad looks around the casita again briefly. He hands Michael a card. "Call my cell on this card if you see something else or have more problems." They thank him and he leaves. Michael and Rita adjourn to the back portal to smoke. Rita tells her closet smoking story to Will while Michael makes fun of her. They speculate about the break-in until Will gets up to leave. "Some of us have to work for a living." Michael thanks him as they hug before he leaves.

30 Clue 2

Michael and Rita sit on the portal while she smokes another cigarette. They are both still feeling the trip from Battle Mountain. The break-in is almost too much. Michael decides to spend the night in his parents' house. He thinks about cleaning up the glass on the floor at the back door. He decides to wait until the morning. He gets his Marine-issued Beretta M9 that he keeps by his bed and puts it in his toiletries bag. He is spooked. He grabs an extra loaded clip. He locks the casita back door and puts a chair in front of it. At the main house he and Rita barely kiss each other good night. He is to sleep in the guest room down the hall from Rita's room.

His room has a bathroom too, but only a shower. Michael puts the folder from the dining table, the cabochon from his pocket, now in its bag, and his Beretta in the drawer of the nightstand next to his bed. He gets in bed. About fifteen minutes later, just as he is dozing off, he hears Rita coming down the hall. She comes into his room slowly, looking at the bed. "Are you awake?"

She doesn't wait for an answer. "Can I get in bed with you?" He moves over to the right side. "Yes." She gets under the sheet saying, "I'm spooked already, so if you wake up suddenly it won't matter." Without another word she slides under his arm and puts her arm across his chest. Michael puts his arm around her. No dreams, nothing but undisturbed sleep until morning.

When they awake, they visit their respective bathrooms and brush their teeth. Then they meet back at Michael's bed to plot their next move. Their plotting was followed by a very close consultation. They end up with Rita lying on Michael's back, her head resting on the shrapnel scar. She is outlining his rose softly with her hand. Her other arm is pinned under his chest.

After showers and peanut butter and jelly sandwiches Michael says, "I want to talk if you are good with it." Rita looks up. "Is it about you and me?" Michael smiles. "Yes, but not in the way you may be thinking. This is more about helping me with something I have going on. I feel that something brought us together. Maybe it was fate or luck. I've known you what, ten days and I feel like..." He stops. "Too weird?" Rita nods her head slowly yes. "It's weird, but I feel the same way." Both are quiet. Michael breaks the silence. "I want to show you something. Let's go to the table."

They stand at the dining table. Without saying anything, Michael pulls the treasure hunt calendar to them. It has the folder from his room on top of it. He tells Rita about Mort and his relationship with him. He was not only his grandfather, but one of his best friends. "He was a character. He loved magic, riddles and mysteries. He even took me on the stupid-ass Santa Fe Ghost Tour when I was twelve because he was buddies with the guy who did it. We did it a couple of more times together." Michael slows down. He thinks about his words. "Before he died, Mort apparently set up a treasure hunt for me to find what I think may be the missing twenty pounds of Lander Blue."

Rita sits down at the table in front of the calendar. After a few seconds, "Seriously?" Michael anticipates her reaction. "I am not totally sure. You can judge for yourself." Looking at him she says, "The hunt is the reason you came to Battle Mountain." Michael thinks to himself, she's sharp. "Clue two was in the cemetery there." She has a curious look on her face. He picks up the folder and removes the copies of the newspaper clipping and Mort's letter that were in the box buried in the well house. Clue 2 is paperclipped to the letter.

Michael lays each item in front of her on the table. "There are two more cabochons like the one I showed you too. They are in a safety deposit box with the original letter and clipping." He tells her about how he and Will retrieved the box from the well house after Mort's mysterious last message. He puts his finger on July 13. "This is when the twenty-four-day time period started. I am not sure what happens if we don't find the treasure by August fifth."

Rita looks at the newspaper clipping first. She reads the entire article. Michael tries not to hurry her. As soon as she stops reading, he gently pushes the letter in front of her. "Clue one, in the middle of the page, is how the hunt started. Mort made a recent trip to Vegas. I think that's when he and his buddy Easy set up Clue two." Rita is ignoring him. She unclips Clue 2 and lays it on the table. She is holding the letter with both hands looking at it intently. "I would have liked Mort."

She mouths Clue 1. "You figured this out?" He smiles. "Will and I, some pot and beer, Googling and some wasted time." Michael adds, "As you saw, there are three more clues to solve according to his letter." She gently smooths Clue 2 with her hand on the table. She then picks it up and reads it out loud.

When she is done, she pauses and asks, "Mort didn't like your dad. What did your parents do that prompted him to set up the hunt?" Michael tells her about the mutually unsatisfactory relationship Mort and Mel had. "Yes, it was pretty weird. I quit worrying about it a long time ago. I didn't care for my dad that much either. He didn't like me because of the relationship I had with Mort. Hamilton's and money bound our family together."

Michael is quiet for second. He finally sits down at the table. "This is good for me to talk about this." He shifts his feet looking at the table. "I got the impression that Mort thought Mel was to leave Hamilton's to me. My parents redid their will right before they died. They knew then they were to sell Hamilton's and not leave it to me. It looks like they wanted Hamilton's sold to spite me after they died. Really nice. They probably thought they would outlive Mort too. It really pissed Mort off I think."

Looking at him, "Why didn't Mort just give you the treasure?" Michael tells her about Mort's last message. "I never got to ask him. I do know he loved riddles. We competed for who could come up with the best riddle while I was in Afghanistan. He sent me a handwritten letter each week for four years." He softly taps his finger on the table. "My guess is he thought this was our last competition. He knows I will figure this out." He stops. "Now we are going to figure it out, if you will help me."

Michael pulls Clue 2 in between them.

It is natives' heart of the country: *Gallup, New Mexico is titled the Heart of Indian Country.*

Lots of posts, but not much fence there: *It is comprised of many trading posts.*

The biggest lunch boxer stands guard: *There is cabochon made from a shard stolen from a mine in a lunch box prominently displayed in Bruce Magnum's Trading Post front window in Gallup.*

Find the holiness of the guarded throne room: *Find the hole in the bathroom wall at Magnum's Trading Post.*

Michael gives it a minute, "I searched "heart of the country" and eventually found Gallup, New Mexico. It is considered the Heart of Indian Country. That makes sense. Mort knew lots of traders and craftsmen in this area." He smirks. "The posts line is typical Mort. I haven't been to Gallup in a while, but it's mostly trading posts." Rita smiles. "I get it." Michael puts his finger on the third line of the clue. "This is where I stopped, because I had to give someone my undivided attention."

He reaches out and grasps her hand. They sit for a minute staring at the clue. Rita gets up and goes to her room. She returns with a laptop and sets it on the table. "Not to change the subject, but I haven't heard anything from Hugo. I hope the video and message to his boss settled him down. That said, I know it's not over." Michael hears, "Big fucking mistake" under her breath.

They talk about what a "lunch boxer" could be. Some searching on the Internet reveals what it is. That afternoon they call trading posts in and around Gallup to see if anyone knows about a lunch box piece of turquoise. They are unsure about the stands guard part. No one they talk to knows anything about it. After they call all the trading posts they find searching online, they agree that a trip to Gallup is necessary.

They spend the rest of the afternoon speculating about what "Find the holiness of the guarded throne room" might mean. "Toilet" comes up when Rita searches synonyms for "throne." Almost under her breath she says, "Maybe Mort put the clue in the bathroom in the store where the lunch boxer stands guard. Toilet does keep coming up." Even quieter she quickly adds, "Maybe." Once again, they agree a trip is necessary.

It is Rita who has bad dreams that night. At midnight she suddenly sits up moaning and scared. Michael instinctively grabs his gun out of the nightstand. She immediately apologizes, "I was dreaming I was burning in my trailer." He gets up and comes around to her side of the bed, sitting down beside her. "You are doing my work for me. I am sorry. You are not going to burn up, but let's go smoke." Rita relaxes. She throws on a short robe from a chair next to the bed. They sit on the back portal and listen to the sounds of a quiet Santa Fe midnight.

The next morning, they drive to Gallup in Michael's Jeep. They cruise old Route 66 through the stirring town. Everything about the town shows wear and tear, but it works. Old trucks and cars with reservation license plates already line sections of the streets. They park on South First Street. There are many trading posts in the adjacent blocks. They split up and start walking the streets looking in each trading post at the displays.

About thirty minutes later, Rita gets a call, "Come to Bruce Magnum's Post one block in on South Third." About ten minutes later she shows up. Michael is standing in front of a store window smiling. On display is "The largest natural lunch box turquoise cabochon on display in New Mexico. American Mine, Old Hachita, New Mexico, 1882." Michael excitedly says, "Don't know if it is guarding anything, but the lunch box part seems right." Magnum's is closed until tomorrow.

The next morning, they drive back to Gallup. They are excited. They have talked it out, so they are both quiet for most of the ride. They are ready to see if their hunches are correct. They stop and get coffee in Albuquerque before starting the ride west. Arriving in Gallup, they park in front of Magnum's about ten minutes after it opens. They go in and are greeted by a friendly short Indian woman. "Can I help you?" She is folding white, beige and black woven wool blankets. She stops folding and walks toward Rita. She stops suddenly when she sees her Lander Blue bracelet. Rita sees her staring at it. The woman softly asks, "I don't mean to be personal, but is that Lander Blue?"

Michael seizes the opportunity. He butts in, "I am sorry, but do you have a restroom I can use?" The old woman points to the back of the store as Rita starts talking. Neither is paying attention to Michael as he goes to the back of the store in search of the bathroom. He goes into the small very used, but clean room. He latches the door. The window to the alley is slightly open. He can hear cars on the next street over. A garbage truck is coming his way in the alley. A young woman who had just come into the store with her husband starts knocking hard and pleading to get into the bathroom.

He sees the hole in the wall and wonders if this is what Mort meant by "holiness." He reluctantly leaves the bathroom. The knocking woman does not even wait for him to be clear of the door before she starts past him. Her hand is on the door to shut it as soon as she is in. He doesn't even have time to give her an indignant look. He walks back to the front of the store. Rita is laughing. She is still talking with the old woman. Michael waits until she is done and looks at him. He calls her over to look at a rug he is holding up.

She excuses herself and walks over to him. He tells her about what he saw in the bathroom. He explains why he didn't have time to check the hole in the wall. He feels awkward about going back. She needs to go to the bathroom and check the hole. They smile at each other. Rita grabs his hand and squeezes it. She tells him about Magnum's Lander Blue bracelet that his wife told her about. The knocking woman finally comes out of the bathroom. After a couple of minutes, they are the only ones in the store again. Rita raises her voice. "I'm going to the bathroom too." She heads to the back of the store like she owns the place.

Rita locks the door. She takes the opportunity to pee. She sees the hole in the paneling as she washes her hands. Under her breath, "I guess I am going to have to stick my fingers in there. Wish I had a glove." She sticks her second and third fingers in the hole feeling downward. Nothing. She wiggles her fingers upward feeling a plastic bag. She can feel a thumb tack holding it in place. She pulls it gently and it comes off the stud. She pulls the bag through the hole. She takes a long breath and thinks how horrible it would have been had she dropped the bag in the wall cavity. She puts the thumb tack back in the stud like it belonged there. Clue 3 is in her jeans pocket.

She rejoins Michael. She grabs his hand and whispers, "This really is a treasure hunt. I have clue three." Michael is relieved and asks her, "Did you happen to ask the woman if she knew Mort?" Rita looks at the woman across the store. "No. We talked about our Lander Blue bracelets." Michael approaches the woman. On a hunch that she knows Mort, he introduces himself as Mort's grandson.

She introduces herself as Mrs. Magnum. She asks about Mort. Michael informs her that he died. "Oh my. Bruce will be upset. They were such good friends, a pair to draw to." After a short exchange about Mort, Michael asks casually, "Do you happen to know anything about twenty pounds of missing Lander Blue turquoise?' Lulla smiles. "I've heard that story for forty years. Traders laugh it off. They love the story though. Lots of them believe that someone has it. If that's true, somebody could be very rich if they wanted to sell it." Michael and Rita try not to look at each other. It is the end to a perfect morning in Gallup.

31 Cozy and Hugo / Bad Guys Lurking

Cozy has isolated himself in his apartment. For the past week he hasn't spoken to anyone who doesn't perform a service for him. Cromley has been trying to reach him about signing Slipper's divorce papers. He also worries it's because of Oralynn's death.

Cozy imagines there will be a restraining order accompanying the divorce decree. "Fuck'em." It gives him pleasure knowing that he cheated on Slipper. The detective has left another message too. This bothers Cozy, as he knows he will have to reply soon. To heighten his anxiety, he left a message with Teddy's mother to have him call. He has not heard from him. He hopes something is not up with that little fucker.

Cozy has been providing discreet courier services for a presumably wealthy Santa Fean. He neither sees the client nor communicates directly. He is called by a gallery on Canyon Road. He picks up instructions, which are sealed in an envelope at the front desk. The packages are picked up at night at the gallery and delivered following the strict instructions. An envelope with a generous amount of cash is waiting at the gallery after each delivery. Cozy knows he is carrying paintings. He is not sure whether a new owner or an insurance company is paying for them. Maybe both.

On Wednesday morning the tracker alerts him that Michael's Jeep is on the move. It is heading toward Gallup again. He saw it was there the day before. He cleans up quickly and heads to Gallup too. He keeps the Tahoe's windows rolled down as he speeds west. He parallel parks across the street from Magnum's. He sees the Jeep parked in front. The dot on his phone is blinking bright red. He slides down in his seat out of habit about fifteen minutes later when Rita and Michael emerge through the front door. Cozy chuckles as he takes another swig from his flask. They have no idea who he is. Why is he hiding?

He waits until they are out of sight. He crosses the street and goes into Magnum's. It looks like most trading posts in Gallup. So much cheap stuff that it hides the good stuff. Seeing nothing unusual, he turns and starts to the door as Lulla comes out of the back. Cozy doesn't stop. He leaves and heads to Earl's. As he pulls into the parking lot, he sees Michael's Jeep. He decides to drive to a dive Italian place in Albuquerque where he sometimes meets customers. He checks the tracker app while he is eating. The Jeep is heading east out of Gallup. When he checks later in the afternoon the Jeep is back at the compound in Santa Fe.

Cozy sits at the small dining table in his apartment that afternoon. He doesn't feel like drinking anymore but does anyway. He thinks about Oralynn's comment about a treasure hunt. Mort mentions a treasure hunt in his letter. Maybe there is a treasure hunt. Maybe Magnum's is part of it?

The girl's car plates are registered in Nevada. He has learned enough about Lander Blue to know the mine was in Nevada. He is starting to think that her being with the Hamilton kid is not coincidence. He wants to be optimistic, "What if that is what they are doing?" He closes his eyes and leans back in the creaking chair as he finishes the last shot from another bottle of Four Roses. He nods off wondering how many clues there might be.

About eight miles north of Cozy's apartment thirty-three-year-old Deputy Sherriff Hugo Benson lies on his bed in a room at the El Rey on Cerrillos Road. He arrived late the night before. It's been three days since he received the threatening email from Rita, at which time he ran the Mercedes plates and traced the car to Michael's parents' house in Santa Fe.

The Lander County sheriff told him, when he asked for time off, "You fuck around with that young woman again and you're gone. Have a good vacation." He knows the sheriff is glad he requested time off. The asshole didn't even ask what he was doing. Hugo decides he doesn't care. He knows he is stalking Rita. He knows his common sense has lost out to his jealousy and anger. He wants to make her come back to Battle Mountain. He wants to beat the shit out of the guy she is with. They deserve to be tormented.

When Hugo looks in the mirror, he sees a special man who should be desired by all women. Several in the limited dating pool in Battle Mountain found out how special he was. As with them and eventually Rita, his possessiveness and short fuse drove them all away. His arrogance would never let him admit anything other than he was the one who ended the relationships. Rita is the exception. She has not given him a fair chance. He is not used to the torment jealousy brings.

He can't believe she is now with some guy that just happened through town. He sees her Volvo parked in the Hamilton compound garage when he goes by mid-afternoon. He parks up the street and strolls by the front of the compound. He sees the blue Mercedes in the garage too. The plate matches. The Jeep in the drive must belong to the guy who is causing him so much grief.

Late that night his anger about Rita trying to blackmail him with the video is fueled by too many tequila shots at Evangelo's. He drives by Michael's. The Jeep and Volvo are parked in the drive. He circles the block a couple of times. He parks almost in the same spot Cozy did. He crudely scribbles a note and folds it in half. He slowly walks into the compound with a bat close to his leg. He keeps it in his car specifically for breaking out windshields. He breaks the front windshield out of Rita's Volvo. He leaves a note under Michael's Jeep's wiper. "Fuck you Hamilton. Fuck you Rita. Fuck your video. I'm gonna get you."

32 Clue 3

The next morning when Michael gets the paper, he sees Rita's car. Disgusted, he removes the note from the Jeep's windshield. He takes it inside and shows it to Rita. She immediately goes outside and looks at her car. "I was afraid of something like this. The motherfucker must have run your mother's car's plates to find me." They decide not to call the police. Neither thinks that Hugo is the burglar from the night before, but they both know he broke her windshield.

Michael gets a broom from the garage. Rita tries to take it away from him. "Let me do this. You have nothing to do with this shit." He stops, but does not give her the broom. "I got this. You didn't do it either." He sweeps up the glass and puts it in a black plastic contractor bag. He puts that in the garbage bin. She is staring at him the whole time. He can't tell who she is mad at. He puts the broom back in the corner of the garage. As he is coming back toward her, he says, "You can ride the broom until your windshield is fixed."

Without saying a word, she closes the distance to him and puts her left hand on his left cheek. She holds his head gently and stretches. She kisses him softly on his right cheek. "Asshole." Michael smiles. "Let's take your car and get the windshield replaced." He throws a heavy packing blanket from the garage over the driver's seat. He looks at the blanket-covered seat. "They can clean the inside at the glass shop."

Michael decides to deal with Hugo differently now. When they return from dropping off her car, they discuss Rita posting the video anonymously on a popular Black Lives Matter Facebook page. Rita is not sure about this. Michael assures her, 'Hugo is here. He will keep dogging us until we can confront him. Involving the local police at this time will not help. His type will come to us." Rita is not used to being the aggressor. "You mean bait him?"

Michael looks straight at her. "Yes. I will be with you all the time. Hugo needs to be more forcefully told to leave." He turns and leaves her alone. She realizes how pissed she is at Hugo. This son of a bitch won't leave her alone. He's stalking her fifteen hours from Battle Mountain. The tone of her email does not match her confidence in the confrontation strategy, but she hits send. The email includes a link to the Facebook video, a taunt, "Should I send this to the sheriff?" and a warning, "Leave us alone, bitch!" She slumps heavily back in her chair when she is done.

Mid-morning, they sit down at the dining table. They look at Clue 3. For the first time Rita wonders if Michael will share the turquoise if they find it. She daydreams about having millions of dollars. She wonders if he suspects she's there because she wants part of the treasure. She wonders sometimes herself. Everything has happened so fast. She thinks of the movie, *Romancing the Stone*. A chance meeting leading to crazy adventure and romance. Their story is like this, except the stone is turquoise, not emerald.

Clue 3 is another series of riddles.

> It's black and white and red all over: *A corny old joke. The answer is a newspaper. The local newspaper is the Santa Fe New Mexican.*
> OLDP 8 was 8 before you: See the *8th story of the Old Prospector (OLDP) series written by Mort in 1982. Michael was born in 1990.*
> The YP is real: *The Young Prospector (YP) and hero in the story, Herculano Montoya is a real person.*
> 005237 shows the place: *This is the negative number of a picture in The Palace of the*
> *Governors Archives showing Herculano in front of the American Turquoise Company Muniz – Tiffany Lode Mine.*
> Love to see your face: *Go to this mine.*
> At the base: *Dig at the base of the sign.*
> Expected sign: *A NO TRESPASSING sign.*
> Start a mini-mine: *Dig there.*

They recognize the first line as part of a corny newspaper joke. They decide to assume it is the local Santa Fe newspaper. Michael says the next line under his breath. "I bet the "eight" before "you" means nineteen eighty-two. Eight years before I was born." He rubs his chin. "That line is typical Mort." He is unsure about the rest. "We need to go to the paper. Look at papers from nineteen eighty-two." They continue looking at the handwritten clue. Rita points out the OLDP and YP may be related, "Whatever the YP is, it's real." She says "real" louder. She immediately smiles. They decide to clear their heads and go eat green chicken chile enchiladas at Maria's for lunch.

That afternoon they go to the *Santa Fe New Mexican's* offices. The building is low, dark brown stucco and nondescript. The entrance is lined with old and new newspaper dispensers. They introduce themselves to the receptionist. They explain that they want to look at newspapers from 1982. The online archive does not go back that far. They are unsure exactly what they are looking for. She tells them to have a seat. She disappears for a minute. She returns. "Please follow me." She takes them down a hall into a small room with brown boxes arranged on tall shelves. The years are marked on the shelf in chronological order below each batch.

There is a big black machine that looks like a giant computer screen sitting on a table in the middle of the room. There is a slot in a box under the screen to insert the microfiche sheet. The receptionist takes down a box labeled 1982. She pulls out the first sheet and inserts it in the slot. Each sheet has approximately seven days of newspapers. She shows them how to navigate the sheet. "It's like reading a paper using a microscope. Please keep them in order by month. I am sorry, but our reader is old. There is no search function. You have to look at each sheet." She takes a step back. "I'll be up front if you have any questions. Good luck." She leaves the room.

They pull the two chairs at the table in front of the machine. Michael enthusiastically says, "I've never used a microfiche reader before. Guess we start at the first." He begins scanning around the sheet the receptionist inserted. After a minute they figure out how the newspapers are arranged on the sheets. An hour later, Rita is looking at June newspapers. There it is on the feature page of the June tenth paper: "Installment 8 from the Old Prospector – The Young Prospector and the Woman Miner." Underneath the story title is "by Mort Hamilton." Two full pages are dedicated to his story. "What a cool guy," Rita murmurs. In silence they read the story together on the microfiche reader screen. It seems to take forever.

The story is about a determined, beautiful young woman being bullied by a mean nearby property owner for her turquoise claim in 1860. Her name is Suzy. Almost predictably, she has developed a passion for turquoise mining. Her pursuit is very un-womanish for the time. A young prospector comes through town and helps her fight the villainous property owner and his worthless sons. They fall in love and turn her mine into the best turquoise claim in the world. They both laugh at the end. Rita pushes back from the machine. "I love it. It's so shmaltzy. The woman is Suzy."

They focus on the line in the riddle "The YP is real." They decide that YP means the Young Prospector. They get to the last paragraph of the story to see his name is Herculano Montoya. The story is the perfect miner's fairy tale told by the Old Prospector. Without waiting to ask if the pages can be printed, Michael takes a series of pictures of the story with his phone. He checks. The pictures are good enough to read. They carefully arrange the loose microfiche pages and put them back in the box. They thank the receptionist as they leave. "We found what we were looking for. Thank you."

They immediately go back to the compound and Google Herculano Montoya. In the first round of hits there is a picture of him from the Palace of the Governors photo archives. Michael is excited. "He is real." They go to the picture in the archives. The negative number below it is 005237. "We got it. The picture was shot in nineteen thirty-seven." The description below the picture, "Herculano Montoya of Cienega at the American Turquoise Company Muniz - Tiffany Lode Mine near Turquoise Post, Cerrillos." Michael claps his hands. "Clue four is located at this deserted mine I bet."

He takes a breath. "The rest of the clue sounds like there is a sign at the mine. I bet the next clue is buried near or below the sign. We will have to go there to check this part out." He sits thinking then he says, "I have no idea where this mine is. It's been closed for a long time I imagine. Who would know where it is?" They take a smoke break on the back portal. When they come back into the house, they start looking for information about the Muniz-Tiffany mine.

They find that Tiffany, the New York jewelry company, bought turquoise from five mines in an area called Turquoise Hill. The Muniz mine appears to be the one in the Herculano photograph. Rita finds the recorded claim for this mine in the New Mexico Mining Office online archives. Michael writes down the recorded coordinates for one of the claim's corners. He smiles at Rita. "I used coordinates all the time in Afghanistan. We can find this." The afternoon was gone. They had not even noticed the shadows starting to engulf the courtyard.

That evening Michael uses the mine's coordinates to find its approximate location using Google Earth. County Road 57 will get them within hiking distance. It is in Waldo Gulch. He is sure the mine is on private property. They will have to deal with that. The next morning, they leave for the Cerrillos area with a printed aerial view of the mine area, hiking boots, gloves, the shovel and a cautious optimism that they might find another clue.

The drive to Waldo's Gulch down Highway 14 is beautiful. The morning is still cool. They keep the Jeep's windows down. Rita keeps looking at the clue. She is not herself. "You okay? You seem preoccupied." She quietly says, "I'm just worried about Hugo doing something. He's still around you know." Michael continues to stare ahead. "I know. He will show up. It will be all right." Rita is unsure why he believes it will be all right. "I'm sorry you are having to be a part of this. Maybe I should just go back to Battle Mountain. I can settle with him there. I don't want him to do anything to you or your place. Especially you."

"Good, that's the way you're supposed to feel. Please don't leave." He looks at her this time. "Unless you just really want to. I would prefer you stayed here and continued to have sex with me." He is smiling big. She reaches across the console and hits him on the arm. She is smiling now. They leave the main road and turn onto a gravel road that looks like the one shown in the aerial view. The road crosses the gulch and meanders through small outcroppings of faded red rock.

They soon come to a rusted gate on the left side of the road. They see a small metal sign with "TIFF Ameri" in faded turquoise letters barely visible. The rusted lock on the gate has been punctured by a large caliber bullet. It is still defiantly clasped. They pull off the road and park. They grab their gear and start on a barely visible trail which begins on the other side of the gate. They walk on the trail hoping it is the right one. After about ten minutes they stop and look around. They are paralleling a bluff that is eroding into the gulch. The sun is reflecting off the white dirt and already creating eerie shadows as it is shaded by some of the rock formations on the other side.

"We might as well be in Nevada. This is some rough terrain." Rita laughs. After another ten minutes on the overgrown trail they see a hole in the side of the bluff. To the right of the opening is a hand painted NO TRESPASSING sign on a post. They slowly walk to the sign. They both are looking around. Michael puts his hand on the post. "This looks like an expected sign." He unfolds the shovel and starts digging at the base of the sign. At about the same depth as Clue 2 he hits something. He finishes digging with his hands. Soon he is holding another pill container. He extends it toward Rita. "Clue four, I hope." She pops the top and takes a plastic bag out. She unfolds the perfectly folded piece of paper inside and reads it to herself. "It's Clue four."

33 Bad Guys, Minus One

Cozy arrives at Waldo's Gulch about fifteen minutes after he sees the red dot stop moving. He drives by Michael's Jeep parked on the side of the road. There is no cover to park anywhere close. The gravel road goes around a small hill about three hundred yards ahead. He drives around the hill and parks on the side of the road. He grabs a pair of binoculars out of his trunk. He uses them sometimes when he is tailing someone. They are good enough to allow him to read lips. He carefully climbs over the barbwire fence and hurries up to the top of the small hill. He lies down at the top. He is breathing hard as he looks across the gulch below.

He is surprised to see Michael and Rita walking along the bluff a couple of hundred yards away. The sun reflecting off the bare white bluff edge makes it hard to see them sometimes. He trains the binoculars on them as they stop. They are talking and looking around. They start walking again. He looks ahead along the bluff and sees a NO TRESPASSING sign in front of a hole in the bluff. It is several hundred yards ahead. He knows that is where they are headed. He takes a moment to roll on his back and catch his breath.

He watches them as they approach the dark hole. He watches the kid dig a hole at the base of the sign and take something out of the ground. He hands it to the girl. She opens it. She looks at a piece of paper, refolds it and puts it back in the container. They high five and then hug. Quickly they turn and start back to the Jeep. Cozy jumps up. His breathing is almost normal. He runs down the hill traversing the downward slope back to his car. Not knowing where the road leads to the west, he three point turns around roughly. The dust from his passing has settled by the time Michael and Rita get back to the Jeep.

Once Cozy gets back on paved road on his way into Cerrillos he calls Teddy and is surprised when he answers. Teddy is hanging with his girlfriend again. He jumps when his phone rings. He sits up on the couch and answers knowing it's Cozy. He has avoided him for two weeks. He waves off his girlfriend. He hoarsely says, "Hey." He hears Cozy, "Hey jackass you been avoiding me? I'm gonna get into your mother if you don't start paying better attention. You call me back when I leave a message."

Teddy says enthusiastically, "Hey, I have been busy with a new job. You know, with a landscape service." He is lying. Cozy knows he is squirming. "We need to meet." Silence, then Teddy, "For what?" Cozy gruffly snaps back. "Beeeeecause I want to talk." Cozy hears heavy, shallow breathing. He ignores it. "Meet me Sunday evening at seven o'clock at the Sierra del Norte trailhead." Teddy hears three beeps as Cozy hangs up.

Two weeks earlier Teddy had seen the article in the paper about Oralynn's death. He went to high school with her younger sister. The sister went away to college and then stayed away to work. They haven't communicated for several years. He got to know Oralynn during that time at family gatherings. He thought she was nice. She listened to him. He is surprised to see she jumped. He was startled when he read the estimated time that she jumped, late Wednesday night, July fourteenth. He immediately thinks about how he picked up Cozy that night at the bridge where she committed suicide.

When Teddy gets off the phone, he starts talking to himself and pacing. "Oh shit. What the hell. Shit. This is too much. It's gotta be a coincidence." He freaks, even though he has no idea how or why Cozy might be involved in Oralynn's death. He knew Cozy's story was lame at the time, but so is Cozy. "This is not cool. Now he wants to meet. This is not cool." His girlfriend sits on the other end of the couch staring at him, thinking about leaving.

Cozy splurges and picks up a burger to go at the Blackbird in Cerrillos. The high-ceilinged old saloon has good burgers. It is a favorite for bikers cruising the Turquoise Trail. As he is exiting the front door the Jeep pulls up on the other side of the street and parks. Michael and Rita are talking. He puts his head down and goes to his Tahoe parked two cars down on his side of the street. As he drives past the Jeep, he looks the other way. Michael glances up as the black Tahoe passes.

His eyes are drawn to the adobe colored Albuquerque Police Department parking sticker in the upper right windshield. He continues watching as the Tahoe turns right onto the main street. He thinks,

"That's the police dick from The Pantry." He forgets about it as Rita gets out. "Come on, I'm hungry." She waves the pill container with Clue 4 at him.

Back in Santa Fe Hugo leaves his room at the El Rey and drives by the compound several times during the day. It looks deserted. The garage door is closed. He is pissed. He obsesses about the video posting. The BLM account has contacted him by email. His Facebook account has been blocked. It took about three hours before the Lander County Sheriff's Office received a call about it. He has a message on his phone from the sheriff, "You are fired Hugo. Pick up your personal items when you get back from your now permanent vacation." There is a pause. "We are going to get sued because of you, asshole." This abrupt end to his Lander County law enforcement career is not how he envisioned it would be.

That evening, Hugo foregoes the margaritas and goes directly to tequila shots at Del Charro. After four shots he is feeling taller, smarter and meaner. The bartender suggests he slow down. He decides to leave. He drives straight to the compound and parks in the same place he did two nights ago. The Jeep is the only vehicle parked in the drive. He knows he is not going to get Rita back. He has no job. His tequila-induced pity party has left him with nothing to lose. "How about all the windows this time?" He grabs the bat from the passenger's side seat and heads to the Jeep.

Rita and Michael are sitting on the back portal when they hear the first whack of Hugo's bat. Michael jumps up and heads around the house to the drive. Rita follows him. Hugo has taken out the driver's side windows when Michael starts yelling at him, "What the fuck are you doing, asshole?" A motion sensor light comes on. Michael starts toward him even though Hugo has the bat. Rita rounds the corner in time to see him closing quickly on Hugo.

Hugo has the bat ready, but he is not expecting the fighter that is coming at him. From the back Rita sees the Marine that took out the rebels. Hugo takes a swing at Michael with his bat. Michael sidesteps it easily and closes fast with a kidney punch from the side. Hugo cringes and drops the bat. He turns on Michael and pulls a pistol from a holster on his belt. He stands pointing it at him.

Out of the shadows Rita's voice, "Put the gun down Hugo. We can talk. Leave him alone." She steps out of the shadows. Hugo turns and points the gun at her. "You wrecked my life. I got fired. Everybody hates me on Facebook." Michael is immediately on him. He grabs his arm as he waves the pistol around. Hugo fires the pistol twice at the ground. As the casings hit the concrete drive loudly, sparks fly as the bullets ricochet into the bushes leaving white depressions in the concrete.

Rita watches Michael get him down. Michael violently brings his elbow up into his chin, knocking his head back. He has his arm with the pistol with one hand and the other is around Hugo's throat. He turns the gun into his chest. "Stop what you are doing. You are gonna die if you don't." As if he doesn't hear, Hugo tries to point his pistol at Rita again. Quickly, Michael points the gun into Hugo's chest. Hugo's engorged face is turning blue.

With Hugo's own finger trapped on the trigger, Michael forces him to pull the trigger. The gun explodes in one big hurrumff into Hugo's chest. The sound rips through the quiet night. Hugo is limp. Michael quickly gets up like this is something he has done before. He has blood on his shirt and face. He looks at Rita. She is scared and shaken. They are both quiet. Lights are coming on inside houses down the street in both directions.

Michael opens the garage door and turns on the outside lights. He looks at the Jeep's broken windows. "More glass to clean up." Without saying anything, he goes in the casita and washes his hands and face. He changes shirts. He spreads the bloody shirt neatly on the floor so the police can see it. He calls 911. Then he calls Cecil Soledad's number. When he reaches him, he tells him what has happened and asks him to come. Rita stands at the entrance to the casita staring at him while he makes the call. He isn't aware she is watching him.

She has now seen the fighter. She has seen a man she despised die at his hands. No woman would argue that the asshole lying in the drive in a pool of blood didn't deserve it. What she has seen scares her, however. She has never been around anyone like Michael. He was almost emotionless in this situation. In an unexpected way, it reassures her. Underneath the apparent calmness, this boy is a pretty fearless badass. A siren gets louder and louder as it gets closer. Soon a couple of cop cars and an ambulance arrive.

Waiting in the driveway they identify themselves. Rita points to Hugo, "He is, or was, a deputy sheriff from Battle Mountain, Nevada. He is an ex-boyfriend. He has been stalking me here in Santa Fe." She shows them a picture on her phone of the broken Volvo windshield. The two cops look at each other. Rita tells them about the note and him breaking the windshield out of her car a couple of nights ago. "He said he got fired when he was raging at me tonight. He may not be a deputy sheriff anymore."

Rita tells the video story. "He is a known asshole." It sounds stupid to her now. She tells them about the fight, how Michael was defending them. He didn't have any choice. She walks over to the new white pockmarks in the concrete driveway. She points at them and angrily says, "This would have been us if Michael hadn't stopped him!"

Detective Soledad arrives about ten minutes later. He gets out of his car. He looks at Hugo's body. He goes straight to Michael, "What the hell is up with you? You are a magnet for trouble." He stands and looks at him. His tone softens. "You okay?" He pulls out a pad. "Tell me the story again." They finish talking about five minutes later. He writes down a couple of things. Soledad confers with the two cops that talked to Rita. The cops give him the pistol in a plastic bag.

Their heads are nodding as they separate. The EMS attendants put Hugo in a bag. Rita hears the zipper as they close it. Through the shock of it all she still thinks "Good riddance asshole." The attendants put him on a stretcher and wheel him to the ambulance. Soon they are on their way to the hospital. The cops leave too. Michael turns the outside light off. Rita, Soledad and he adjourn to the casita to talk.

Rita tells the detective the sordid story of her relationship with Hugo. She tells him about Hugo trying to set fire to her trailer. "With us in it!" She tells him about the video and what they did. "Maybe not the smartest thing." Taking full credit for posting the video, she says, "That's on me." She looks straight at Soledad. "The asshole wouldn't leave me alone. The sheriff was no help. I thought it might stop him." She looks at Michael. "I am sorry that Michael had to be involved in this." She tells Soledad about the Facebook group in case he wants to watch the video. He writes it down.

She shows him the picture on her phone. "He broke my car windshield out with a bat, probably the one in the driveway." She gets the threatening handwritten note and shows it to him. Cecil looks at Michael. "He fucked with the wrong guy. I looked up some things about you that help me understand how this went down." He stands. "I want you on my team." He looks at the floor. "Downtown may call you tomorrow about this. I will turn in what I know. Looks like a jealous asshole got in deeper than he wanted. He paid for it." As he walks through the casita door, "Hope not to hear from you soon. Good night." With his gloved hands he picks up the baseball bat from the drive. He puts it in the back seat of his car.

The silence and darkness in the compound settle them. Michael gets a water hose from the garage as a wrecker arrives to remove Hugo's car from where he parked it. The pulsating yellow lights on the top and back are irritating. He washes the pool of blood off the drive. It is only a bad memory as it washes into the earth at the edge of the drive. He looks at the drive with a flashlight. The concrete is stained, but this will do for now. He doesn't really feel like doing anything else. Once again, as with each time he has been in a kill-or-be-killed situation, he wonders if there is something wrong with him. He hopes this doesn't become part of his dreams like the rest.

Two days later a short story in the newspaper on page four refers to Hugo as a former law enforcement officer from Nevada. He was stalking a woman who was visiting Santa Fe. He was caught breaking out car windshields by the former girlfriend and current boyfriend, a decorated former Marine. He died in an ensuing struggle. His death is ruled a justifiable homicide.

34 Clue 4

Michael and Rita resume sitting on the back portal in the dark staring into the courtyard. They sit quietly for a couple of minutes. Someone in the neighborhood has a pinon fire. The smell is faint, but identifiable. "That was pretty gutsy stepping out at Hugo like you did." Michael stretches out in his chair. "I served with guys in Afghanistan that would not have done that." He waits to let his comment sink in. "Your friend in Battle Mountain said you were the smartest person there. I have to wonder though." He reaches over and affectionately rubs her shoulder. Referring to what Soledad said about him, "I want you on my team."

Rita puts her cigarette out. "I was hoping the distraction would give you an opening to do what you did." She looks away and then looks back sadly. "I am sorry I put you in this place. You don't deserve this." Very quietly, almost under her breath, "I wanted you to kill that son of a bitch. I have been worried about going back." She looks straight at him. "I know that's horrible. It's especially bad because I'm not sure I could have done it myself."

They sit for a minute. Michael softly says, "That's a good thing. I hope you never answer that question. I have answered enough for both of us." A group of jabbering tourists returning from a quintessential evening of green chile chicken enchiladas and strong margaritas walks by on the sidewalk on the other side of the courtyard wall. "Is it bad that I don't feel anything for Hugo, other than he won't bother us anymore? Is it bad that I don't miss my parents?" He takes a puff. "I miss my grandfather." The questions hang, as there are no answers.

Rita breaks the silence. "Guess it is what it is. I'm just going along with what comes right now. Melon is probably right about letting it come to you." She leans back and stretches her legs out. "I hope it is a good thing." It has been a day. The high was finding the clue in the morning. The low is obvious. They both know Hugo's death would not have happened if he would have backed off.

They sleep together, but on separate sides of the bed. They are both uncomfortable and restless. In the morning, Michael brings Rita coffee in bed. He stands looking at her. "Long night. I didn't sleep enough to have a bad dream." She sits up and rubs her eyes. She smiles and reaches for the cup. "Good morning. Thank you." Her sleep shirt is down over her shoulder. She adjusts it. Her smile relieves Michael. She starts again, "I am so sorry for getting you into this situation. I never thought it would end this way."

He sits down on the side of the bed by her feet. Without acknowledging her comment, "I've been looking at the treasure hunt countdown calendar. We are going to be able to do this. Let's go for a hike. Maybe it will make us both feel better. I know I need the air." Even though the treasure hunt clock is ticking, they decide to go for a hike at Kasha-Katuwe Tent Rocks National Monument. They take the Volvo with a new front windshield. After they turn by the giant earthen dam at Cochiti Lake, the Indian service road into the park seems to go forever.

They park and start up the Slot Canyon Trailhead. "My grandfather brought me here several times. Believe it or not we would hang out in the slot canyon where we are going. On the way to the top of the plateau he would stop by this giant ponderosa pine and show me card tricks." They walk along the sandy trail with Michael in the lead. Rita stops when she sees the "Watch for Rattlesnakes" sign as the trail veers off to the canyon. Michael smugly points out, "You Nevadans aren't the only ones with rattlesnakes."

White boulder-capped hoodoos pop out of the ground everywhere along the trail. They line the sides of the plateau they are hiking around to get to the trail to the top. The hoodoos look like cones with rocks balanced on them. They walk under some that are a hundred feet tall. Rita stops and takes a couple of pictures with her phone. She has Michael stop. She puts her head next to his and takes a selfie of them with the white cliffs in the background. "Our first selfie." They are holding hands as they enter the slot canyon. Soon Michael is in the lead again, as only one person at a time can fit in the slot.

They come to a giant pine in a wash. It is a cool and shady spot. Michael motions for Rita to sit on a giant root spanning the trail. He pulls out a deck of cards and turns to her. They are laughing at the silliness of what he is doing. He has her pick a card and put it back in the deck. He shuffles the cards and says again, "Pick a card." She draws a card and flips it over. It's the card she picked earlier. "How did you do that?" He turns and starts walking. "I'll never tell."

After the six hundred-foot ascent to the top of the plateau, they sit on a rock ledge at the end of the trail. The morning is clear and no one else is around. They take in the "money view" of the three mountain ranges and the Rio Grande River Valley. Rita sighs. "This makes me feel small." They scoot close together. As if she had been waiting for the opportunity, Rita says, "Are you okay with me still being here? I don't know what I am doing here really. I want to help you find the treasure. Is that what you want?"

Michael puts his hand on her leg. "I find something with you that I haven't found with anyone else. I feel like fate had a hand in it. Even the Hugo part." A light wind rushes down the valley stirring the nearby juniper. Its new grown light green tassels bob happily. Michael looks at the expanse in front of them. "This is silly, but I hope the myth of turquoise and the happiness that can come with it is true. I like to think Mort had it. I saw him rub Suzy's stone so often. Somehow I think it gave him comfort." Rita asks, "What are you going to do with the money if the treasure really is twenty pounds of Lander Blue?"

He puts his arm around her. With his index finger, he turns her head and kisses her gently. "If we don't solve Clue four, we won't have to worry about it." They sit and watch the thunderheads forming over the Jemez range. Rita takes note that he said "we." She is still unsure how he feels about her being with him. He has been so gentle and loving that she knows it is more than just sex. She has never believed in fate. She rubs her bracelet and feels the familiar warmth on her wrist.

After spending Friday night worrying about Cozy's threatening call, Teddy calls the Santa Fe police Saturday morning. He is unsure about what exactly he will say, but he is spooked and wants help. He gets transferred to workaholic Detective Cecil Soledad, who is still by default the detective on duty. Two tours in Iraq as a Marine under Bush senior cost him his marriage. Two years ago, a drunk driver took his only child. At forty-eight years old he is tested and mangled, but not at all lost, though his twenty-eight-year-old son's death broke his heart.

His family holds him out as a war hero. He was the real deal. No supporting role for him. He led a small field group that was responsible for finding and apprehending bad Iraqis. No one really knows for sure what he did as he has shared only limited details with one of his cousins who was also in Iraq. Neither talk about it much. They all affectionately call him, "nuestro valiente heroe," ("our brave hero"). He loves to work. He is completing a tedious manpower report when his desk phone rings.

He picks up and hears, "Hey. Who is this?" Cecil waits. "Who is this?" There is silence. Then, "Hey. Let's say I'm just somebody familiar with cops. I have a little drug history, but I'm clean now." Cecil, "So." Teddy is finding this difficult. "Hey, I got some information about a bad cop. She was a friend. She didn't do no bridge. Hey, I got a problem with my safety." Cecil doesn't understand. "You may have to get a restraining order. No matter, you are going to have to come in and talk to somebody. Nothing can be done until you do that." Teddy is frustrated. "Hey, I told you man, I got a problem with my safety now." Cecil hears the phone click as Teddy ends the call.

After eating a green chile cheeseburger and spiced fries from the Lotaburger on Guadalupe, Michael and Rita settle at the dining room table. Without missing a step Michael nonchalantly pulls a chair out for her as he passes the table. Smiling, he motions with his head for her to sit down. He gets the folder with the clues from his bedroom nightstand. He unfolds the handwritten paper and places Clue 4 on the table in front of her.

A cracked green leather chair: *The cracked green leather chair at Mort's desk in his study at his house.*
Memories of being there: *Michael would sit in the chair pretending he was running a company as a boy. He would talk with Mort there as a teenager and young man.*
Breakfast at Tiffany's was his claim: *Truman Capote wrote this.*
Our mugs hiding there in a frame: *A picture of Mort and Capote when he came to Santa Fe in the early 1980s.*
The missing piece is surrounded by mines: *A two-inch by two-inch piece of the picture is cut neatly from the lower right corner. It is lodged in a crease of a folded map showing the location of several southwest turquoise mines.*
Most memories from past times: *Most of the mines shown are closed.*
Check all that pulls out: *The folded map is in something that pulls out—the drawer of Mort's desk.*
Till you have no doubt: *Keep pulling things out until you find it.*

Michael gets a bottle of water for each of them from the kitchen and sits down beside her. "I think I know about the first two lines. I am not surprised this clue is in Santa Fe. I have no idea when Mort hid the clues in Gallup and Cerrillos. It makes sense he went to Battle Mountain when he and Easy took off. Not bad for an eighty-two-year-old trickster. Lots of walking. I imagine he got tired." He thinks sadly that maybe the wear and tear was part of the reason Mort didn't survive the virus. "I am pretty sure the green chair is in Mort's study. I used to sit in it and pretend I was the boss of my own company. This clue may be easier than the others. I think we need to go to Mort's house to solve the rest of it."

At Mort's house Michael pulls his Jeep into the drive and parks in front of the house. Rita gets out. "This is like your parents' compound." They go around the house to the backyard. She follows him to the well house entrance. "This is where it all started." The hole he and Will made in the middle is still visible, though the spiders have recreated their web city in the left corner. He describes how he and Will dug up Clue 1.

The gazebo in the yard is shady and inviting. Though overgrown, Mort's back courtyard is alive with blooms too. They enter the house through the back portal door. The house is musty from being closed. "I haven't come over here often enough." They open a couple of windows in the kitchen and adjoining den. Rita follows him down the hall into the master suite. It is huge. It has glass doors opening onto the back portal. Michael opens another window. They go into Mort's study. Behind the large dark oak desk is a cracked green leather chair.

Michael opens the shade concealing the big window facing the front. He meticulously cranks the metal frame casement windows out. Immediately a light draft of air begins flowing through the room. He goes to Mort's desk, pulls the chair out and sits down. Rita sits down in an old brown leather chair in a corner against the wall to the left of the door. He lays Clue 4 on the desk as he says, "I Googled Breakfast at Tiffany's."

He smiles faking surprise. "Surely this has no connection to us visiting the Tiffany mine where the Tiffany colored stone was mined." He gets serious. "Anyway, the story is written by Truman Capote. My guess is it's a picture of Mort and Truman Capote. I have no idea why or when. He mentions in a frame, so my hope is it's a picture that's out in the open somewhere here in the house. Think we need to find the picture."

They look around the study. Several black and white photos

autographed by native craftsmen are hanging on the doorway wall. Nothing with Mort in it. The rest of the room is mostly floor-to-ceiling bookshelves filled with books. A row of seven drawers, three shelves up runs along the wall across from the desk. Michael gets up. "Why don't you check the front of the house and I'll check the back. I hope the picture is hanging or sitting somewhere in this house. He pulls up a picture of Truman Capote on his phone and shows it to Rita. After looking she does the same.

Five minutes later Rita calls from the den, "This might be it." In a cluster of black and white pictures of Mort with different celebrities is a picture of a much younger Mort with a shorter stocky-looking man wearing a starched white shirt and a white Panama hat. Michael looks at the picture of Capote on his phone. "This might be it." He picks the frame up by the top. It is faded like the rest, but not as dusty.

They go back to the study. He sets the frame down on the desk and gently undoes the hasps holding the picture in the frame. He turns it over leaving the white mat and the glass on top of the desk. The bottom left corner of the photograph has been cut off.

He turns the photo over. In faded ink in the upper right-hand corner. "Visit to Hamilton's Sept. 10, 1981." There was Truman Capote's autograph on a piece of paper folded behind the photo. Michael sits holding the autograph. "I guess maybe Mort just wanted me to know about this. This step seems unnecessary." He looks around and Rita has wondered off down the hall, looking at things with drawers. He thinks for a minute more. She returns to the study. "There's a lot of things to pull out in this house."

He looks up preoccupied. "Yes. This is where I get confused." Rita purses her lips. "It sounds like maybe it's in a drawer or something that pulls out." Michael retorts quickly, "We are assuming it is a drawer. We are assuming the clue is here in the house. The part about being surrounded by mines that are closed makes no sense." Rita is anxious to do something. "Let's start looking anyway. It will be fun to go through some of Mort's stuff." She looks at him and smiles. "Won't you have to at some point?" Michael looks at her. "I guess I hadn't thought about it, since I haven't heard what Mort wants to do with his compound. I am unsure about it. Cromley didn't say anything about it when we spoke. At the time I thought it was weird to ask."

They both look at the drawers across the back of the room. Michael suggests, "You start on that end and I'll start on this end." An hour later they have found nothing in these drawers. They take a break. They step outside into the cooling late afternoon air. They sit at the table in the gazebo as the sun starts down. As if talking to himself, Michael says, "I think it's here in the house. I don't know what Mort means by surrounded by mines. We just need to keep looking."

They walk back into the house and turn on the lamps in the den and study. The rooms seem smaller. They go back into the study. Michael walks to the end of the shelves and pulls out a book. He holds it out to Rita like a magician verifying his prop is real. As she looks at the book an 18-inch wide by three-foot tall section of the shelves automatically swings open. No one would know the three-foot deep cavity extending into the pantry in the kitchen was on the other side of the adobe block wall. Rita laughs out loud. Without finishing her sentences, "How the hell, why would Mort? That is so cool." She sticks her head in the musty-smelling hole.

Michael smiles as he lightly pushes the section back in place. "Mort's bullshit. I never knew him to keep anything in there. I wasn't sure it would still work. He loved gadgets too." He shakes the book at her playfully before replacing it carefully in its weighted position. They hear the sensitive spring reengage on the other side of the books.

Michael sits in the armchair at the desk. They are looking at each other. "When I was little, I would think about getting in that hidey hole and disappearing. I couldn't figure out how to open it from the inside." He is playing with the drawer pull on the desk. He realizes what he is doing and opens the desk drawer. In the very back corner under several rubber banded bundles of cancelled checks, old pens, rubber bands and paper clips, is a folded piece of heavy paper.

Without thinking he takes the neatly folded piece of paper out of the drawer. The paper is thick, dry and yellowed. The old pens falling back into the drawer make a loud noise. He starts to unfold the paper. Rita is at his right side now. He stops, gets up and turns the overhead light on. She waits. She touches nothing. He returns to the desk and gently unfolds the paper. It's an old color map. Someone has marked and labeled by hand turquoise mines in Nevada, Arizona and New Mexico. The Capote picture piece is snugly wedged in the centerfold. The last clue is neatly handwritten on it in small letters.

Outside Mort's house Cozy parks on the street near the driveway entrance. He woke from a nap, checked the tracker app and saw that the Jeep was at Mort's house. He has been sitting in his car for an hour.

He wonders if he can make it through the entrance to the shadows of the house without anyone seeing him. Maybe he can look in a window. There are no people on the street. He slides out of the Tahoe and starts toward Mort's. He is in the driveway entrance when the lights in the house go out. Shortly Rita and Michael come around the corner of the house laughing, heading to the Jeep.

Cozy knows they can see his silhouette. He turns abruptly and almost runs back to the Tahoe. There is no other choice. He doesn't want to wait until they leave as they will go right by him. He turns his head pretending to be doing something as he starts the Tahoe. He knows they are watching him. There is just enough light for Michael to see the Albuquerque Police Department parking sticker as Cozy drives by still looking the other way.

35 Too Coincidental and the Last Clue

As they climb into the Jeep Michael says, "Did you see the guy at the end of the drive? He was coming this way. He stopped and went to that black Tahoe that just went by." He doesn't wait for Rita to say anything. "That's the third time that I've seen that Albuquerque cop parking sticker and that car. The guy was in Cerrillos when we were." Rita responds quietly as if others might hear her, "I saw him. Really more his silhouette. He did leave quick like he didn't want us to see him. He was purposely looking the other way when he went by too."

Michael starts the Jeep. He tells Rita, "I should have followed him. It's too late now. Maybe I should tell Soledad about it? I hadn't wanted to mention the treasure hunt to him." He stops before they pull out on the street. "I wonder if the break-in is related?" He looks both ways on the street and pulls out before answering his own question. "That's crazy. How would anybody else know about what we are doing? Unless Mort told someone else? Cromley and his assistant and Will and you are the only other people who know anything about the hunt. Cromley's assistant isn't in the mix anymore according to the newspaper. Pretty weird. She committed suicide."

With the last clue in his shirt pocket, they arrive at his parents' compound. Michael is smiling as they walk to the front door. "I already got this one after one look, I think. Mort slacked off for this last one." They change into their bed clothes. Michael decides to call Cecil. After pleasantries and an apology for bothering him in the evening, he gets to the point. "Since the break-in at my casita we have seen this guy several times. It's like he might be following us. It's too coincidental." Cecil asks logically, "Did you see the guy's face?"

"I saw him be an asshole at The Pantry the first time I saw him. He is white, maybe fifty. Slicked back hair. Have to say I was watching the poor young waitress more than him. He left quickly." Michael realizes that The Pantry sighting was before Mort's hunt had begun. He and Will were on their way to find the box in Mort's well house that morning. He tells Cecil, "We were walking out to the parking in the back when I did see the asshole get in a Tahoe that had an Albuquerque police parking sticker."

"It was the black Tahoe. New Mex plates, but don't have the number. There's an adobe colored police parking sticker on the front window on the driver's side. Unsure what to think about that." Michael apologizes again and thanks him. After he disconnects, Rita joins him at the dining table. She sits down hard in one of the chairs and pulls her knees to her chest. "I'm too tired to eat. I hit my wall." She asks Michael if he told Cecil about the treasure hunt. Michael shakes his head slightly. "No. It's such a stretch to think that this guy would have anything to do with that, but why does he seem to be following us?"

They are both mentally exhausted. He shows her the last clue which is neatly handwritten in black ink on the back of the picture piece.

Ten years old: *Mort built a gazebo at his house when Michael was ten years old.*
Screws: *The deck boards were screwed down.*
Smiles: *Screwing screws with the electric screwdriver made Michael smile.*
Middle: *Look in the middle of the deck.*
Under: *Look under the deck.*

That is Clue 5. They adjourn to the back portal. Michael calls Will to tell him they found the last clue. Will is in Denver at a paint show. He wishes he was there. Rita hears Michael say, "I think it's under the deck of Mort's gazebo. Gonna find out in the morning. Take it easy dude. See you in a couple of days." He ends the call with Will.

He turns to Rita. "Get this, we may have sat on the treasure today." He explains to her, "When I was ten, I helped build the deck for Mort's backyard gazebo. I loved screwing the screws in with this old electric drill. I annoyed my parents talking about it." The pot is slowing him down. He takes a pensive look out at the courtyard. "I remember Ernesto. He was this old Mexican carpenter. He had just a few teeth. But what a smile. I wish I had a picture of him." He thinks to himself, "Of all the fond memories I have of the old man, I mention his teeth."

As a kid he thought Ernesto was interesting looking. He continues nostalgically, "He let me help screw the boards in place. He showed me how to apply just enough pressure without stripping the screw head. That nice old man is gone now." His voice drifts off. "He had the kindest brown eyes to go with his smile. I don't know for sure, but I bet someone was lucky to have him as a father."

Michael relates how Mort had already laid about six planks each way starting at the center of the twenty-feet by twenty-feet deck when he got there that morning. "I was there with him until dark the night before. Mort may have buried the treasure after I left or before I got there early the next morning. I rode my bicycle to his house early. I didn't even tell my parents." He pauses to take a puff. "Ernesto was still drinking a cup of coffee on the back portal." Michael smiles now, understanding why Mort didn't wait for them to start.

Twenty years ago, Mort orders a metal box with a lid from the local feed store. The day he picks it up he removes the mysterious leather bag from Hamilton's safe. He takes the leather duffle bag and puts it in a black garbage bag. He places this in the metal box he buries between the middle rows of deck posts. The box is located at the center of the deck. Because there is no spacing between the boards, seeing the lid between the cracks would take more than a casual look.

As the quiet is settling around them for another night, Michael's phone rings, startling them both. It's Cecil. "So, I've been thinking about your call earlier. I was just wondering who your lawyer is." Michael thinks this is a strange question as he answers, "Burt Cromley. He's been our family lawyer forever. Why do you ask?" As if he anticipates the question, Cecil answers calmly, "I've been working on something else and I am looking for connections. I don't have enough to even say anything about it. Catch up soon. Thank you." Michael sits rubbing his hands together. Soon he realizes that he and Rita are thinking the same thing. "Maybe we should tell the detective about the treasure hunt."

36 The Bag in the Box

Michael is quiet and absorbed when they get in bed. Rita drifts off to sleep wondering what he is thinking. She sleeps for about four hours before she wakes, hot and clammy. Her shoulders and back are tight. Somehow during this block of sleep, she has become disappointed in herself. The weight of her guilt feels like it runs through her whole body. Ruminating about whether part of the turquoise is hers has worn her out. She sits up, realizing if there is a bag of Lander Blue, it really isn't hers. She knows that it was Mort's and he is giving it to Michael.

She pushes the covers off and stares at the ceiling fan thinking, "Why don't you get up and turn it on?" Suddenly she realizes that most of her angst is not about the turquoise, but about her relationship with Michael. She has only known him for nineteen days. He is so different. He is not pushy. He is great in bed. He doesn't push that either. What will happen when the treasure hunt is over? Will she go back to being a waitress at the Battle Mountain Diner? At least she doesn't have to worry about Hugo anymore. Maybe she should sell Suzy's bracelet and move on. Pay her debts and start over again.

She is about to get up and go sit in a chair in the den when Michael rolls over and stretches his body sideways against her. He gently puts his arm across her chest. He feels her warmth and removes his arm. He doesn't say a word. He is doing it in his sleep. She smiles. She turns her back to him and pulls his arm back across her chest. As if he absorbs the heat, she feels cooler. She inches her body into the shape of his body as she falls back asleep.

The next morning, they are up early. Michael is in the garage gathering tools for the work ahead of them. Rita makes coffee. He tests an electric screwdriver that has been charging all night. As they sit drinking coffee on the back portal, Rita asks him, "How do you think your life will change after today if there is ten million dollars of Lander Blue?" He replies, "It's all happened so fast I haven't really processed it.

There has been so much bad." He turns and looks at her. "And then so much good, I hope." As crazy as it is, he woke up this morning thinking he might be in love with Rita.

They are anxious to get started. As they are leaving the house for Mort's, Cecil calls. They sit down on the back portal so Michael can talk. Cecil doesn't get into it with him, but he has been focusing on the police parking sticker. The day before, he had called the Albuquerque Police Department. He identified himself and said he is working on a case in Santa Fe and that he ran across MacFarland's name. He asks what they know about him. He is transferred to a talkative desk sergeant who knew him when he was active. "He is freelancing now. Think he is getting divorced and having rough times. He is doing work for a law firm somehow connected to his wife."

The Sergeant does not know the firm's name. Cecil asks the Sergeant if "Cozy" was asked to leave the department? The sergeant lowers his voice slightly, "Funny you know one of his nicknames. He wore out his welcome here. He pushed the chief to a bad spot. Honestly, none of us were sad to see the son of a buck go."

Cecil's instincts are telling him something is there, but exactly what is not clear yet. He has methodically arranged the coincidences in his mind. Oralynn's death, the call he got from some junkie kid, the parking sticker Michael keeps seeing and the compromised detective working for the family lawyer are brewing.

He starts the conversation with Michael, "Is there any reason you can think of why the guy with the parking sticker might be dogging you?" He takes about five minutes and tells Cecil about Mort and the treasure hunt. He ends the story. "The last two times I saw the sticker Rita and I were solving clues. How did the guy know we were there?" Cecil continues without specifically acknowledging his question. "Did Cromley know about the hunt?" Michael thinks about the answer and replies, "I imagine. He told me I had twenty-four days to find the treasure after I told him Will and I found the first clue in the well house."

Michael pauses then continues, "I got the feeling that neither Cromley nor his assistant knew all the details. He didn't mention any others. Maybe he didn't tell me all he knows either. Mort's stuff is at his office in a file." As an afterthought, "I have not gone back to talk with him as the hunt has been taking all my time and has been productive. I only have a few days left." He doesn't tell Cecil that they hope to retrieve the treasure this morning.

Cecil gets off the phone. He thinks to himself, "Now add a crazy treasure hunt to the mix." He calls Cozy next. As expected, he doesn't pick up. This message is less polite. "Call me. I need to talk with you. If you want to meet for a cup of coffee that will work too. Call me." Cozy's lack of response is suspicious, just because of the lack of cop to cop courtesy, if nothing else. The mounting coincidences feed Cecil's suspicions. He knows there is more to what is going on.

Rita and Michael may be anxious to get started, but they are hungry. The buy chorizo burritos at a taco wagon on Early Street. They get to Mort's about nine o'clock, as the sun is warming things up. They park in front of the house in the drive. Michael gathers the tools from the back of the Jeep. They walk around the house to the gazebo. Together they move the table and chairs to the side of the deck. They are ready to see if they have the last clue right.

Michael places the battery-powered screwdriver and two pairs of gloves on the table. He hopes Mort's garage will have any other tools they might need. They try looking between the cracks in the middle of the deck. They can't see anything. Michael thinks about the moved chair that he and Will saw when they found the box in the well house. He tells Rita about it. "Mort sat here when he buried the box in the well house. I bet Mort sat here many times after he buried the treasure, if in fact it is below us. I wonder if he thought about it each time. It's like he wanted it close, but unknown to everyone else."

The deck surface has aged to a dull gray finish. Fourteen screws later, the middle plank is loose. Michael gently pries up one end up with a crowbar he keeps in the back of his Jeep. As he lifts it, little chunks of wood stick to the joists underneath. They have had years of shrinking around each other. He tells Rita, "There was lots of dancing and partying in this gazebo. As a teenager I would come by Mort's gatherings sometimes. He loved it. Several of his local crew would be singing and drinking tequila. Mort used to call that crew the "Geriatric Gang."

Once the board is loose Rita picks up the other end. They turn it over on the deck. The bottom is perfect, except for the few missing chunks every two feet. They each take a couple of steps to the middle of the deck and look down into the eight-inch-wide gap. They almost bump heads trying to get a better look. Both look up smiling. Michael wants to hug her. He wonders if she feels the same.

They take up five more boards running perpendicular to the joists. They each have the same number of screws to remove. Rita takes over for a couple of boards. Each board coming up reveals more of the buried box. The whir of the screwdriver sounds like a swarm of bees every fifteen seconds. Soon there is enough room for the rectangular lid to be raised. Nineteen days in and Mort's treasure hunt may be ending. They stop and stare at the lid. Michael looks up to the sky. "Hope this isn't all a joke."

The soil comes up to the lower edge of the lid. It is white, packed and dry. There is a crack all the way around the box where it has shrunk away. Michael takes a deep breath and gets on his knees. He reaches down between the joists and grabs the four-inch long raised metal handle. The top doesn't budge at first. He jerks hard and it comes loose with a crunching sound. Rust fragments from the edge of the box that clung to the lid scatter onto the deck and onto the contents in the box.

The box contains something inside a black garbage bag about the size of four shoe boxes. The bag is wrapped tightly with duct tape. Rita is on her knees beside Michael. They grab the plastic bag as best they can and clumsily pull it out of its twenty-year-old coffin. Michael carries it to the table and gently puts it down. Both are sweaty and quiet.

Michael goes into Mort's kitchen and gets scissors. When he returns with the scissors, they sit down on opposite sides of the table with the bag between them. He pulls the plastic up from the contents as best he can. He gingerly works the scissors, cutting and then pulling back the wrapping until a brown leather duffle bag is exposed on the table.

Once again, they stop and stare at each other. Michael unzips the bag and peers at the contents. He slowly looks back up and then at Rita. "So, this is what I hope ten million dollars looks like." He moves out of the way and motions with his eyes for her to come see. Rita spreads open the top of the bag and looks at the contents, "I think this is it. I can't believe we found it." There is bottle on top of the contents. It is wrapped in a 1976 *Santa Fe New Mexican* newspaper. A partial front-page headline reads: "Hamilton's Opens on..."

Michael takes the bottle out of the bag and carefully lays it on the table. On the outside is a handwritten taped note. "Enjoy for me and Suzy. We missed having this in 1973." Michael takes the newspaper wrapping from around the bottle of 1972 Stags' Leap Cabernet Sauvignon. He folds the old newspaper carefully and sticks Mort's note on the top of the folded newspaper. He stands the wine bottle on it. The wine had been placed atop a bag full of rough shards of turquoise. Each shard is wrapped in white tissue paper. Each shard reveals a thick band of Lander Blue.

They each undo a couple of shards and set them on the table. Rita moans humorously and caresses one of the shards as she holds it against her chest. "It might be a couple of twenty-five-carat cabochons." She holds it out for Michael to see. He smiles. He has one just like it in his hands. It is Lander Blue shard after shard. Some bands are three inches thick. Some bands run six inches through the shard.

Their eyes meet. They empty their hands and embrace. Michael has never felt the desire to kiss anyone like he does at that moment. He holds Rita firmly against him and closes his eyes. Their lips touch. They both realize quickly how dry their mouths are and cut short their kiss attempt. Their eyes lock again. Without saying a word, they laugh, and both know it is okay. They sit for a minute more. Michael slumps in his chair with his feet straight out. His head is on his chest and his eyes are closed. Rita asks him playfully, "Are you praying?"

"I was really thanking Mort. I was thinking about how much effort it was for him to set up the treasure hunt. I kept his last message, the one that started this, on my phone. He was not doing well at the end." They sit silently and stare into the courtyard. "He knew I would find it. He knew I would have to learn about turquoise because of the clues. I know that was part of his plan." Michael calls Will and leaves a message that they found the treasure buried beneath the middle of the gazebo deck.

37 Cozy's Move / Plan B

Cozy is tired of fucking with this. He is not prepared mentally or physically this morning. He could tell by the tone of the third message left by the cop that he is a problem. He is drinking black coffee and hating the light coming in the dirty kitchen window. He is hung over. He thinks about selling a couple of pistols from his handgun collection. Take the three grand and go to Mexico. Leave all this shit behind. Slipper is on his ass to sign the divorce papers. Cromley left a message that their business relationship was over because of his treatment of Slipper. Cozy sees on the tracking app on his phone that the Jeep is at Mort's. "Shit!"

He's come this far. He might as well check it out. "Maybe whatever these little fuckers are doing is close to over." He cleans up as quickly as he can. The shower makes him feel a little better. He drives by Mort's and sees the Jeep in the driveway. They must be in the house or in the back courtyard. No shades are up. He parks further up the street this time. He takes the low trail in the trees along the river. He thinks of it as his getaway route as he gets closer to Mort's.

He walks quickly to the corner of the house. He stops and looks around to see if anyone is watching. He moves through the overgrown chamisa and apache plume. He can see Michael and Rita in the middle of the gazebo. He stops and stoops down. He watches them retrieve the wrapped bag from the middle of the deck. He watches Michael unwrap it. He wonders to himself if this is the treasure. He sees them unwrap two shards. He decides to make a move. He will have to rely on his instincts and the element of surprise from here on.

After they sit down at the table with the bag, Cozy pulls out the 1911 with the worn wood grips and short silencer. He quickly approaches them and points the gun at Michael. "Stay seated." They both look up, startled. Michael starts to get up looking at Cozy incredulously. "Who the hell are you?" Cozy points the pistol at him. "I said sit down." He then points the pistol at Rita. Michael slowly sits back down. Cozy is still unsure about what is in the bag. He holds the gun on Michael and steps to the bag. He looks in it. Seeing the shards of rock wrapped in tissue paper he says, "This bag is literally full of rocks."

Michael's phone pings. Cozy looks at him nervously. It's a text from Will that Michael doesn't bother to check. "Back in town early. Be to Mort's soon." This time Michael yells at Cozy. "Who are you? What are you doing? Are you the guy with the Albuquerque police parking sticker?" Cozy is quiet. He backs up a couple of steps knowing he has the drop on them. He thinks about how to make this go down.

Getting another car for the trip to Mexico can be done through an acquaintance who has a used car business on the way out of town. He can tie this pair up in the house and no one will know about this until he is in Mexico if he is lucky. He can work with the fence he knows from Mexico to get money in exchange for whatever the rocks are.

Feeling more comfortable with the situation, "Your grandfather was something. I saw the last clue to this hunt, or whatever it is, in a letter at Cromley's." He pauses and looks at them waiting for a reaction. "So, it appears the treasure is the mythical twenty pounds of turquoise." Michael moves to the edge of his chair. "Have you been following us?" Cozy smugly replies, "I tracked your stupid ass." Michael is visibly agitated now. "What does that mean?" Cozy continues smugly, "I mean I used technology." As soon as the word is out of his mouth Michael springs up at him. Preferring not to use his gun, Cozy pulls out a 2.8 Million Volt Tactical Security Stunner from a scabbard on his waist. It is turned to full power. Just like a couple of junkies before him, he hits Michael with it just as he gets to him.

Michael fights the shock at first, but then crumples to the ground with a surprised look on his face. He is paralyzed. Cozy quickly rolls him over on his belly. He jerks his hands back one at a time and puts a pair of handcuffs on him. He pulls out a knife. He starts cutting off a piece of Michael's shirt to stuff into his mouth. Michael's eyes close and he passes out. Rita is in shock. Without considering anything other than running, she grabs the bag of turquoise and bolts for the house the moment Cozy starts cutting on Michael's shirt. Cozy finishes and roughly stuffs the shirt piece in Michael's mouth.

Rita is shaking. She tries to focus on herself, not Michael. She decides to hide the bag in the hiding place in Mort's study. She runs to it. The room is like they left it when they solved Clue 5. She sees floating dust in the air where the sun is coming through at the blind's edge. Michael was so impressed with himself when he showed her the hidden compartment. She was sure he never thought it would be used this way. She pulls out the book. As hoped, the shelves pop open. The bag just fits in the opening. She pops it shut looking at the door to the study. The book is back.

She is heading for Mort's bedroom and the door to the side courtyard. She meets Cozy in the hall head on coming from that unfortunately unlocked door. She tries to kick him in the crotch. She starts screaming. She grabs both his wrists and sinks her fingernails into them. He is so surprised he almost drops the gun. She runs the other way. He starts to shoot her in the back. He looks at his wrists. He catches her at the back-portal door. He grabs her and gets her on the floor. She can smell the dust in the worn rug he is pushing her face into.

He rolls her over, sitting on her. He takes the gun and shoves it under her chin. "Where is the bag?" Rita fires back, "Go to hell piece of shit!" Cozy pulls her hair jerking her head sideways. Her mouth involuntarily comes open. A couple of downtown hookers experienced this same treatment when he was shaking them down and setting a trap for their pimp.

The doorbell rings, then there is a hard knock on the front door. Cozy gets up, watching Rita. He drags her to a standing position forcing her into the kitchen. He throws a towel in her face. "Get the blood off your mouth and answer the door. If you don't get rid of whoever it is, I will shoot them. Then I will go out to the gazebo and shoot your boyfriend. You can watch, bitch."

She takes a second to compose herself. She wipes her mouth and throws the towel on the floor in front of Cozy. She goes to the door. She looks at Cozy standing out of sight in the hall. He still has the gun on her. She looks through the peephole. It's Will.

She slowly unlocks the deadbolt and doorknob. She opens the door about two feet. "Hey stranger. How was your paint convention?" Will takes a step toward the door. "It was good. It was a bunch of old guys that make paint turn into money. Lots of fun with them." Will stands in front of her waiting to come in. "Where's Michael? I got his text. Pretty cool."

Rita is terrified. She cannot think of anything else to say. "Will, you have to go. Now! Michael will call you soon." She shuts the door quickly. Before the door is closed securely, Will starts knocking again causing it to push open. Rita stands there looking at the door. She bolts toward it and screams at Will to run. Almost instantaneously Cozy is behind her. He pushes her forward and knocks both legs out from underneath her at the same time. She falls in a heap to the left.

She watches in horror as Cozy positions himself in front of the doorway with his pistol pointed at Will. Will starts in, sees Cozy with the gun and instantaneously dives to his right. Two bursts erupt from Cozy's pistol. Will falls on the portal. One arm is laying in the doorway. The muffled cracks from the 1911 make the dogs bark next door.

Will moans loudly as Cozy quickly drags his body inside. He slams the door shut. Rita sees that Will is shot below his left shoulder. It looks like he was hit only once. His quick reaction may have saved his life. He is bleeding through his shirt now. Cozy looks at him. He looks at Rita like it's her fault. "This has gotten weird. Gotta go. It's time to go." Like he didn't have her attention, Cozy slaps Rita across the face with his open hand.

He gets his face real close to her stinging cheek. She feels the silencer in her ribs. "Give me the bag." She is rubbing her chin. "Fuck you. I don't have it. Find it, shithead." She looks at Will. He isn't moving. He has turned his head to her. He is looking at her, but his eyes are glazed. She can tell he is not able to do anything. She hopes he can hear so that he can tell someone what happened. As their eyes part, Rita hopes that he makes it.

"Plan B." Cozy grabs her hair thinking to himself that there was never really a "Plan A." He jerks her upright and looks around the room as he puts the pistol in her ribs again. "You're coming with me then. We're going to my car. I want to shoot you so bad. Don't fuck with me." They both look at Will. His eyes are closed now. His shirt is soaked with blood. They exit through the front door and walk awkwardly and slowly down to the river path.

Cozy forcefully pushes and drags Rita back to the Tahoe. For a moment he thinks of carrying Oralynn. The doors click open as they get within twenty feet. He is practically lifting her off the ground with the pistol when they arrive. He takes a roll of tape out of a plastic crate in the back. Rita sees rope, a couple of pairs of handcuffs, several knives and a folding shovel in the crate.

Cozy feels like people are watching them. He is sweating. He pushes Rita around to the passenger side. He opens the door and flips her around. He grabs both arms hard and tapes her hands behind her.

He shoves her into the seat. After she is seated, he roughly forces a small rag into her mouth. He forces her mouth shut. He puts a broad piece of tape across it. Part of the rag is hanging out of the tape. He tells Rita to settle down or she will suffocate herself. He pauses. "Or I will suffocate you if you don't." He pushes her over against the door when he gets in. They leave Mort's without the treasure.

Cozy doesn't speak to her as he drives to a metal building in an industrial park on the south side of Santa Fe. It is in a row of three other buildings. The weeds are grown up around it even though it isn't very old. Cozy knows if somehow the local cops determine he is the kidnapper, they will go to his apartment first. He uses this building to facilitate transactions sometimes. It is owned by a friend that he does favors for. He has confidential access anytime. The owner never asks him anything.

Plan B includes holing up here with the pain-in-the-ass girl until he can get the bag from Michael. Then it's off to Mexico. They sit in the car in front of the building. The street is deserted. Rita is trying to breathe regularly through her nose, so she doesn't choke. Cozy calls a fence friend just to make contact. "I might have some product, but I am not sure yet. Expensive quality turquoise, I think. Wanted to make sure you are still working."

They are parked in front of a nondescript faded blue metal entrance door. When Cozy drags Rita out of the car, they can hear movers talking about how to load a truck one building row over. He pushes her up to the door. He pulls out a key and unlocks the cheap lock. He pushes her inside. He looks back at the cul-de-sac. Nobody. He quickly closes the door. He drags her over to a metal chair in a corner. There is a table and chair in the other corner. He shrink-wraps her to the chair. He pulls the tape from her mouth. "That will get the hair off your upper lip." He pulls the rag from her mouth.

She takes a deep breath and coughs loudly. Tears are streaming from her eyes. She is staring at him. Cozy asks, "What's in the bag?" Rita taunts him. "What kind of thief tries to steal something when they don't know what it is? You figure it out." He moves close to her. He bends over and gets in her face again. "No matter how this little adventure ends, I may just shoot you and leave you in an arroyo." He stands up and turns his back to her. He paces for a second, rubbing his chin with the end of the silencer. He turns back to her. "You are gonna get your boyfriend to get the bag and swap it for you." He pauses. "That is if he thinks you are worth it."

Cozy laughs and stuffs the rag back in her mouth. He goes to the back of the building and opens a wide overhead door. He departs through the opening as the south breeze blows into the stuffy building. In a minute the Tahoe pulls into the building. He gets out and closes the door. The chain rattles smoothly as it descends and hits the concrete floor with a bang. He goes to the desk and gets on his phone. Rita tries to relax. She is very thirsty.

38 Reverse Tracking

Michael feels an unbearably sharp pain when Cozy hits him in the stomach with the almost three million volts. It's like his brain is hijacked. The pain stings like unimaginable hell. The stunner's electrodes damage or kill the nerve endings at the point of contact. The voltage delivered through those electrodes creates the pain. Sustained contact causes spasms and a doubling up effect. Cozy knows these effects are more pronounced when the recipient is surprised. He also knows the pain fades eventually if the recipient doesn't have a heart attack. Usually they recover.

Michael comes to. His abdomen is tingling fiercely. The remaining electricity in his body is slowly dissipating. His head hurts. His eyes slowly focus as he tries to sit up. He remembers Rita running to the house as he watched helplessly. Coming out of the electrically induced fog he feels his hands cuffed behind him. He panics. "I need to get into the house. Where is Rita?" He assumes Cozy has taken the bag and is gone.

He twists his arms and slowly inches them down behind his butt. He pulls his legs slowly to his chest while continuing to pull the chain under his butt. He stretches his arms as much as he can. His backward arm loop is big enough for him to get his legs through. Unexpectedly his mind flashes to the morning he joined Rita doing yoga. He realizes that he connected with her at that moment.

He quickly removes the shirt stuffed in his mouth thinking, "I'm gonna get this motherfucker." He slowly gets up and steadies himself on the back of his chair. His adrenaline kicks in as his anger rises. His head is clearing. "Focus. What if the guy is still in the house?" He slows down. He forces himself to stand straighter. He considers the disadvantage he is under with the handcuffs on. He makes it to the door. He looks at the windows. Nothing has changed.

He slowly opens the door. He waits a second. He is breathing regularly now. He opens the door the rest of the way. He looks inside the kitchen. He sees Will lying lifeless in the entryway. His shirt is stuck to his chest. Michael instinctively mouths "medic." He wonders how much blood Will has lost.

He supposes Will is shot in his torso, but he doesn't know where. No Rita. He quickly goes down the hall. He is unsure what he will do if the guy is still here. He looks in each room. No Rita still. He quickly returns to Will. He sits down and cradles him in his lap as he dials 911. He has a pulse. He looks at Will's face. "Hang in there, bro. We got this." Michael squeezes his hand. Will opens his eyes. His lips are dry and stuck together. Michael wants to get up and get him some water, but he's afraid to leave him. "You've lost a lot of blood dude. You are holding together good though."

Michael squeezes his hand again. "I think the bullet went through. I don't think it hit anything important." He smiles weakly at Will. "The ambulance will be here soon." Before he finishes Will whispers, "He has her. He knocked her around. She tried. She didn't tell him where the turquoise is. She's something." With that he closes his eyes and lays his head back. "I'm nauseated. Sorry. Gotta lay back." Michael wants to ask, "Where is the turquoise?" Instead he calls and tells Cecil what happened.

He is sitting with Will's head in his lap. His hands are on both sides of Will's wound when the ambulance comes. Michael has determined that he is shot once in the shoulder area. He thinks about all the people he saw shot in Afghanistan. He remembers a coonass named Justin in his platoon. He was fearless and funny. He really trusted him. They became good friends. Michael remembers cradling him the same way that bad day. Justin didn't make it.

The attendants load Will quickly. They are efficient and quiet. A serious-looking EMT with a shaved head hooks up the IV as Michael watches from the end of the ambulance. He sees the name Andy on his scrub top when he steps out of the ambulance toward him. "Not many shooting victims for me. Your friend has lost a lot of blood. The pressure on the wounds may have saved his life." He smiles politely and turns. He hurriedly goes to the driver's side of the ambulance. The lights come on and the siren wails as they start the drive to the hospital.

After the ambulance leaves, Michael sits down on the front portal steps. Rita is gone. The guy took her. It makes more sense now. He doesn't have the bag. He is sitting with his head on his chest. The handcuffs shine in the light. Cecil hurries out of his car when he sees him. "I heard they just took your friend to the hospital." He motions for Michael to extend his hands. He unlocks the cuffs and they fall on the concrete. Neither reaches to pick them up.

Cecil sits on the step beside him. Quietly, with his hands on his knees, he asks, "What did the guy look like?" Michael tells him, "It's the guy I saw at The Pantry. The Albuquerque police guy." He describes him. "Did he say anything worth remembering?" He describes how the guy just appeared and shocked the shit out of him. Rita ran into the house with the bag they found. Will got shot he thinks just by coming over to see what was up. He shows him the text from Will. Wrong place, wrong time. Rita is kidnapped. The turquoise is probably somewhere in the house. He stares into space. To himself he vows, "I'll swap it."

Michael remembers Cozy standing and talking before he rushed him, getting shocked for the effort. "He said some things that made no sense. He said he saw the last clue in a letter from Mort. I asked him if he had been following us." He looks directly at Cecil. "He said I tracked you. I asked the smug bastard what does that mean? He flippantly said, I used technology." Cecil doesn't say anything. Michael leans back on his elbows. He feels how bruised and sore his wrists are.

His riddle-solving instincts kick in. He starts framing these comments in his mind as riddles. As usual he starts pairing key words first. "Tracking technology" popped into his mind easily. He thought of money bags with trackers that his group sometimes escorted for delivery to warlords in Afghanistan. He stands and starts walking toward the Jeep. "I'm gonna see if this fucker put a tracker on my Jeep."

He gets down on his knees on the passenger side of the Jeep. He slides under on his back a couple of feet and feels along the frame. Cecil hears him say, "Damn. Got it." His fingers hit the magnetized case on a lip of the frame as if he knew where to look. He slides out holding the black box. He stands rubbing the dirt from it. He starts back to Cecil. "You know anything about trackers? Pretty sure this is connected to a cell phone app."

They go back and sit down on the steps. Michael tells Cecil about a guy in his ops that could reverse-track active trackers. The Afghan rebels would put trackers on U.S. provision trucks. They would wait until they were isolated and raid them. Several traps using drones with guns and bombs were set because of the reverse tracking. When he is done, he asks Cecil, "Do you know anybody in your force or in the area that could do this?"

Cecil smiles slightly. "Ajax Brimley. He is an ex-special ops guy from early-on in Iraq. Our tours overlapped, but we didn't. He is the unofficial tech guy at the station. He should have enjoyed a vacation in prison after his return from Iraq. He hacked into a Pentagon account and made some noteworthy contributions to some of his favorite charities. Not a dime for himself. It took the FBI a year to find him. He was such an asset in the field in Iraq that they swept the charges away."

Michael and Cecil meet in the parking lot at the police station. They take the tracker to Ajax. They enter a small room in the middle of the building with no windows and one door. Upper cabinets line the walls. Each pair is padlocked. All surfaces are clear and clean. Ajax is sitting at a desk in the middle of the room. He reminds Michael of Walter in the Big Lebowski. He is a crew cut fireplug, complete with aviator eyeglasses with yellow lenses. He thinks about asking him if he has seen the movie. Ajax opens the small black case in front of them. Without any emotion and in a monotone voice, "Give me a couple of hours to make a couple of phone calls. I think I can reverse track the signal to get the cell phone number." Michael thinks to himself, "So much for the Walter theory."

In the same dead pan voice, Ajax explains that live GPS tracking devices require a monthly subscription. Since the tracker transmits data over a cellular network, the owner usually will have a credit card or address on file for the automatic monthly payment. Not to mention, these trackers all have serial numbers. The manufacturer can activate or deactivate the device using this if they want to. He adds quietly, "I can too."

Ajax looks down and then up with a serious look on his face. It's obvious he wants them to leave. "If I get the phone or account number, I can find the phone." As they start walking out of his room Ajax raises his voice just slightly. "Cecil, listen to me. After the phone is located, I am going to turn the tracker off. Not sure how this will affect your guy. The other thing, he may see that it is at the police station right now." Ajax lets that sink in with them. Michael turns. "I don't give a shit. Please do it as fast as you can. We have nothing else right now."

He and Cecil talk as they walk out. Michael is thinking about Rita again. "I don't know what to do about Rita." Cecil reassuringly tells him, "If he has her and not the turquoise, there will be a call soon. There will be." He has a hang-in-there look on his face. "You think she has her phone?' Michael doesn't answer directly, but says, "I'm going back to

Mort's after I visit Will. I'll look at everything again now that my head is clearer." Cecil lets him know. "I have to go to court down south when I leave here. I'll be in touch later this afternoon. Text if anything happens."

Michael wonders about the tracker showing that it is at the police station as he gets in his now untracked Jeep. "Fuck him." He keeps thinking about Rita on the drive to the hospital. He suspects she put the bag in the hiding spot in Mort's study when she ran into the house. He pulls into the hospital parking lot with a headache. He is dehydrated. He gets a bottle of cold water from a vending machine in the stairwell. He takes a big swallow. He sits down on a step as the water goes down his throat. He shudders from the cold almost uncontrollably. He takes another swallow.

Will's room is on the third floor. Michael knocks lightly on the door. He pushes it open. Will is propped up with tubes coming out of his nose and chest. His eyes are dull, but they brighten when they see him. He softly says, "I was worried about you." Michael takes his hand avoiding the taped IV. "You are worried about me? Shit. I am so sorry." With an attempted smile Will says, "You better be. My parents just left. They are pissed that I will have to miss work for a few days." He stops and looks at Michael seriously. "Another time I owe you. The doc said the pressure you applied probably saved my life there at the last." Michael shrugs. "It's the other way around. You wouldn't be here if it wasn't for me. I owe you."

He leaves about fifteen minutes later. He wonders how much therapy they will all need when this treasure hunt is over. He foregoes the stairs and takes the elevator to the hospital lobby. He heads back to Mort's. When he gets there, he heads straight to the study and pulls the book out. The bag is fit snugly in the compartment. He leaves it. It seems anticlimactic. He is sure that Mort never envisioned his best friend getting shot and the woman he is falling in love with being kidnapped as part of his grand adventure.

He goes out the kitchen door to the gazebo. He sees the removed boards. He sees the open box in the middle. How could something so cool turn into something so crazy? He picks up the bottle of wine, the newspaper and the note still on the table. He puts the bottle under his arm. He does not see Rita's phone. He goes back into the house, walking into each room checking all the windows and outside doors to make sure they are locked. The front door is the last to be secured. He sees the dried blood on the front portal concrete where Will went down.

Cleaning it up will have to wait.

He gets back into the Jeep. He heads back to his parents' compound to eat something. He sits staring straight ahead before he starts the Jeep. He wants to remember everything he can from what happened a couple of hours ago. Someone he doesn't know has been tracking him without his knowledge because the guy read a letter in Mort's file at Cromley's. He knows about the treasure, but not what it is.

All he can do is wait. He feels the anger, fear and frustration boiling inside him. He slams the Jeep's steering wheel. As with many times before, there is no place to put the anger. He knows it will pass, but the fear and resultant frustration will end only when Rita is found safe. The loss of the turquoise is not what is on his mind. The loss of Rita is.

39 No Deliberation Necessary

Michael parks in the drive of his parent's compound. He goes directly to his bedroom in the house. He isn't as bloody as Will was, but the bottom part of his tan shirt has dried into a pink nasty color. He takes his bloody clothes off first. He gets a trash bag from the kitchen and puts them in it. He takes a quick shower. He puts on long pants and a long sleeve shirt. He puts his worn military issue boots on. He gets his Beretta that he has been keeping by his bed in the house since the break-in. He decides to drive the Mercedes.

He parks the Jeep in the garage after he pulls the Mercedes out. He heats up some Ramen noodles. He takes the hot bowl of noodles to the back portal. A cold Gatorade from the refrigerator is a perfect complement. The electrolytes help. He drinks another cold bottle before he finishes eating. He rubs his still-tender stomach but feels better.

For the first time since he and Rita sat at the gazebo table, he thinks about the turquoise being worth ten million dollars. He could be rich. He has dreamed about having money. He realizes that in this dream he never thinks about what he would spend the money on. His mind wanders to thinking about how much his life has changed since Mort's treasure hunt started. It's not just the hunt or even the turquoise. The change is Rita. Maybe in some cosmic way the Lander Blue was meant to be their connection. He stands and stretches.

His phone rings. "Hey it's Cecil. The guy is Cozy MacFarland. Ajax got his account from the tracker. He's an ex-cop with local history. That's why the parking sticker." Cecil clears his throat. "This is where it gets weird. He works or has worked for your attorney, Burt Cromley." Michael starts to say something, but Cecil continues, "We are waiting to hear back from the phone company about his phone's location. Ajax has turned the tracker off."

A longer pause. "I am having Rita's phone location traced too." He tells Cecil that he didn't see her phone at Mort's house, so he bets she had it. He tells him that the bag of turquoise is at Mort's. Cecil is still at the trial. He promises to let him know if he finds out more. He will send a patrol to check Cozy's supposed residence in south Santa Fe, though he knows he will not be there. They hang up.

Plan B was more eventful than Cozy anticipated. He sits down at the desk. He massages his fingernail-tattooed wrists. There are three piercings on each. The blood has dried in a uniform pattern on each. He has not checked the tracking app for several hours. He opens it and finds that the tracker is dead. It has been almost three weeks since it was activated. He wonders if maybe the batteries died. He doesn't consider that Michael may have found and deactivated it.

He takes Rita's iPhone out of his jacket pocket. He thinks about the call he is about to make. He wants to get this over with. He is now having to drag himself through the motions. Under his breath, "You better get your mind in this. Find the joy, baby. You gonna be shed of Slipper and rich enough to lead a good life under the guise of a rich guy hanging on a Mexico beach." He thinks out loud, "The best yet. Everybody can kiss my ass." If things go like they should, he will be across the border before anybody knows what has happened.

He finds Michael's number in her contact log. He looks at her photos. Almost every photo the last three weeks is a selfie with this guy. Not a lot of calls to anyone. Several yoga apps. He sits and drinks from a plastic bottle of water. He clears his throat loudly to make sure Rita is looking at him. He sets the bottle down on the corner of the desk so she can see it. He hopes she is thirsty.

Cozy makes the call. Michael answers, "Where are you?" He hears, "The bag for the girl. It's that simple." He hears Cozy walking as his heels scuff the concrete floor. He hears a moan and muffled coughing. He can tell Rita is on the phone. Without waiting, "Are you all right?" Rita's mouth is so dry she can barely talk at first. "I'm in a metal..." Michael hears a pop close to the phone. He stiffens. In a second, he hears Rita say, "I'm okay." He can tell she is scared. "I left the turquoise in the hiding place in Mort's study." She stops and swallows hard.

Softly, "Know you have to decide about the swap." Cozy is back on the phone. "No cops. No guns. No bullshit. This can be simple. I tie you up and take the turquoise. I leave you two love birds to be found after I am long gone. Call me when you leave old man Hamilton's. I'll text another number to call." Cozy is silent. "I really want to shoot your girlfriend." He disconnects.

This is how he thought it would go down. He heads to Mort's to retrieve the bag of Lander Blue. He thinks about calling Cecil. As suspected, Cozy kidnapped Rita because he couldn't find the bag. He parks in front of Mort's and runs to the front door. He unlocks it and heads directly to Mort's study. He retrieves the bag and places it on Mort's desk. He sits in the green leather chair and stares at it.

Ten million dollars is a lot of money to kiss goodbye. He thinks, "Slow down and focus." He considers replacing the turquoise with rocks from Mort's yard. Lots of risk with that. Cozy saw a couple of the shards when they were on the table in the gazebo. He would probably be able to tell the difference if he looks. He dismisses that idea.

He figures he doesn't have a lot of time before Cozy will get suspicious. His thinking changes to Rita. His raw desire to protect her is all he feels. He has never felt that way about anybody. "She's worth it." He stands and has his hand on the bag's handle when his phone rings. It's Cecil. He pauses. Should he pickup? He doesn't want to lie to Cecil. He decides to wait. When he sees Cecil has disconnected, he listens to his long message. Cecil is still at the trial.

The message starts after Cecil is quiet for a second. "Ajax found Cozy's phone, but he is not sure Cozy is with it. Seems like he would be. The phone hasn't moved for a couple of hours based on how far back he can see. It's at 8401 Avenida Christina. It appears to be a warehouse tucked into an old industrial park east of the country club at the end of the street. I am hesitant to rally the troops because of the unverified situation."

Louder and stronger, "Leave it alone for another hour. I will meet you there. No hero bullshit!" He pauses. "We also traced Rita's phone. It is at the same location as Cozy's." Cecil ends. "Did you hear me? I'm heading back now. I will see you someplace near the building. Call me when you get there."

Michael thinks about calling him back and telling him about the call from Cozy. He does not want to wait. Surprise might be the key to saving Rita. Fifteen minutes later he is driving down Avenida Christina in the Mercedes. There are metal buildings lining the street. He sees 8401 at the end. The parking in front is empty. There is only the front door facing the street. He makes the cul-de-sac. He parks two buildings north. He looks around before getting out of the Mercedes.

The sun is in his eyes. There is not a lot of cover around the building. The back of each building is surrounded by an eight-foot-high chain link fence. He might as well go down the middle of the street. If someone is watching, there is no cover. Same thing for the end building. The plan is shaping up to be him taking an unprotected walk to the building and knocking on the door. Rush the bastard. Guns blazing. He adjusts his sunglasses. Too much risk. If he's not going to try and take Cozy, then he might as well wait until Cozy calls with further instructions. The front door is it. He does not want to wait, period. He decides to go knock on the door and see what happens from there.

He gets out of the Mercedes remembering leaving his group and searching the top two stories of the building they were trapped in that day in Afghanistan. He was looking for holed up rebels thinking they would ambush his crew later. Even more unnerving was his looking for boobytraps at the same time. He remembers Melon appeared behind him from nowhere, soon followed by Henry. They went through thirty rooms together.

His insurance will be that he doesn't have the turquoise with him this trip. As a precaution he leaves the Mercedes keys on the pavement behind a newly deposited Miller Light can near the driver's side front tire. He stands for a minute. Too risky, but it's what he has.

He starts toward the door. No gun, no nothing. Cecil Soledad is going to kill him, if he survives this. He is sure he will be frisked. Lots of random thoughts. He gets close to the door. He thinks about Cozy's 1911 with the silencer. He fucking shot Will. He will never forget the shock Cozy gave him. He is as ready as he will ever be. He knocks loudly on the door. Anyone on the street or near the building could hear it. He waits about three feet in front of the door with his hands away from his body.

About fifteen seconds later the doorknob turns. Cozy peeks out around the door edge. He sees Michael. He opens the door quickly. He points the pistol at him. He motions him in the door with the gun. Once he is in and the door is shut, without saying a word, Cozy frisks him. Satisfied, Cozy stands back. "What a surprise. How did you find me?" Then, "Where's the bag?" Michael looks around. He can smell dust. It is hot. The vents on the roof are open but no air is flowing. He sees Rita sitting shrink wrapped to the chair. Their eyes meet, but she looks drained.

He sees the overhead door. There are no other windows in the building. It's the front door or the overhead door. His gaze falls on Cozy. He sarcastically replies, "I used reverse technology." He looks around some more. "The bag's nearby. I wanted to make sure my girlfriend is okay. I'll do the swap if you will leave us alone. I'll get the bag and bring it to you."

Cozy wants it to end. He doesn't really want to kill either of them, at least for the moment. What he says does not reflect this. "I'm gonna be waiting on the other side of this door when you come back. I will have this gun jammed under your girlfriend's chin. You fuck with me and I'll take both of you out. I win, you both lose. Get it?" He looks at Rita and starts toward her as Michael opens the door and exits.

The sun is going down as he walks slowly back to the Mercedes. He looks back at the faded blue door. It is closed. Cozy is not looking. The sun is getting lower, but there are no lights coming on in the industrial park yet. He thinks about his training, about techniques for taking out an armed assailant when you are unarmed. He is glad he did not wait for Cecil. He grabs the bag out of the trunk. He puts it on the hood of the car. He looks inside. One last look. "This is it." He picks up the Mercedes keys and puts them in his pocket. He hopes he will need them to drive away from this. He starts back to the building.

Cozy drags Rita to the middle of the building. The legs of her chair make a screeching noise as he drags it across the concrete. He locates the desk chair about eight feet from her. He waits until he sees the front door start to open to put the silencer under her chin. Michael opens the door slowly. He is holding the bag in front of him as he reenters the building. The door slams shut. He sets the bag on the floor about ten feet inside the building. "Let's do this asshole."

Dangling another pair of handcuffs, Cozy motions for Michael to come over to the other chair, "I'm gonna fix you up too." There is a roll of shrink wrap on the floor next to the chair. Michael is looking at Rita as he starts walking toward the chair. He sees the tape over her mouth. She is flushed and having trouble breathing. Her hair is matted to her head. He wants to go to her, but his training tells him to focus on the task at hand.

Cozy is watching him closely. As he moves away from Rita to take care of Michael, he turns his back to her slightly. With a huge grunt, Rita pushes with her feet, tipping her chair over right into the back of his legs causing him to fall forward. Michael closes the last eight feet, hitting Cozy full force as he is trying to get up.

40 Twenty Pounds Later, Again

Cozy is whipping the 1911 up as Michael hits him. He winces as Michael delivers a body blow to his ribs and grabs for the gun. Cozy has it around enough. He pulls the trigger. At that range, the 45 slug pushes Michael away from him. Blood shows on his shirt instantly. They hear the bullet ricochet off the building somewhere. Michael immediately puts his left hand on the wound. He can tell that the slug has gone through the fleshy part of his side.

As he is grabbing his side, Cozy hits him in the face with the pistol grip. Michael does fall backward this time. He catches himself with his hands as he hits. His nose is now bleeding too, but he immediately starts back up. He slows and sits on the concrete looking at Rita as Cozy is towering over him with the gun pointed at Rita. He has splattered blood spots on his pants and shirt. There is a long silence. Michael breaks it, "Take the fucking bag and leave us. Wrap me. I give up. Just take the fucking bag and leave!"

Cozy is pissed. He is sweating. The knees of his pants are dirty, along with the dried blood spots. His hair is wet, revealing a bald spot. He has a small cut bleeding on his gun hand. "I ought to shoot both of you for the trouble." Michael stands with a go to hell look on his face. Cozy aims at his crotch. "I'd think long and hard. Getting shot there might be worse than her getting shot." As soon as he gets the words "shot" out of his mouth the front door bursts open and slams hard against the wall. It's Cecil. He rushes into the building about four feet with his gun drawn. He is looking the wrong way.

Everybody is startled. Cecil turns around just as Cozy settles the 1911 on him. He fires twice hitting Cecil in the chest. It sounds like two loud spits. Cecil is thrown into the closed door. As if planned, he slides down on the floor sitting perfectly with his back to the door. His head is on his chest. His eyes are closed. This is it. Last chance for brute force. Michael jumps up and heads for Cozy one last time.

He catches Cozy's arm this time before he can get the gun turned.

They both slam to the floor. The silencer is helpful for masking noise, but the gun and can are too long to maneuver this time. Michael grabs Cozy's arm and brings it violently across his rising knee as it hits Cozy right between the legs. The gun clatters off to the far wall. His hand-to-hand instructor would have been proud of that move.

Cozy is wiry, however. He is not a stranger to protecting himself in close quarters. They separate and both head for the gun against the wall. Michael is half running, half crawling. Cozy is closer and gets there first. He grabs the gun and has it on Michael. Michael stands, clutching his side, realizing this may be the end. He survived Afghanistan and now he is going to die at the hands of a bad cop who fucked up their treasure hunt. Rita starts rocking her chair loudly on the concrete.

Michael starts yelling crazily, "Why can't you take the bag and go? Leave her alone. Take me, leave her alone. Who the fuck are you? You don't know us." Cozy's eyes switch from him briefly. He looks at Rita rocking. From the door they hear, "You're done motherfucker." Three shots, two-tenths of a second apart, rip into the side of Cozy's torso as he looks at Cecil. It's too late for him to get his pistol up this time.

Cozy twists as he tries to stay up. Blood is coming from his mouth before he hits the floor. Cecil lowers his arm. The pistol is still tightly clutched in his hand. This is the third man he has shot in his career. His back is still against the door. He is looking at his chest while he is unbuttoning his shirt. He picks two 45 slugs about three inches apart from his bullet proof vest. He is grimacing and smiling at the same time. He looks at Michael. "Hoped I'd never test this. Thank God it works." His eyes automatically look up to the ceiling.

Blood is gushing from Cozy's side now. Cecil is on all fours struggling to get up. Michael goes to Rita. He can see the relief in her eyes. He gently pulls the tape from her mouth. She opens her mouth as wide as she can. He pulls the wet wad of shirt out. Her nose is snotty and running. She sucks in a giant breath with her mouth wide open. Tears are coming fast now. Michael turns to Cecil. "Do you have a knife?" Cecil nods no. Michael starts at her waist using his car key to methodically rip and pull the wrap from her body. Soon her arms are free. She is soaking wet under her shirt. She asks for the bottle of water Cozy did not finish. Anything wet.

Soon the last of the wrap around her top is off. She raises her arms away from her body. She tries to roll out of the chair. Michael grabs her hand and holds it for a second. "Hang on." With that he pulls the shrink wrap around her legs. She is free. She gets on all fours too. She rolls into a fetal position then slowly stands. She immediately throws her arms around Michael. He winces as he hugs her back. She grabs him like no other woman ever has before in his life. It feels like she is absorbing him. He pulls her in close with his right arm.

They hear Cecil calling 911. He gives them the address. Michael looks at Cecil over Rita's shoulder. "Thank you." After they separate, Rita says to Cecil, "I'm gonna make sure the bastard's dead." Cecil and Michael watch her bend over close to Cozy's graying face and say something. She then kicks him with as much strength as she can muster right in the spot where he shocked Michael. She turns and looks their direction, but her eyes are seeing past them. Her face muscles relax. She drops her gaze to the floor. She goes to a chair and sits down hard, "I need more water." They are all relieved to hear sirens in the distance.

Michael opens the blue front door. He remembers Cecil leaning against it after he was shot. That was his low moment. He thought it was over for all of them. He sticks his head out and smells the dry air. He feels the cool breeze that comes with Santa Fe nights. Security lights from the adjacent buildings are on. He is almost doubled over as he walks back into the building. His hand on his side is covered in blood. "How did you know to come barging in?" he asks Cecil. Cecil looks at Rita and then back at him. "First, you never called me back. Then I saw the Mercedes and no you. I've been around you long enough to know how you operate."

He pauses. "I gave you the address because I feared if you waited, you might lose the turquoise and the girl." He looks at the floor. "I'll never admit it. I warned you. Thought you could decide what to do." He smiles slightly. "I hoped I would get here in time to save you if you needed it." Michael extends his hand. They lock eyes and shake without another word.

Rita is still slumped in her chair. She is listening to their conversation. Hoarsely, looking at Michael, "How did you know where we were?" He sits in the other chair. "Cecil's guy reverse-tracked a device that Cozy put on my Jeep. Found his cell account and tracked his phone." He weakly smiles again. "I was serious when I told that asshole I used technology." He looks at Cozy's body. "They tracked your phone too, just to let you know for future reference." They weakly smile at each other.

Cecil butts in. "He was supposed to wait for me. He couldn't." He has a serious look on his face as he looks at Rita. 'We are all lucky, but you are especially lucky. Your boy here was to trade that bag for you." He stops talking abruptly. He glances at the open doorway. The sirens are close. "Let me see what the hell I almost got killed for." He picks up the bag from the floor. He takes it over to the table in the corner bending backwards as he walks. He is carrying the bag with both hands as his bruised chest muscles are tightening.

Michael joins him at the table. He unzips the bag and opens the sides. He takes a couple of the shards out and unwraps them. He lays them on their paper jackets on the table. He looks at Cecil, "My hope is that each one of these is worth fifteen to twenty-five thousand dollars each. This bag may be worth ten million dollars." Cecil laughs out loud. Michael continues, "Each shard has a thick dark Lander Blue turquoise deposit waiting to be revealed to the world." Without saying a word, Cecil closes the bag and sets it on the floor between the desk and wall. He walks toward the door. Michael goes to a chair and sits down.

Two police cars and an ambulance are now parked outside. An EMT worker comes in the door and looks around. He is followed by two policemen. They all are looking at Cozy's body in the pool of blood. Cecil identifies himself showing his badge. He tells them immediately that he is the one who shot the guy on the floor three times. He points to Rita and then Michael. "They witnessed it all." The EMT goes to the door. "Bring two gurneys." He turns back. "Who is the first one to go to the hospital?" Without looking or waiting for anyone to answer, Michael winces and gets up heading for the door. He sits back down. "I'll take the gurney."

All the lights in the building are on. It feels small now to him. With great effort he gives his keys to Cecil. "Please move the Mercedes to the front of the building and lock it. I have another set. I'll get the car when I get out." He trails off licking his lips. Rita sits and watches them. She is about to pass out. The EMS crew had water on the wagon. She has poured some of it on her chest. They are to hook up an IV to get some liquids back in her system when she gets in the ambulance.

After a short discussion, the EMTs decide not to wait to take her too. Michael is stable, in the ambulance, but he has lost too much blood. They call a second ambulance for Rita and Cecil, if he wants to go. As Michael is loaded on the gurney, Rita makes eye contact with him. She mouths, "Thank you." She sees his eyes close as she says, "I love you."

41 Plan B Aftermath

The night shift is abuzz with speculation when news of the situation reaches the police station. Chief Flores leaves a dinner gathering at his house to come to the crazy scene. It isn't every day that one cop shoots another cop. He is concerned about the press. It was reported that a retired Albuquerque cop did not make it. He also has no idea what is going on other than Soledad, the workaholic, is the one at the scene.

On his way to the building in the industrial park he passes the second ambulance on Airport Road. He imagines it is headed for the hospital. After he told the dispatcher he was going to the scene, the dispatcher texted Cecil to tell him that Flores was on his way.

After Rita is loaded in the ambulance the two policemen return to their cars. The building is empty except for him and Cozy. Cecil drags a chair back to the desk. He places the bag back on the table. He sits and looks at the leather duffle bag like it is going to say something to him. He looks inside again. "Humph. Still looks like a bunch of rocks." How did he get involved with these damn people? Neither said anything about the bag. Understandable, but he is literally left holding the bag. He smiles at his unheard joke.

He did not mention the bag to any of the responding officers. Chief Flores is on his way. He picks the bag up and walks to the overhead door. He raises it. He peers out the door at the night. He sees stars. He is still alive. He gently places the bag to the right of the door against the building wall. The decision he just made feels right. He shields his eyes from the security lights on the next building and looks around one more time. He lowers the door quietly.

He mutters to himself, "Life can be simple. Sometimes the world is not as perfect as we would like." He thinks about how he never had the opportunity to do anything like this for his son. He saw what Michael went through for Rita and the turquoise. The kid was willing to swap the whole damn thing for the girl. She's something to draw to as well. Give these gutsy kids a leg up. Let them take advantage of something that was dealt their way. "Besides, I don't want the responsibility. Michael can decide how to deal with his treasure." He quickly walks back to the desk and sits down.

In about five minutes Chief Flores enters the door slowly. The first thing he sees when he comes in the door is a pool of congealing blood on the floor. Ripped shrink wrap is scattered by a chair. He sees a gurney against the wall with a black body bag on it.

He has been a New Mexico cop for three decades. He drank with Lester "Cozy" MacFarland at state police functions over the years. He knew Cozy was considered aggressive back in the days when cops didn't wear cameras and answer for their tactics. He was nice enough but had a bitter streak. Especially after a few drinks. He goes over to the bag and unzips the top. He looks sadly at Cozy's face. He zips the bag back up. He turns as Cecil approaches him.

Cecil's shirt is open. His bullet proof vest is visible. The Chief pulls the right side of Cecil's shirt back. He rubs his fingers on the two imprints left by the 45 slugs. They smile at each other. "You okay?" Cecil replies, "I will be. It just hurts like hell right now. I have talked to the patrol officers. Hate it, but there wasn't another choice." The chief looks at Cozy on the gurney. "Why didn't you call for backup?"

Cecil quickly answers, "There wasn't time. When I knew what was going on it was past time to act." Cecil looks at the floor and shuffles his feet. "The hunch was that MacFarland was dogging the young pair. They were on a treasure hunt." He stops and catches his breath. "It was a treasure hunt set up by Mort Hamilton before he died. You know Hamilton's on the Plaza? He was Michael's grandfather."

The Chief looks around the empty building. It has a bad feel. He thinks about the steak that he left on his plate to come to this musty metal building. He looks at Cecil. "A treasure hunt, huh? Let me see your report before you submit it. Focus on the shooting part." He turns and walks to the door. "Go to the emergency room if you need to." He is gone.

Cecil breathes deeply when the Chief leaves. Maybe he should have called for backup. He will embellish his story more in his report. The focus will be on shooting Cozy. He thinks how ironic it is. Michael and Rita are at the hospital for their troubles. Neither has the treasure. He does. The processing begins. Cecil feels his adrenaline surge with the thought. For the first time, he thinks about how close all of them came to dying. It will take a while to shake this off.

After a lone EMT in an old faded ambulance picks up Cozy's body to take it to the morgue, the two patrol cops leave. Cecil gets the bag from outside the overhead door. He puts it by the front door. As he sets it down on the floor, he thinks about coming to, leaning against this door and hearing Cozy. He remembers waiting for what seemed like forever before he shot him. He walks to the Mercedes parked on the street and pulls it up to the front door. He gets the bag. He looks around as he opens the trunk. He puts the bag in and closes it. He locks it. He pockets the keys and stands looking around. His chest hurts like hell, but he is standing upright for another day.

He calls the station and has a patrolman in the area pick him up at Michael's parent's compound. He parks the Mercedes in the drive close to the garage and locks it. He is the only person in the world who knows that the turquoise is in the trunk. The patrolman picks him up shortly and takes him back to his car. He doesn't even go back in the building before he gets in his car and leaves.

Michael wakes up in a start. He moves his arm and feels the intravenous drip taped tightly to the top of his wrist. He needs to pee. Where is Rita? Where is the Lander Blue? He didn't even think about it when he left the warehouse. His room has a bathroom. He swings his legs over the side of the bed. His head hurts. He feels the tug of the eight stitches on the front and back sides of his body. A clean shot thru the flesh of his side. He will be going home in two days and should mend fine. No broken bones, but plenty of bruises.

He wheels the drip into the bathroom with him. He shuts the door. He looks at himself in the mirror. His hair is greasy. His eyes are hollow. Quite the prize. He pees and washes his hands for a long time. He puts water on his face and swishes some in his mouth. He is smiling when he finishes. He wants to go see Rita. He starts out of the bathroom. Sitting in the chair by his bed is the most beautiful sight he has ever seen. Even with the black eye, scratches on the left side of her face, cut lip and bruised swollen wrists, she is beautiful.

They smile at each other. Rita walks over to him. She gently puts her body against his, careful to not hurt him. "I'm so glad to see you." She kisses his cheek and turns his face gently to hers. She kisses his lips and holds his head between her hands. "We made it. You have the treasure." Michael looks pale. He heads to the bed. He sits down on the edge.

"That's the thing. I'm not sure exactly where the bag is. I don't know if the police took it or if it's still there. Surely not." He looks paler. "I felt so bad when I left, I didn't think about it. Did you see it before you left?" Rita shakes her head. "I'm sorry. I fainted right before the second ambulance arrived. I didn't think about it either. I was thinking about not throwing up." Michael starts to look for his phone. "I need to call Cecil." Rita puts her hand on his leg. "Call Cecil. I bet he has it."

He calls Cecil. No answer. He leaves a message for Cecil to call him back. He is clutching his side. He is filled with anxiety that something has happened to the turquoise after all they have been through. He realizes that being alive and having a very alive Rita in the room with him makes the loss almost palatable. But not quite. His phone rings. It's Cecil. "Wondered when you would call. You okay?" Michael responds quickly, "Yes. I think so. Do you know what happened to the bag?"

There is silence on the other end. "I guess I didn't think about it. Maybe I should go back to the building." Michael's heart is sinking. It's been a full day since Cecil set the bag behind the desk in the warehouse. It is probably gone. "I'll call and let you know if I find it." When he hangs up, Cecil feels kind of bad. Michael is in no shape to have his chain jerked like that. He thinks about how he used to mess with his son like this.

He texts Michael about two minutes later. "Last clue. You can find the blue junk in the blue trunk. Good luck." That's it. He sends the text, smiling. He is proud of himself for thinking to text a riddle. It seems a fitting end to the whole crazy treasure hunt. Michael laughs out loud when he gets the text. He reads the riddle to Rita. The color immediately starts coming back into his face.

He thinks about how he gave Cecil the keys to his mother's blue Mercedes so he could move and lock it. He lies back on the bed. "That bastard. It's in the trunk of the Mercedes." He texts Cecil, "THANK YOU! Your riddle was great. Where is the BLUE Mercedes?" He gets a text back quickly, "Your parents' driveway." Michael texts back, "I owe you. Will catch up soon."

That evening Michael wakes from a nap. Rita is sitting dozing in the chair by his bed. He clears his throat. She opens her eyes and stretches. "Hey. Glad you napped. I went to the house. The Mercedes is there. I found the other set of keys and moved it into the garage. It's all locked. Your Jeep is in the drive." She takes a breath and flashes a big smile. "I checked. The junk is in the trunk too. You have the treasure." The look on his face gives her pause. "Be happy. You did it." Michael swings his legs over the edge of the bed, touching the floor with his feet. He is no longer in a hospital gown. He is wearing a pair of baggy Isotopes shorts.

He sits staring at her. "We did it." He tells her "we" with his eyes too. He starts again, "I have thought about this a lot. I want you to understand that no matter what happens with our relationship I want to do this." Rita is unsure what he is saying. She starts to ask. Michael interrupts her, "I want to split the treasure with you. Less a couple of shards. It might have been yours had Mort not met Suzy." Rita is silent. She covers her mouth with her hand. "You were willing to swap it for me." A tear rolls down her left cheek. She quickly wipes it away.

She returns the serious look. "I have never felt the way you make me feel. You treat me like I am equal. You want me to be okay and the sex is pretty good too." She gets up and sits by him on the bed. "I will take it, if we can be partners. I also want very much to stay with you here." Michael smiles as he turns to face her. "I hoped for the last part more than anything." They shake hands gently.

They sit silently a while longer. Rita finally says, "I went to Will's room. He seems much better. His shoulder and chest are pretty bundled up. He's in and out. He is to be in the hospital several more days. Both of you guys are in such good shape. It really helps." Michael is relieved. "Good deal. I owe him too. I'll go see him tomorrow."

On the twenty-fourth day and the deadline to complete the treasure hunt Rita has the compound ready for Michael's return. She picks him up in the Mercedes. He pats the trunk as he slowly walks around to the passenger side. They had visited Will that morning. He has two more days before he can leave the hospital. Even though he is groggy, he complains that he needs to get back to work because he needs the money. Michael and Rita agree he will be back to being Will again soon.

They sit holding hands looking into the courtyard. Michael is restless. "You want to look at the Lander Blue?" He laughs. "That is, if you will get it out of the trunk." His phone rings. It's Cromley. He wants Michael to come to his office so he can deliver the rest of Mort's instructions. They set up an appointment for ten o'clock the next morning. Michael has no idea what other instructions Mort may have given Cromley. Maybe it's about his will.

As they sit and watch the sun start down, Michael remarks, "Cozy never knew what the treasure was that he died for. He tried to kill Will and Cecil. He probably would have killed us. To me it's weird he was willing to try to kill people for a thing he didn't even understand the value of. Something he thought was worth money, but he didn't even know what it was."

He hears his phone ping. It's a text from Cecil. Attached is an image of a letter from Mort to Michael. The text says, "Retrieved this from Cozy's phone. Think this is how he knew about the treasure hunt. He had your addresses in his phone too. He also had a new tracking app on his phone."

42 The Letter and Being Nice

The next morning Michael gets up early. He takes a shower and replaces his bandages. The stitches are beginning to stick against his shirt, so he knows he is healing. He is anxious, but not sure why. He arrives at Cromley's office early. His new assistant, Celeste, stands when he comes in. She introduces herself. He has a seat. About three minutes later Cromley comes out of his office. He smiles and extends his hand to him and invites him into his office. As he passes Celeste, Cromley asks her to get Mort Hamilton's file.

Michael sits down in front of the desk as Cromley makes it to his chair. He puts on his glasses and opens the file. He places an envelope and Mort's will out on his desk. He puts the file aside. "Do you want the known or the unknown first?" Michael hesitates. "I'm not sure." Cromley interjects, "Let's go with the known." He hands Michael Mort's will. "You get everything Mort had. His house, his money, his collection." He stops. "For real." He laughs. "Any treasures he might have claim to."

They look at each other knowing that the treasure reference is Mort having fun. Cromley holds up a piece of paper with handwritten numbers on it. "This is the combination to the safe in the master bedroom closet. Can't imagine what is in there." He lays it back on the desk.

"I'll have Celeste make a copy of his will for you." He hands Michael the envelope. "Mort instructed me to make sure you got this letter the twenty-fourth day after you found the box in the well house. That was yesterday. I figured today was close enough." Michael picks up the letter. His name, Michael Hamilton, is written on the front in Mort's handwriting. Cromley hands him a tarnished letter opener. There are two blank pages with a handwritten letter sandwiched in between.

My dear Grandson, if you are reading this letter, please know I am smiling. I bet you have already found the blue treasure. In case you haven't, the last clue is at the bottom of this note. You may or may not know yet that you are a rich man. The value of what you have cannot be measured in the millions of dollars it is worth.

I hope the treasure hunt has opened your eyes to the magical world of turquoise. Suzy opened my eyes to life. Along the way, I fell in love with turquoise. I hope you do too.

Ten years old.
Screws.
Smiles.
Middle.
Under.

The letter is signed, "Your loving Grandfather, Mort Hamilton." Michael puts the letter down on the desk in front of him. He rubs his eyes. He sits straight up on the edge of the chair. He thinks about how Rita has opened his eyes. Cromley breaks the silence, "I guess this makes sense to you?" Michael nods. "It does. More than when I came in here for sure. Here's something that doesn't."

He shows Cromley the photograph of the letter he just opened and read. "This is from the guy, let me back up." He tells Cromley about Cozy and the kidnapping. The brutal showdown after they find the treasure. "This photo came from Cozy's phone." Cromley looks at it not knowing what to expect. After a brief look, he stands. Both hands grip the edge of his desk in front of him. He asks about the date on the photograph. Michael tells him. Cromley sits down hard and loudly in his chair, causing Celeste to come to his door.

That evening, Michael and Rita go to Michael's new home. They walk through the house to the gazebo. Everything is just like they left it. They sit at the table. They talk about moving their things into the house. Without discussing their feelings regarding the move, there is agreement to get out of his parents' compound and stay in his new house tomorrow night. It seems natural to both. Michael calls Will. He is to get out of the hospital after lunch tomorrow. Michael tells him, "I'll be up to see you in the morning before you check out."

As he gets off the phone with Will, Cecil calls. "Hey it's Cecil." Michael enthusiastically replies, "I was hoping you would call." Cecil goes first, "Couple of interesting things. A guy called the station a while back. He called to report something, but he chickened out. He called back yesterday after he saw in the paper that Cozy was dead. He tells me about picking the asshole up at the bridge the night Oralynn supposedly committed suicide. He knew her."

Cecil takes a breath and a swallow of something. As if chiding him, Michael asks jokingly, "Are you drinking?" Pensively, Cecil says, "Yes. A lot." He takes another swallow and continues, "I also got a call from your lawyer, Sherlock. Thanks for showing him the picture of Mort's letter. We talked about how Cozy would have somehow had to get into Mort's file without permission to have taken the photograph when he did. He thinks Oralynn found out and confronted him. Cromley thinks this makes more sense than her committing suicide." He takes another swallow. "No matter what, another life wasted. Got to go. Glad you are okay."

Michael quickly says, "Before you go, I know you are not feeling it right now, but Rita and I have something here at the house for you. I'll send you a picture in a while. I will have it for you when you retire or want it." With great sincerity Michael says, "I owe you for more than being a cop. You saved my life." Cecil is quiet. They end the conversation agreeing to catch up soon.

Cecil disconnects with Michael. He doesn't want to put it off anymore. With a sense of duty, he calls Oralynn's mother, "Mrs. Lowry. This is Detective Soledad. We have talked several times. I just want to let you know that we have enough evidence to change Oralynn's death from a suicide to a homicide. I know it doesn't bring her back. I am once again so sorry for your terrible loss."

He holds his phone away from his mouth and takes another swallow. His next statement is maybe the most important to both.

"You were right about her Mrs. Lowry. She didn't take her life." He is quiet. The old woman sniffles and clears her throat. "At least I know I will get to see her in heaven." He hears muffled crying and a soft "Goodnight." Cecil disconnects and lowers his head thinking about seeing his own son. He takes another swallow from the half empty Crown bottle.

As the courtyard fills with shadows, Michael and Rita go into their new dining room and turn on the light. They draw the shades. Rita places the duffle bag on the table. They take out every shard. They unwrap each and lay it out in five rows across the tabletop. They stand back. Even in the dim light of the dusty fixture over the table, the bands of blue glisten and shine. Michael holds her hand and says, "So this is what ten million dollars looks like."

They hug and laugh. Michael hovers over the rows of raw turquoise. "Let's find the one to give to Cecil." They each look. They agree on a stone with a band that is thick and concentrated. The black matrix is visible like in no other shard. The band sticks out of the stone. Rita comments, "Suzy must have gasped when she got this one. There are collectors who would kill for this rock."

Michael picks it up and sets it to the side by itself. He takes a photograph of it with his phone. He and Rita put their heads together and he takes a selfie. He texts both pictures to Cecil. "Thank you my friend. We will save your shard until you want it. Catch up soon."

Michael knows Will is an early riser. He arrives at the hospital the next morning as they are serving breakfast. He slowly opens the door to his room. Will sees him and starts to sit up. He is dressed already. His shoulder is in a sling. Michael smiles big at him. "Going somewhere?" Will replies, "God I hope so. I'm going crazy." Michael comes over and sits on the edge of his bed. "I was thinking, you never got to see the treasure you got shot for." Will smiles but doesn't understand what Michael is trying to say.

Michael continues, "It's a bag full of these. Each one is worth between fifteen thousand and twenty-five thousand I hope." He unwraps a shard he pulls from his pocket. He holds it out to Will, who takes it and looks at it. He immediately rubs his hand on the dark blue deposit protruding from one side. He holds it out for Michael to take back.

Michael looks at him. "You are my best friend. You almost lost your life because of me. You were there when I started the hunt. This is really a bribe so you will keep being my friend." Will predictably replies, "It's not necessary." Michael cuts him off standing up. "I know. Save it please. Love you dude." They hug gingerly. Both grimace thinking the other can't see. Michael smiles as he leaves. "Glad you are going home. Catch up tomorrow."

On his way back to his new house he stops at the bank. He closes the safe deposit box. Later that morning he and Rita open Mort's safe for the first time. It is a large walk-in space with shelves of pots and turquoise jewelry. Each item is tagged with a card identifying the artist and year it was made. Michael makes room for the new additions. He puts the box with Mort's original letter, the Las Vegas newspaper clipping, the three cabochons and Clue 1 in first. He sets the duffle bag now weighing about nineteen pounds in a corner. He places Cecil's shard on a high shelf.

Michael stands back and looks at the safe contents. He turns and looks at Rita sitting on the side of the bed watching him. He thinks about the life represented by the collection on these shelves. He sees a dark brown leather binder standing upright by itself at the end of one of the shelves. He removes it. The leather is dry and rough. He unzips it and opens it on the shelf edge. He finds a hand-drawn map. In the middle of squiggly lines showing hills and gulches is a X. Written above the X is "Sky Stone 79 Mine." There is a worn business card for Winston Sky Stone, Geologist, Lapidary and Miner, paper-clipped to the map. On the back of the card is written, "M. Hamilton – you own part of this claim now. I know it's here like I told you." The initials WSS are underneath with the date August 4, 1984.

Behind the map is a newspaper article. Michael sees that Winston was murdered taking a large find to the safe at his rock shop. The turquoise was never found. The mine was closed. His murder was never solved. Michael picks up a small stone wrapped in Kleenex lodged at the bottom of the binder and rolls it in his fingers. Without unwrapping it he knows it is from this mine. Michael laughs softly to himself. "That damn Mort." He has his back to Rita. He closes the binder and puts it back on the shelf smiling. "For another day."

The next day they happily occupy Mort's house. They spend the week working on the compound. They set up the master suite first. That night, after they passionately celebrate their new abode, they both go to sleep knowing the Lander Blue treasure is tucked away in the safe in the closet next to them.

The next week they repair the gazebo deck. Michael sprinkles a palm full of Mort's ashes into the metal box. Each thanks Mort with a moment of silence while they look at the open box. Michael shuts the lid securely. He smiles as he screws the boards back down, just like he did when he was ten years old. They clean up the back courtyard. Michael makes an appointment for the following week with Butch Doring at the Turquoise Museum. The rest will come. As per Mort's request, they host his crew Friday evening in the gazebo.

43 THE SENDOFF

The sun is going down. Small white lights outline the railing around the gazebo. Pinon is burning in a blackened clay chiminea off to the side. The light breeze teases attendees with the smell. Michael, Rita, Will, Cecil, Busy, Bruce, Lulla, Omar and Cromley stand around the table which has been placed back in the center of the gazebo. Michael starts telling the group the treasure hunt story by pointing at the well house.

When he and Rita finish telling the story, Michael says, "Everyone attending tonight was involved in this adventure." Bruce and Lulla hug and laugh. Lulla snorts, "Now we will never get that hole fixed in that old bathroom." Omar wonders how he was involved. Michael explains. "If my parents would have left Hamilton's to me, Mort might not have thought it was necessary to come up with the treasure hunt. Maybe the Lander Blue would never have been found. At least until the deck was demolished someday." Everyone laughs.

Mort's simple silver urn is sitting near the edge of the table. There are photographs of him positioned around it. He is smiling in every picture. Once again Michael gets everyone's attention. "Welcome Mort's geezer friends." Pausing for effect. "That's what he called you all." Everyone laughs again. Michael continues, "Mort requested this gathering. He wanted each of us to touch his urn and say something about him. He said it doesn't have to be nice." Everyone laughs again. Michael holds up the wine bottle that was in the duffel bag for the group to see. He shows them the note. "Enjoy for me and Suzy. We missed having this in nineteen seventy-three." The group is quiet. He softly says, "We are going to, Grandfather."

He carefully uncorks the bottle of 1972 Stags' Leap Cabernet Sauvignon, imagining the story this bottle could tell. He has checked the price online. At two-thousand dollars, it is the most expensive wine he has ever had. He lets it breathe for a minute. He pours a small amount in a crystal wine goblet from Mort's stemware collection. He smells it and takes a sip. He smiles. Without saying anything else, he pours a goblet for each attendee. The group toasts Mort. Busy says, "Goodbye old friend." Bruce adds, "It was a pleasure, you character." They all take a sip. They take turns touching Mort's urn and toasting him. They each tell a short story about him to lots of laughs and some tears.

Michael has not had a bad dream since he met Rita. He thinks about the irony of something so well-intentioned turning out the way it did. As with most things, there is bad that comes with the good. He feels Suzy's stone against his chest. It is warm. He looks at Rita. He is hopeful for the future.

In the early Fall Michael and Rita return to Battle Mountain. They leave some of Mort's ashes at Suzy's grave. They watch the sunset after leaving more ashes at the Lander Blue mine. Two days after they return to Santa Fe, they surreptitiously drop some of Mort's ashes on the sidewalk in front of Hamilton's former location on the Plaza. The following Sunday afternoon they visit the Santuario de Chimayo and place some under a tree out back by one of the acequias. The rest of Mort's ashes are in the safe to be buried, one day far in the future, next to his grandson.

1. Is it believable that Mort fell in love with Suzy in such a short and tumultuous time?

2. Is it believable that a chance meeting like Suzy's and Mort's could have such a positive influence on Mort's life? If you believe it did, which had the most influence, Suzy or the twenty pounds of Lander Blue?

3. How did Mort change from when he is introduced to when he dies? What about him doesn't change?

4. Is Mort's guilt-driven relationship with Mel as only a business partner believable?

5. Is it believable that Mort, as a Grandfather, could ignore his own son and wish Michael, his grandson, was his son?

6. Why did Mort not do something with the remaining turquoise until he set up the treasure hunt for Michael?

7. What symbolism did the treasure hunt have related to Mort and Michael's relationship? Was it a way for Mort to say goodbye?

8. Was Oralynn's attraction to Cozy believable due to her personality and family issues?

9. Is Michael's reaction to Mel's and Darlene's deaths realistic? Was Michael's relationship with Mel the same as Mel's relationship with Mort?

10. Is it believable that Michael fell in love with Rita in such a short time?

11. Cozy tracked Michael and Rita knowing they were looking for a treasure of some kind that he convinced himself was worth a lot of money. Is it realistic to think he would pursue something, even commit murder, not knowing what the treasure was?

12. What was the worst thing Cozy did in the story?

13. What was your favorite treasure hunt clue riddle?

14. Cecil does not mention the turquoise treasure after the event in the warehouse. Does this seem like a reasonable compromise for a lawman to make? What does this say about him?

15. Rita posted the damning video of Hugo on Facebook. Did she use Michael to get rid of Hugo?

16. Did the chapter about the Turquoise Museum in Albuquerque, New Mexico make you want to visit it?

17. What was your favorite place or thing in Santa Fe or New Mexico mentioned in the story?

www.ingramcontent.com/pod-product-compliance
Lightning Source LLC
Chambersburg PA
CBHW010746310726
48980CB00004B/376
* 9 7 8 1 6 3 2 9 3 4 7 5 8 *